Papal Glow

Papal
Glow

Blake Wallin

maudlinhouse.net
twitter.com/maudlinhouse

ISBN-13: 978-0-9994723-4-7

Papal Glow

Contents

The importance, in historical mythology, of the Napoleonic character probably derives from the fact that it is at the point of junction of
the monarchical, ritual exercise of sovereignty and the hierarchical,
permanent exercise of indefinite discipline. He is the individual who
looms over everything with a single gaze which no detail, however
minute, can escape: "You may consider that no part of the Empire
is without surveillance, no crime, no offense, no contravention that
remains unpunished, and that the eye of the genius who can enlight-
en all embraces the whole of this vast machine, without, however,
the slightest detail escaping his attention." At the moment of its full
blossoming, the disciplinary society still assumes with the Emperor
the old aspect of the spectacle. As a monarch who is at one and the
same time a usurper of the ancient throne and the organizer of a new
state, he combined into a single symbolic, ultimate figure the whole
of the long process by which the pomp of sovereignty, the necessarily
spectacular manifestations of power, were extinguished one by one
in the daily exercise of surveillance, in a panopticism in which the
vigilance of intersecting gazes was soon to render useless both the
eagle and the sun.

Michel Foucault, *Discipline and Punish*

In his fantasies of domination and power, he began to identify with
Napoleon. He admired this man who had rained fire and blood
upon Europe and killed hundreds of thousands of people without
even a fig leaf of ideology, faith or political conviction. Unlike Hitler,
unlike Stalin, the only thing Napoleon believed in was himself. He
had succeeded in establishing a radical separation between himself
and the rest of the world, and considered others mere tools in the
service of his imperious will.

Michel Houellebecq, *The Elementary Particles*

Things could be so different now
It used to be so civilized
You will always wonder how
It could have been if you'd only lied

Depeche Mode, "Policy of Truth"

<u>Introduction: Genesis (1808)</u> – an historical satire

1.

—I understand a pupil wrote it, but you have to understand your role in this dormitory…

—Am I to be neither seen *nor* heard? They already barely see me.

—Mr. Livery, it's a matter of showing them how *best* to use these gifts they have.

—He drew a goat next to it!

—Then he is clearly reading the commentaries on the material. He earns high marks and knows how to use that first word of the sentence, clearly.

—I tried to show him that the war reading was not meant to engender such language.

—Did you *cane* him?

—I really didn't think it was my place…

—And I don't think it's my place to strip you of your rank, but I might do that.

At this point Mr. Livery had hit a standstill and was staring at the sentence scrawled in chalk in front of the two dignitaries. Why teach the child what he seemed to already know? That the world was baseless and ugly and he had found a place in it within himself to comment on its baseness should be celebrated, Livery thought.

Dr. Eaves dropped a teabag into his tea more delicately than Livery expected and began to think aloud that this was what the war with the French was leading them to.

—I would blame Alexander Pope or Jonathan Swift, but are they relevant anymore?

—Pope will always be relevant, proclaimed a righteously offended Livery. —If only because he shows the world what needs to be shown to the world.

—Yes, but one could say the same of Swift.

—Swift hates humanity, said Livery, and the best course of action for this young man [pointing to the scrawled sentence] is the path Pope has set out.

—Yes! exclaimed Eaves. —We must at once thrust this young chap into the papacy!

—That's not half of a bad idea, replied Dr. Eaves to himself.—But we need to murder his entire family and pay his classmates to bully him.

Livery looked at the chalkboard more wistfully than he would have liked to, and in that moment he realized that it would be the easiest thing in the world to murder the child's entire family, pay his classmates to bully him, and thrust him headfirst into a rich papal glow. The devil in the room was what was written on the wall, scrawled in script so miniature as to be seen only through squinting, script that read: HUBRIS IS THE BENEFACTRESS OF MY MASSIVE THROBBING COCK.

The tired schoolteacher knew the boy was doing right by his country, but he needed to be doing right by God, and—what amounted to the same—himself. And the schoolteacher needed to do right by all those people as well and give this boy up for holy adoption. Could he be so blind as to not see the signs of the coming of the one to save the world from its masculine dredges through its ultimate nadir and usage? This boy needed to be shown the *right* way to display masculine pride and toxic masculinity.

2.

The marks on the skin of the land around Bernard's estate were soft. Etched into the surrounding landscape, they carved circles and figure eights through the heather and barley that had become staples of the vast land they had owned since the War of the Roses. Bernard knew only to keep the land—at the behest of his grandmother who for some reason kept that dream alive—but not how to do so.

So he set up charters with local farmers as soon as his father died (unceremoniously) leaving a battlefield he was on the front lines for. Apparently someone had not told his father that turning your back on your enemy is neither the best idea nor the most apparent. Why his father had done that stumped Bernard to no end, and the part of him that wondered whether it had been a suicide attempt had to be squashed daily.

The farmers took shifts alternately throughout the growing season, and sometimes he would have long conversations with whoever wasn't stationed on the fields of heather that day. Lately, though, he had wished the growing season were stronger, as the ratio of work to conversations was growing shorter. Today a Gaelic one named Ailen was talking his ear off about granular agriculture.

—It's about the *seeds,* said Ailen. —If we don't trust ourselves to use the seeds right, how will they trust themselves? If we treat the soil the way we would be treated instead of how we *think* they need to be treated, then our crops will be doomed to failure.

—We live in a fiking moor, Bernard shot back. —Everything we grow is doomed to failure except the crops that for some godforsaken reason grow naturally.

Ailen sat back in his chair and petted Bernard's dog, which flitted between the legs of the table like a sled-runner and started nipping at Ailen playfully. The dog—Argyle—began to yelp and emit excited noises at Bernard and Ailen alternately, darting back and forth between the table and the more spacious kitchen.

—Bernaard, drawled Ailen. —What has this dog done today?

—It was out in the moors, Bernard replied. —Why?

Ailen tried to lift Argyle's upper jowl, but the dog yelped a reply. —How long has he been this excited, Ailen eventually let out.

—Lay off him, will you? Bernard said wearily. —The dog's just getting over a fever.

—When was the fever?

—About two days ago. He's been positively giddy ever since.

Ailen got up quickly and started searching the kitchen for a rifle. —You need to shoot this dog.

—I don't have a rifle in the kitch—wait what? Shoot my dog? Have you lost your mind?

—This dog is going to do the same if you don't shoot it.

—Oh Christ is my dog mad?

—It looks like your dog is mad.

—The only guns I own are in my room and on the practice range, and I'm not about to shoot my dog in my own house.

—Hope you've had practice recently, then. I'm a pacifist, but you have to know these things.

Bernard grabbed his coat, cursed, and tried lifting Argyle, but the dog snapped up at him, the harsh work of his jaws so distant from the look in the dog's eyes, a look suggesting just sheer pain.

Bernard nodded, and Ailen opened the door out into the vast moorlands.

The dog bounded in the direction of the shooting range almost as if it knew, or at least as if the part of itself that was not taken over by the disease still knew and was dragging its disease-ridden body into the only place that would offer what was left of the dog peace.

Bernard and Ailen walked down the hill, and it struck Ailen that Bernard must have been experiencing the opposite: adrenaline in his veins, health in his system, and sheer moral ambiguity in the fibers of whatever was left of him as a man.

Bernard raised the rifle until the dog was in the sight, and then put the gun down.

He raised the gun again, and then put it down again.

He raised the gun a third time, and shot his target as the dog was mid-leap, and some of the blood from the hit lightly dabbed the tarpaulin target behind the dog.

They were silent for a while as the wind tried to cleanse the surrounding area.

Ailen eventually asked Bernard why he sent his son to a boarding school instead of helping out at the farm.

—I just shot my fiking dog, Ailly. Jesus.

—No, said Ailen laughing. —It's just that you don't seem very religious. Neither am I very much, it just made me wonder.

—It really makes *me* wonder why you're not respecting the solemnity of the occasion.

—You shooting your dog?

—Aye.

—Just seems sad to me.

—I'm right going to aim at you if you don't stop.

Ailen was quiet from that moment on, reflecting on the dog lying between the targets and the two men. Bernard had a look on his face that suggested indigestion, but of the moral kind, and the dog looked like it hadn't been thinking properly before the death but was finally, in its last moments, thinking right again. Ailen didn't know what he looked like but he imagined it looked something like shite, just heaping moments of shite—it characterized his life up to this point anyway.

—He's doing well at Wensley, said Bernard eventually.

—What in Christ's name is Wensley?

—Where my boy Leo is.

—Ah, right. Godspeed then.

<u>**Part One: Bullying (1807–1809)**</u> – a bildungsroman

1.

The truth of the matter is that Leo was only allowed into the prestigious boarding school once he turned eleven, while most of the boys entered the fray a year earlier. The school would not let him enter earlier because, for some reason psychology hadn't figured out yet, Leo remained developmentally challenged socially, and, if the school was ever falsely accused of giving a damn, it looked like a good time to start caring.

The headmaster of the school, Dr. Eaves, had given express instruction to the school-teachers to be delicate but firm with this boy, that he would be a challenge, that all their hopes for him would eventually assuredly be dashed, etcetera. The walls of Eaves' office were lined with the aura of his achievements, but to be completely honest that fad had not yet picked up speed, so his office remained a gloomy affair with one diploma hanging directly above his seated head, and of course a desk—curiously shorn of any noticeable materials.

Leo's parents—Bernard and Anna—brought Leo and his twin sister Liza to Wensley during a rainstorm. The rain was never the point of the journey, but almost became that after Leo tried to unsuccessfully jump out of the moving carriage, opening the latch of the door so gingerly he made Liza, who thought he was bluffing, giggle with mirth.

After the foiling of the plot, Liza felt mildly betrayed that Leo would 1) try to escape their parents' clutches without her, and 2) do something so potentially dangerous anyway. She eventually settled on a thin scowl over poking her tongue out, a move she thought fit the situation better and fit how much she was willing to let Leo know his action affected her.

—This carriage was not made for that, Leo, sighed his mother Anna.

—Right, Leo snapped back. —It was made for carrying the bourgeoisie.

—Oh God, Bernard sighed. —Is he babbling nonsense again?

A moment passed, wherein Leo knew the word he had uttered would be the harbinger of some new undefined era, but it was also a moment for Leo to collect whatever was left of himself to collect in a carriage ride he knew his parents couldn't afford.

—Is that German? asked Liza finally.

—Ja, Leo emitted, lying.

The cabby turned around for a brief second to examine if there was a runaway German youth still in his carriage, but, after finding no evidence to support this theory, turned back around, slackened the reins, and gave them a good thwapping against the two horses' hides.

—This hackney isn't suited for such talk, the coachmen said without turning around.

—Excuse me! said Leo. —We can't hear you with the rain! Sorry, can't hear!

Anna ran her fingers along the pleats in her capacious skirt. She was happy to be off the moors for more than a minute, but was increasingly uneasy about the trip: if her premonition was right, they wouldn't accept Leo again this year, because his beloved sister Liza was always preventing him from succeeding. It didn't look that way from the outside, believe you her, but when Liza looked at Leo faux punching Liza from across the carriage, she knew tearing them apart would do Leo a world of good.

Bernard lifted up the window curtain of the coach with his right index finger and looked at the rain hitting the puddles amassing on the uneven sides of the road. The drops lifted back as soon as they hit, as if they weren't just drops in the ocean of the English countryside, but instead like they had a purpose other than to keep time while he waited on whether Leo would be accepted to the boarding school finally and put him and Anna's minds (mind?) at ease. He didn't know what to do at this point, and he didn't want to go back to their erstwhile farm in any case.

Liza deflected Leo's fake punches and then signaled she was quite done playing by turning to the window, lifting a curtain, and looking out her side of the carriage. Liza never looked down at the ground much, as she knew it and it didn't really affect her daily life in any way unless she was walking and something was in her way, and even then she didn't pay much attention to it other than avoiding the obstacle. So she looked at the trees instead, bare ones, little knubbers of doubt she could examine. Little ones trying their best in the world but ultimately coming up short because of their surroundings. She didn't make the next, obvious connection, but it was there nonetheless.

Leo turned to Liza and then Anna and smiled before following the suit of Bernard and Liza and looking out at his dreary surroundings. He didn't look at his father, out of (what will become to him later, inexplicable) reverence. He had met Dr. Eaves before, during his last entrance examination attempt, and he didn't exactly relish the opportunity to either see the man again or retake the test he'd already failed three times. If he had been at most two years older, he would have had the ability/presence of mind to be able to discern the true reason for the boarding school: to separate him from the sister he loved so much. But he just looked at the somehow-trampled grass lining the poorly paved road; it looked like a fresh hell.

—We've hit enough bumps on this road to revive the Roman Empire, said Bernard stupidly.

The other three looked at him blankly for a second and then all burst out laughing.

—Because … because they had better roads, stammered Bernard.

—Ah yes, said Anna, wiping a tear away from her. —We all know about your views on the rise of Christianity in Britain, dear.

—Father, said Leo innocently. —Why am I being sent to a religious school?

—Because there are no others, was the reply from Bernard.

—Why would a school be set up on the premises of a relatively recent system of thought?

—He's doing it again! Bernard exclaimed to Anna.

—He means no harm honey. It's just his imagination.

—I wish he would imagine something more productive. Maybe then—

Anna quickly pointed out a bunny in the woods. —Look Leo: a bunny in the woods…

—So it is, said Leo, not going over to look at the bunny but instead remaining in his seat.

2.

When they got to Wensley, the coachman hobbled off the carriage and nearly fell on his face, much to the joy of Leo and especially Liza. The lion sculptures flanking the steppes appeared to be having an identity crisis, as if they weren't sure whether they were entirely gargoyles that served a purpose for letting water out, or just merely decorous attachments to the steppes.

As soon as Leo thought this, however, he was sprayed with water that shot out in spurts from the left lion's mouth. His parents offered him a hanky and a kerchief, respectively.

—Don't worry about that, said Eaves, magisterially descending his own staircase. —The left one likes to spit water at people.

He winked. —The right one just bites.

—We heard you the first time, said Leo bitterly.

—Excuse me? You should be kinder in front of your namesake.

—What, the lions, the bravery they represent, or the inverse of it that you represent?

—Yes, yes dear, he said it last year, we're well aware, Anna said tiredly.

Dr. Eaves sighed. —Let's set you up for your exam. Maybe you'll liven the place up, he said looking around at the weather. Liza briefly mentioned that Leo could brighten up any room, to which she received a light punch from her brother Leo.

The room that held the exam bore no trace of the elegance of the building's façade. Like Eaves' office, it held a plaque with only the name of the school on it, just above a grandfather clock. The rest of the room was barren except for the desk in which Leo sat for the two hours the test was supposed to take him.

Questions flew by him and answers appeared in front of him instead, in their place. It didn't take him two hours; it took him an hour and ten minutes. He spent the remaining time checking over his answers and looking at every facet of the desk in front of him. A sentence had been scrawled into the desktop's upper right corner. Leo leaned forward and read the words GOD SAVE ME and, in the lower left corner, GOD SAVE HIM, BUT GOD DESTROY ME.

Leo decided not to bring up this embarrassing token to Dr. Eaves, as much as the latter's reaction would be sweet to Leo if he didn't get into the school. But he may have passed, and independent of that, this harbinger of doom seemed like it would be better enjoyed silently to oneself, like a prayer. Leo wasn't sure how religious this school was, but he figured no school was too religious for him; no school could get to him. It was this confident secular prayer that he said as he opened the door into Eaves' office and handed him the exam.

Leo went back to sit with the other three and found himself exhausted enough to fade into a sleep that lasted until a much more chipper than normal Anna poked her son awake with a smile, and Leo opened his eyes to see Dr. Eaves standing in front of him majestically.

—Congratulations young man, said Dr. Eaves. —You've passed.

—Praise God, said Bernard, drawing a blush that elicited a different reaction from Eaves, but one Eaves quickly dismissed to get to the matter at hand.

—Yes, your scores were quite remarkable.

—Thank you, sir. I'm excited to begin.

—That's it? No verbal fanfare?

—Doesn't seem like the right occasion for it, sir.

—He would never- began Bernard before Eaves cut him off.

—He would, Eaves said. —We'll be keeping our eyes on you, but only because we know what potential you have.

—Well at least they're speaking plainly now, sighed Anna.

But Leo was keeping those two conflicting scrawled sentences in his mind, saving them for a later he knew would come, a later he dreaded but knew was the place he would end up eventually, as happens with later.

Bernard grabbed Leo's suitcases out of the car, causing Anna to gasp. —I had no idea, exclaimed Anna.

—Maybe you should think higher of our son, he replied.

—More highly, she said, taking a suitcase from him and almost climbing the steep steppes of the boarding house.

All his roommates had gone to play cricket, so, once they'd distributed Leo's belongings and he was moved in, Bernard hugged him and said something nice, Anna hugged him and said something nicer, and Liza said something positively strange.

I will be with you always, Leo thought to himself using Liza's thought, checking its veracity by looking at her reassuring nod while the semi-thought was occurring.

—Is it a one-way thing? he whispered.

It's a one-way thing, she responded.

—I thought this was a myth.

It's our myth.

Leo started crying at his terrible fortune.

3.

The textbooks the children received were standard issue textbooks, but Leo's were not. Leo's had pages missing, sections cut out, and scratched-out text all over, but littered throughout were the pieces of information he put together himself. All the lacunae in fact had the opposite effect on the young Leo, and he learned to get what was given to him *and* separate fact from the overarching fiction of the books' metanarratives.

When Leo was in his second year, a young boy named Gerry—whom everyone called Grist—would always look over in amazement at Leo's half-assed book, either to reflect on how half-assed it looked or to think more sinisterly about how full-assed destroyed it was. He would ask whether Leo could really learn from that and also to what extent the schoolteachers must have hated the boy.

—Psst, said Grist. —Leo…

—What? said Leo at full volume.

—You able to read your book?

—Yes, said Leo, supremely insulted. —Of course I can read.

—How? Grist laughed. —I wouldn't be able to read that if God gave it to me Himself.

Leo thought about saying that Grist probably couldn't read the unexpurgated version as it was, but decided not to.

—And what would you suggest? Leo eventually asked.

—How about destroyin some-thing they hold dear.

Independent of how touched Leo was that Grist knew learning was important to the young boy, the idea was ludicrous to him and he laughed accordingly, a laugh that drew the consternation of the Latin instructor.

—Is there something funny about the *Aeneid*?

Leo sighed and leaned back in his chair. —Once it's translated there is.

The schoolteacher pushed up his glasses for about thirty seconds before responding in kind, or, at least, of a kind, kind of. —How *dare* you?

Leo thought this as good a time as any to bring up the book issue.

—I dare only on the grounds that I cannot read this cut-up book.

The schoolmaster—people called him Sir Peter—looked imperiously down his newly fallen glasses and stared at the young boy with a magnanimity Leo would come to know well throughout his life.

—Only the pictures are gone, my good sir. Other than that it's in pristine condition.

Leo wasn't sure if the first sentence was true, but the second was not. —Then this translation is terrible.

Sir Peter went to get his cane from the rack near the door, and Leo looked for places to escape but found only faces looking at him with either morbid curiosity or sheer delight, depending. Sir Peter grabbed his most gnarled cane—the veins of it sticking out like some more modern, woe begotten crown of thorns—and proceeded to traipse down the aisle of desks Leo was adjacent to.

—Stick your hand out, Sir Peter requested.

—I'm not sure the circumstances call for it, said Leo, shocked to hear that it was his own voice.

—The measures one must take to maintain virtue are second to none.

Before Leo could parse out what exactly logically bothered him about Sir Peter's statement, the cane struck the side of his hand in all its full-veined glory. —You hit a nerve, Leo gasped.

—Yes, Sir Peter let out. —This cane does have veins, and so does your hand. How quaint.

Leo adjusted to a palm-up position before the next thwack, and as soon as the cane started its descent, Leo quickly moved his other hand to meet the end of it. His left-hand fingers snapped over the middle of the cane, he brought it up to his eye-level, and he slammed his right hand down on the other end with all his might until it delivered its own unique uppercut right to Sir Peter's ersatz jaw.

Sir Peter stumbled back and tripped over Grist's desk, landing on his back on the desk so that Grist had potentially one of the best views ever of Sir Peter's corpulence. —That'll teach you to mess with an authority figure, the man said before stumbling back to his teaching position at the front of the room, still disheveled and not even bothering to get his cane back.

I am speechless, brother.

—I will not punish you for that, Sir Peter stammered. —Not because you deserve a second chance, but because you have made a fool of yourself in front of the entire classroom. I want it to be clear to everyone that this young man has solved *nothing*.

Grist looked towards Leo in awe and asked if Leo was a member of the Thorough Squad.

—No, said Leo at full volume.

—Join soon, or they will bully you mercilessly for not joining, said Grist, although he did eventually concede that his performance during class today might make them think better of it.

4.

Leo wondered very seriously whether he was the Second Coming. He wondered not infrequently whether he was also perhaps the Antichrist.

When this entered his brain space, he typically went for a walk through the school grounds, making sure to bring scissors to clip the fica leaves whenever he felt one of them was looking at him weirdly. It wasn't that he enjoyed transferring the pain of his situation onto another life form, but rather that the life form happened to be in his path when his anger about classmates was in full-force. But he did bring scissors along always, so that gave him pause.

I don't know why you always do this, he and his twin thought together.

But the scissors remained in his right pocket, for as soon as he approached his usual ficus plant, a girl showed up from behind the plant, as if she had been waiting there for him.

—Excuse me, she said.

—You're excused, Leo replied.

—No, I mean, are you the one who's been destroying this plant?

—I destroy many things, said Leo coolly. —But this plant is not one of them.

—Interesting confession, admitted the girl. —But what if the reverse was true?

Leo realized he didn't know this girl's name.

—What if this is the *one* thing you've destroyed in your life? and you've just reserved all your destructive energy for this singular plant?–

—What's your name?

—and then you go your whole life thinking about this *one* plant and how you had this *one* chance to do someth– Sorry, what?

—Your name.

—If you find yourself in the business of harming plants on a regular basis, I'm not sure I should give out that information, the girl replied primly.

Leo shrugged and took the scissors out of his right pocket.

The girl was shocked. —What the hell are you doing?

—Adding another slit, Leo said calmly.

—You'll hurt it!

—I cut diagonally from the center. I don't cut the veins. Always.

—Does that even matter? You sound like a git.

—That's very mean.

That was mean.

—I'm about ready to take those scissors from you.

—Now *that* would be stupid.

The girl lunged forward right as Leo opened the scissors, and cut two of her fingers. She did, however, succeed in dumping the scissors onto the verdant ground below.

—Shite mister, she said. That hurt.

Leo forgot his prior reserve and reached for her hand.

—If you think you're touching my hand you're outta your mind.

—Hold still, said Leo, manipulating the girl's digits around his dexterous hands and fingers.

—Your hands flutter, she said laughing. —Like the wings of a butterfly.

—My name's Leo, by the way.

—Aggie.

—Pleased to meet you.

Leo tried to come up with a reason not to kill this girl and hide the body in this very garden, but was unable to for the duration of the conversation. Something about her struck him as both very odd and very pleasing, and he dreaded this combination, the fear subsiding only when she lifted her gaze from the floor to meet his own, as then there was a new fear. It was all very hard to explain.

No need for explanations. It's 1807…

—How long have you been on the grounds?

—I should say about fifteen minutes at least.

—No, silly, I meant how long have you been at Wensley?

—Since two years ago.

—So that makes you, what? Twelve?

—Thirteen. Old for my grade level.

—I didn't think that was possible here, but I guess anything's possible.

Leo couldn't remember the first time he dreamt about one of his male classmates. The possible explanation was that they simply didn't see the effects of these nocturnal invasions, as he was the only one privy to those. Leo knew they frowned upon it, but suspected some of his male classmates of not frowning upon it, of very much not frowning upon it. And that someone could eventually not frown on it together with him was almost too much for the boy.

You can't let anybody know this about you.

—Robert Hinchcliffe himself, of Sheffield, made these scissors, said Leo.

—The very one.

—1762 issue, one of the first.

—Americer was on the verge of liberation, and we were on the verge of mass production of scissors, Aggie let out.

Leo doubled over, and despite the pain in his gut could not remember the last time he had had this sustained of an interaction independent of the bullies that haunted his very existence at Wensley. It was also then that he realized he was at this school because it was the only affordable one to accept him.

5.

Gant, the main bully at Wensley, seemed perpetually in his last year. Boys and girls notoriously attended only until they applied to Oxford (and occasionally Cambridge), but Gant had failed the test so many times that his family had kept him attending the school either because they held out hope for a breakthrough or, more likely, because they didn't want to see him ever again and were delaying the inevitable.

So Gant trolled the miniature highways and byways that comprised the Wensley campus, flipping bystanders' ascots on a good day and poking them with fountain pens on a bad day.

Leo and Aggie caught Gant on a bad day. As soon as he passed them, he ripped the feather off his most prized fountain pen and threw it like a dagger at Leo, the tip piercing the latter's jacket and coming out the other side like a thrown sword.

Aggie screamed and rushed over to Leo, thinking he'd literally just been stabbed through the chest. Gant cut Aggie off and reached for Leo's shoulder, which he touched to lead Gant away from the gardens and into a nearby outdoor corridor.

—Leo, Gant said. —Good chum, old sport, the alpha and omega, the one who will save us all, etcetera. I didn't know you had a girlfriend, he smiled.

I'm sure he would like to know.

—She's not my girlfriend. I was doing my garden rounds.

—Ah yes, your esteemed *garden* rounds. Tell me, asked Gant. —Why don't you join my gang and you can do what you do to plants, to humans? Humans are so much more elevated than plants and animals, so why don't you elevate your targets?

—Will you stop torturing me if I do so?

—Of course old chap. Young chap.

—How do I know you won't turn on me?

—I won't, honestly.

—I make high marks. Why would I want to jeopardize that?

—Well, I'm not sure. You can either join me and not be bandied about so much and possibly still get into a good school, or not join me and potentially die before you even set foot on Cambridge.

—You're making a compelling argument, Leo admitted.

—God save the queen if it's not a good argument.

—Wait, I'm not sure I understand. If it's a good argument, and you're confident that it is one, why would you wager the queen's life that it isn't? Leo smiled. —Am I to understand you're against the monarchy? The British Empire? The *queen*?

—Join us and find out, said Gant, tap-dancing a jig and then stopping in front of Leo all of a sudden. —Come out and join us.

Leo looked over Gant's shoulder at Aggie examining the torn-asunder ficus plant. Then he looked at Gant again, and said what he had to say, knew what he had to do.

—Yeah I'll join.

Gant got a glint in his eyes, took the feather from the fountain pen out, slit the palm of his hand, and then gave it to Leo who did the same.

—Wait, said Leo. —Aggie already has a cut on her hand, can she join too?

—No, said Gant, glowering. —No she can't.

He doesn't deserve her presence.

6

Leo's roommate Christian examined the choices in his life that had led him to this impasse, and they were few and far between. Fate had been toying with Christian with such regularity that he began to seriously consider singlehandedly starting the English naturalist movement. Everything he wrote committed itself to what he had written previously, and this seemed to Christian like an omen for why he could never achieve anything in life besides menial grades and the negative attention of Gant and the other bullies including, now, it seemed, his own roommate.

Leo bumped into Christian on his way out the dorm room. —I'm sorry, said Leo casually before briefly staring at Christian's mass of books on the floor, thinking for a minute, and then helping him pick up the very last item to be scooped up.

—Oh, it's not a problem at all.

—No, I just don't want you to be late for class.

—I don't think Mr. Livery will mind, laughed Christian.

—If he does, remind him of what I did to Saint Peter.

Christian gifted the atmosphere of the room with a nervous laugh before crossing the doorway and exiting so hurriedly he dropped a portion of his homework.

As soon as Christian had reached his classroom, Leo picked up a piece of paper he'd just noticed on the dorm room floor. —Hallo, said Leo. —What's this now?

It turns out it was a sheet of questions on Hegel's philosophy. For some bizarre reason, they were either true/false or multiple-choice questions—clearly demarcated to work on in the blink of an eye, and not the all-seeing always-open eye of philosophy. No, this eye blinked far too many times for its own good, the test becoming a litmus for how Leo started to view the school in general: easy yet wrong solutions to easier problems.

Leo flipped the paper over to discover that, for each corresponding analytical question, Christian had given thorough arguments for his front-side choices. This may have been what he'd meant two years ago when he had mentioned the *bourgeoisie* to his parents in the coach taking him to Wensley. But he'd be damned if he'd let those trances interfere with his social and—what amounted to the same—academic mobility. So Leo pocketed the slip of paper to hand back to Christian when he got back from class.

As soon as Christian arrived in the doorway of Mr. Livery's philosophy lecture—late—he realized he had left his exam paper back in his dorm room, chilling his nerves so well he had to lean against the door frame for support.

—Fainting again, I see, said a still-distracted-by-Hegel Mr. Livery.

Christian let out a breath before answering that he was afraid he left his homework in his dorm room and did not want to miss the lecture.

—You know what happens next? asked Mr. Livery, glowing with apparent hatred.

—Is that a question?

—We all hope so, for your sake.

—A caning?

—You did go with the question. Good man. [long pause] No, I was thinking the other route.

Christian liked this faux option less than the caning—at least the caning had immediacy and firepower. He wearily went up to the board, picked up a piece of chalk, and wrote a sentence on the board exactly five times, the bottom leg of each capital E connecting via a swirling curlicue with the following line's I, the sentences connecting in a cycle that would haunt Christian for the rest of his life.

I WILL EXAMINE MY LIFE MORE

I WILL EXAMINE MY LIFE MORE

I WILL EXAMINE MY LIFE MORE

I WILL EXAMINE MY LIFE MORE

I WILL EXAMINE MY LIFE MORE

—You see, said Mr. Livery. —It's all about the cycle of history with Hegel, about things returning to their—

Mr. Livery took a long look at the thoroughly crushed and spiritually dilapidated Christian before asking him to please be seated like the rest of the class.

—Why do we do the things we do? he asked the class (and himself). —Love, he answered the class (but not himself).

Gant for some reason picked that day to hang Christian's dirty laundry on the flagpole in front of the administrative building. Of course, he would have to take the British flag down, but he figured that was the price one pays for God and country. He also figured the school might not notice anyway.

Gant rapped on Leo's dorm room door with such force that Leo angrily swung it open and hit a reclining Christian in the forehead sharply. While Leo was profusely apologizing to the departing Christian—who left the room to see about his dorm room war-wound—Gant etched his way into the door frame and pushed his way into the room.

He picked up Christian's laundry basket as Leo tried to convince him not to do this, that Christian had had a bad day, other reasons Gant found pleasure in ignoring.

When Gant made it to the flagpole, his eager lackeys made sure the British flag was down and Christian's dirty laundry was up. Gant looked up at the destruction he had so far wrought upon this young man's life and shed a tear for all the times he could remember not having a psychological reason to bully anybody.

Leo rushed up to Gant et al, but was too late, as all of them had succeeded. Except for Leo, who felt he'd betrayed his roommate, and except for his roommate Christian, who felt betrayed. Christian ran up to Leo and didn't say a word. Leo was looking at Gant with a heat-mixture of sheer hatred, unconditional love, and hurt feelings, while Christian was looking at Leo with the hurt from his brain almost leaving his eyes—Christian didn't bother looking at Gant though.

7.

Up until the blood oath, Gant and his team of bullies approached Leo as one would an animal the opposite of the young boy's namesake. They snuck up on him in the many corridors, and either flipped his ascot or—Gant's favorite—stabbed him delicately with a fountain pen. Gant had mastered the art of the delicate stab, always puncturing just enough to inflict pain but not enough to require medical attention. Leo sometimes watched Gant's methods so carefully that he sometimes didn't even feel any empathetic pain.

Gant grew increasingly less interested in the other tortures that his compatriots seemed so fond of: shaving cream on the face at night (without the accompanying shave), dumping the boy's head into the toilet and flushing (the toilets there were oddly, irritatingly immaculate), and just straight-up waling on him like Sisyphus finally had a free limb to use (the simplicity of the act almost made Gant yawn at this point).

And so it was that the blood oath became the only thing able to assuage Gant's growing boredom, his thoughts swirling endlessly through loops of previous, more thrilling beatings and escapades. The thrown fountain pen body became the last measure of a boy thoroughly spent, his last dogmatic attachment to the bullying schema he held onto, dissipating without an attendant host.

Leo knew about Gant's parasitic nature, but didn't know about Gant's decreased enthusiasm for bullying, so Leo believed he was getting off scot-free. It would be weeks before a chalkboard put him in the right frame of mind for understanding Gant's new-found cynicism.

—Whom shall we torture today? asked Gant, his formality betraying his true feelings.

—Is your heart even in this anymore, Gant? asked Leo after a minute of silence.

Gant scoffed. —As if people had hearts…

—Alright, fine, said an exasperated Leo. —Do you even want to bully someone today?

Gant thought hard about the question before answering that, no, he probably didn't.

—That's not the Gant I came to know through several beat-down sessions… That's not who pinned me to the floor and tea-bagged me so hard something must have been—

Don't.

Leo continued. —Something must have given you a rash, who scaled the heights of the school flagpole to tie my entire stack of laundry to it, with the most delicate items on the top, even when one delicate item tied to the halyard would have done the trick—

—Get to the point, sighed Gant.

—My point is to never lose that spirit that goes against what others have dictated, never be complacently going down a surge of other peoples' thoughts, opinions, and stratagems for your life and the course it should take. We are our own persons, our bodies given to us either by nature or by God, and either way they're a fiking gift. If you don't believe in the sanctity of life, fine, then stop bullying and start behaving. But only through misbehaving will I for one understand the purpose within the sanctity of life in the first place. It's like if someone has a pony, but doesn't train it right. As if someone had a dog that never learned to play. And my prediction is that this type of thinking will become more important politically and socially in the future as new systems of thought crop up and lead some astray. But we will not be led astray, dear Gant, because we have an innate system of thought that will never grow old; we have the keys to the future for which the doors haven't yet been discovered.

Gant stared at an out-of-breath Leo and marveled at the firm resolve the thirteen-year-old showed in the face of adversity. Adversity was getting the ever-living shite kicked out of it, and Leo just stood there smiling over it, laughing. Gant wasn't sure if this was the time to think about the two of them masturbating together, but think it he did; he made a mental note to follow through on that somehow in the future. The boy knew about as much as any of the others about sexual matters but made a lark about how he understood more than the other boys. At any rate, Leo might provide the opportunity for experience in at least one direction.

—You're dealing with the out-workings of an embattled minority, Gant said eventually.

—They teach Hegel here for goodness' sake. Why beat this religious sect when it's down?

Leo gasped for air after his speech, and eventually the lack of oxygen going to his head made him see Gant as a full-grown, naked man.

I'm gonna duck out for a second…

He marveled at the shape of the man's thighs, how the muscles in them twisted and bent at angles he recognized but had trouble locating outside of himself. He wondered how big the cock was, and why male genitalia got its name from just the male of the species. He knew there was no way to escape this cause of his pain, and he eventually decided there was no reason for stopping it, acting as if he could in other words. He knew some of the boys had a similar affliction, but they covered it up the way someone covers a bruise. In this moment, looking at what he assumed to be Gant grown up, he knew he had to both cover it and not, whatever the situation or politics called for in whatever moment he was given. If the moment allowed for sodomy, he figured those moments were ones to be cherished and brought to bear against the other, more concealed moments. In any case, Gant's cock was concealed, but it still looked sizable to say the least.

Leo got on his knees in front of the reclined Gant and tried to put his mouth near what he assumed to be an uncovered, flaccid penis. Instead, he thrust his blissfully lackadaisical head right into the crotch of Gant's trousers.

—Wow, said a rising Leo. —Trouser burn.

Gant gently pushed Leo's head away from his spread legs, kissed him on the forehead chastely, and told him to never speak about this with anyone but him.

Are you two done bullying?

Okay, good, just checking back in.

—We didn't even fuck! screamed Leo into the air.

—Yeah, said Gant. —And we probably won't. I'm afraid you need to be better about this.

—Is that why you've stayed here so long? asked a stung Leo.

—I would be lying if I said it wasn't a benefit, replied a similarly stung Gant.

—I'm sure you just get it in your head to entice every poof who steps onto these steppes.

—You're being unreasonable.

—You used to stab people with fountain pens, exclaimed Leo. —Don't talk to me about reason.

Gant got up, dusted himself off, and parted ways with Leo after saying, —I have reason enough for leaving this conversation. Tooteloo, fucker.

Leo began to cry, but his tears tasted different this time.

8.

Leo had a hard time telling Aggie about the revelation. They had gotten closer, but he still remained unsure how much he could trust her, and eventually decided that he could not.

I think that's wise. No need until you've figured it out.

Leo was about to ask when anybody ever figured it out for certain (and if that logic even applied to him in the first place) when Aggie bounded out into the garden to ask him a question.

—Why is the world the way it is?

—This doesn't seem like the appropriate time. And am I really the person to ask?

—Why is the world the way it is?

Leo sighed, stopped decimating the ficus leaves, put his scissors away, and looked her dead in the eyes to say that no one knows why, and that she should know that by now. Aggie turned away from him and kept walking in the other direction—towards the building where science classes were held—before turning around to face him outright.

Leo began, —The world is so large that even if you could measure it, it would start measuring you more. And it's no way to live your life waiting for the balance to change. Just accept things for the way they are and try to make the best of your situation, that's all you can do.

Aggie looked disappointed and then looked past him at Gant, who was approaching Leo from the rear. She smiled—a smile that looked to Leo (or his projection) curiously like defeat, as Gant placed a hand on Leo's shoulder to make Leo turn around and face him head-on.

—If you and Aggie are going steady, that's super cool, he said, doing that tick where people attempt to diffuse a situation but are unprepared for the emotions in their own statement. Leo took this time to study the Gothic architecture of the science building (which, in a hundred years time, he would have found supremely odd). No gargoyles, but there were buttresses for some strange reason, as it was not a cathedral of any sort. As Gant talked his ear off about how they couldn't do what they had done earlier, how wrong it was, how nobody could know, how they might be going to hell (that one was weird), and how much trouble they'd get in if someone found out, Leo gazed at the buttresses of the science building and imagined sliding down them like a skier—but without skis.

—I think you're making too big a deal out of it, Leo eventually bluffed to Gant.

—I don't think you realize what happened, said Gant, calling Leo's bluff but at the same time completely revealing his hand.

—This is too much gamesmanship; we shouldn't be this concerned about what happened. It happened, it's fine. I agree no one needs to know besides us, but that doesn't mean what happened doesn't have any validity.

—You on Laudanum, mate? What do you mean "validity"? If I had a nickel for every time someone has used validity to justify either evil or complacency, I would *not* be attending this school. I'd be at Cambridge already, even if my grades were gutter-dwelling rat-fodder.

Leo knew he was right, and eventually clapped Gant on the shoulder, as he figured that, if words had no validity for Gant, maybe actions still did. If Leo had taken this line of inquiry further, he would have been terrified to learn that more often than not actions having more validity than words has led to some of the worst political movements in history—and sometimes the conflation of the two. As it stood, and without recent history backing him up exactly, he just remained standing in front of Gant for a minute before Gant looked around, took Leo's hand in his own, and kissed it gently.

—Validity isn't confirmation, he said after his lips left Leo's hand. With that, he took a few steps back, turned around, and left, his steps echoing from the buildings that flanked the gardens and then fading like a cold, whistling breeze that leaves the area.

Leo looked at the science building, and wondered if it had anything to do with his current conundrum. He went up to the façade of the building, touched a bannister, and went up the steps to the door. On the door, there was a note for a lecture on the Biological Reasons for Marriage and/or Statecraft, and the lecture was slated for this evening at seven pm just after everyone's dinner. Leo took the flyer off the door after wondering why the hell it was even just a flyer on a large door in the first place, and then he crossed out all the words except "Biological Reasons for Statecraft" with a fountain pen. He proclaimed it right, bequeathed it so, and started to wonder why anyone on this earth he found himself on ever doubted him.

I doubt you all the time.

He knew Christian would definitely be attending the lecture, but there was no way in hell Leo was going, as he had very important business defacing school property—property that was more permanent than a flyer and would have an impact far beyond his reach, beyond how far Leo even knew his reach and impact extended. What he didn't know (and what might not have fazed him regardless) was that from this moment on it was a matter for the theologians and not the scientists.

9.

The chalkboard loomed large over the philosophy classroom.

Leo scoped out the target long before he stole the chalk or before he mustered up the courage to write what he needed to.

For some reason, he consulted Gant about what he should write, as Gant was sixteen and had been around the vandalism block so many times it could be viewed from space.

Gant told him the words would come to him in time. Then Gant sighed and asked what the concept was he wanted to convey to the school's administration. What big message should they get from what was written? It would need to be subtle, obviously, but also blunt and to the point.

Leo paced his room until the dingy carpet was worn down, and occasionally, until Leo became fearful the shuffling between his standard-issue shoes and the carpet would start a fire.

The only thing Leo was certain of was that the sentence would contain the word "cock" in it somehow. It was a fun word, and nobody would blame him for utilizing it in a good, right, accurate manner. Well, he did hope the administration would blame him at least; they would have to. Or else he would hang his head in shame for the rest of his days at Wensley, hang his head more than he usually did—his chin hitting his ascot.

But, late one December night, he would by the end of the night have no reason to hang his head. For, in the blistering cold corridors, he fingered the chalk and tossed it back and forth between his fingers, the small shadows they gave off in the lamplight thrilling him. He approached the philosophy classroom, and looked at a description of Schopenhauer's philosophical system. Leo knew the philosopher was all the rage right now, but, right now, he had a mission to adhere to that didn't involve worlds or wills. Or, maybe it did, but not to the extent that the philosopher described it in that book. Or, maybe it is to that extent and Leo didn't know it yet. Or, as he finally said to himself, these notes are in the way of my canvas.

He carefully erased the chalkboard, freeing it of more sensible and seemingly intelligible notes. Arguments, craft. Instead, he filled it with a singular sentence, drew a goat to the right of it, and called it a night after softly replacing the chalk and crossing to exit the room. He closed the door quietly and let the words and drawing speak for themselves.

HUBRIS IS THE BENEFACTRESS OF MY MASSIVE THROBBING COCK.   [goat drawing]

When Leo got back to the dorms and entered his room, Christian was nowhere to be found. This suited Leo fine but became worrisome as soon as he saw a note attached to *his* bedpost.

I HAVE GONE TO MEET MY MAKER, PLEASE NOTIFY MY FAMILY.

Leo looked at the paper for a minute, looked up at his roommate's uncharacteristically made-up bed, and looked back down at the paper. Why would Christian make up his bed if he had in fact gone to the lecture tonight? If he'd gone out for a night swim instead, this was an awful way of conveying it; but it took Leo all of thirty excruciating seconds to realize this was not the explanation the world had given him for his friend's actions. Leo had no previous interactions with suicide notes, and so the paper itself left him feeling just confused at first.

Oh, sweet Jesus.

He frantically checked the roommate's belongings for any clues, but found nothing. The only clue he kept coming back to was the point of desperation his roommate had shown when the bullies tied his underwear to a flagpole and lifted it with the halyard. It was standard stuff, but for some reason it really struck his roommate

Christian the wrong way. Leo checked under the covers of Christian's made-up bed, and discovered Christian's sheets were gone.

Oh sweet Jesus.

He rushed over to the flagpole as fast as he could, discovering it again for what he knew would be his last time. Time began to slowly accrete along the edges of Leo's thoughts after Christian dropped from the top of the flagpole.

Leo ran to the flagpole at full sprint before leaping as high as he could and then scaling it for what seemed like hours. When he got to the level of the ever-asphyxiating Christian, he got his scissors out of his right pocket and begun to essentially saw at the tangle of sheets Christian had fashioned into a noose. Eventually, the sheets gave, and Christian fell limply towards the ground, dragging Leo with him. It was all Leo could do to throw the scissors far away from the both of them on his way down and then brace for impact.

10.

Leo came to in the center of a circle of onlookers, kids and schoolteachers who had assembled gravely to watch the two fallen victims. It was odd nobody had touched Christian yet, his body just lying there limply.

Oh Christ, is he not breathing?

—Oh God, Leo let out. —Oh sweet, merciful God. Is he dead?

Leo's cries and sobs caused the circle around him to disperse, and Dr. Eaves strutted through to the center where Leo and—a few feet away—Christian were lying down in varying states of health. The good doctor went over to check Christian's pulse, looked up at the schoolteachers mournfully, shook his head no, and walked over to Leo.

Leo started shouting like a madman for his scissors, or his chalk—or any symbol at all—until the circle dispersed in earnest and the only people left were Leo and Eaves, alive, and Christian, dead. Leo sobbed into the gravel until his nose bled, the tears and blood mixing together for an unholy combination Leo recognized yet again.

Dr. Eaves leaned down to examine Leo, to make sure nothing besides bruises accompanied his person, no reason to involve medical care and the notification of his parents. Eaves took a seat next to the boy, for some reason taking off his pretense long enough to achieve some kind of empathy for what the young lad was going through.

—I understand this is difficult, said Eaves. —But you couldn't have saved him, nothing could have saved him I'm afraid. Some people don't want to live; you should know that: Schopenhauer was up on the philosophy board before your profane message defiled it.

Leo groggily lifted his body and dragged it into the surrounding grass. It felt soft and sweet.

More comfortable crying into the grass, Leo finally started listening to Dr. Eaves.

—We saw what you wrote, and we heard about what you did. We have a plan for you.

<u>Part Two: Murdering (1809)</u> – a picaresque

1.

Dear Ever-So-Increasingly-Less-Little One,

I am overjoyed to hear about you rescuing the kitten from the tree. I'm sure the cat's owners were happy to have their precious feline back safely and in their collective familial arms. Imagine if the poor thing had fallen! The mind asks itself questions the heart can't possibly answer, and sometimes it's the reverse. I can never tell anymore.

Your father has taken to examining the peat bogs with a fine-tooth comb, almost literally. There are days I wander outside to do some menial chore you used to do (not that I'm bitter!) and begin to scratch my head furiously at the sight of your father hunched over the barren soil trying to figure out how best to excavate anything worthwhile. (Honestly, if I were him, I would just call it a day and move to London.)

But then again Liza has become infatuated with literature. First it was harmless, about farming, about tools, about animals, about how the world works. Now (and you know I'm no plebian about these things), the things she reads [extended underline]. Fill in this blank; I dare you. Imagine the worst smut or trash you can think of (or don't—ha!) and then double the amount of smut and trash, and you would be close to approximating the level of depravity her mind engages in on a daily basis.

I think at this point London will be the perfect tonic for her, either to cleanse her or teach her what-for, what it's all for—not in a religious sense, more to get to the point of whatever her life is supposed to be about. We can't be expected to wait for very long on these ultimate questions, no matter the quantity or lack of faith expressed.

More to the point is your description of your lovely classmates. Gant helping you with your Latin homework is a welcome change of pace from when he was just distracting you with cricket, and don't go after Aggie too hard or you might scare her away. The last thing girls want is to be courted too hard, but, on the other hand, it is your world, so go have a good time with it, by which I mean court her and eventually—if she's the right one, and why wouldn't she be—asking for her hand in marriage.

The school sent a letter about you, not about your heroism but about how well you're excelling in your philosophy class. Why a Christian school is teaching Schopenhauer instead of Kant is beyond my imaginative pale, but on the other hand at least it's not teaching Hegel, God Save the Queen. Not that I have any complaints about your high marks. Far from it! If everyone was as studious and hard-working as you are, if everybody maintained the course the way you do constantly, then we'd live in a better world adopted by holy fathers and mothers who would finally deign to have something to do with us peasants.

Ever Your Mother,
Anna

2.

The summer after the suicide, Gant was one of the few students accepted into Oxford.

He spent his remaining days in the repose an Oxford acceptance affords a young pupil: laying about, counting hours, misplacing pens, placing his bullying duties on hold and moving on to bigger and better things. When Leo met him in the newly verdant quad—the summertime playing with any unbiased representation of reality—Gant seemed unfazed by his recent accolades.

—I'm telling you I don't need them in order to be a complete person, said Gant, smiling mischievously. —If I did, I would tell you so that you could follow my example. And we all don't want that occurring, now do we?

No, we don't.

—I suppose we don't, Gant. But why loaf about when there are more important things happening?

—Now Leo, said Gant. —You don't need to tell me we're at war right now. Or some sort of war. Or some sort of us going to war at our discretion. Or our values being under attack. Or, or… Or this thread losing its meaning.

He paused for a bit before snapping his fingers. —Or, I know! Maybe your recusant friends can start attending the Common Prayer readings our chapel holds and maybe Napoleon will vanish into thin air… Sounds like a wonderful solution, now doesn't it? Maybe Napoleon himself will just have a bit of a chat with our pontiffs and decide to just call the whole thing off? No? Well I don't know what to tell you then. (He clicked his tongue at this.) I *can* tell you everybody's looking for answers right now, and I most certainly am *not.* I'm looking to get a fiking education and settle down post-haste. England has no business in the continent's affairs; we have no business because we're too busy with our own businesses, our own little colonies of doubt and redoubling.

Leo asked if Gant was done and the latter assented after wiping off his brow for a good half a minute. —I don't think they'll look for answers from you, said Leo laughing.

—Yeah, said Gant. —But they might look from you. For the answers. They might look for the answers from you. At you they might look for the answers, fike, you know what I mean, Jesus.

—Whoah now, Leo replied, —I'm fine with you invoking the holy authority of our risen Lord Jesus, the Christchild, but only on the grounds that you genuflect first.

Gant got down on one knee and bowed his head before rising up with a vengeance, a vengeance that saw fit to also flip Leo the bird.

—Where in Jehovah's name did you learn that? asked Leo somewhat more innocently than he intended.

Easy now.

—Just a new thing that's going around, replied Gant. —Good luck on your exam. My best thoughts are with you, my very best fiking thoughts.

Leo smiled at the anachronism of everything and waved back at the newly retreating Gant, off to chase his own wants and whims independent of Leo, something Leo was beginning to realize was a beautiful thing in its own right—someone's life being independent of the emotional influence we think we create and organize—something like a beautifully individualized sunset that sets with each person's departure. And Leo almost didn't think these thoughts as he watched Gant leave him for what he assumed to be the last time, but he definitely did during the exam, mulling them about in the mixture of the rest of the unseasonably blistering summertime heat.

3.

Dear Lest-We-Forget-Little One,

Don't be so sad over Gant leaving: he wouldn't want it and you wouldn't be doing yourself a service with your sadness overtaking all your other senses, rendering all your other senses insensate, sensing all the while that there would be better outlets for your newfound grief.

And there you are. You can stall for all the times you'd been blessed by his presence or you can move on and find other people whose presences bless you similarly. It's not a matter of the grief becoming manageable; it's about allowing the grief to become fully realized as its own thing. And this doesn't mean you can't visit him… (Why would you not want to visit Oxford after all?)

Were you not being truthful in your previous letter, the one before that last one? It seemed like you were withholding information, telling it slant, looking at a glass filled with murky water slant-wise. I don't want you to tell me everything, just the things that let me know that it's not being told slant-wise, the little motes of happiness or sadness you're accumulating on your learning sojourn, which will now be sadly continuing into the summer, which is tough, I know, but on the bright side you're experiencing things for the first times, for the last times really, as they will change and morph and never be like this again most likely. These are the best years of your life, so maybe try to show some of that in your letters? Not too much, just enough to let me know you're getting on all right. Alright?

Back to the Gant matter: Let sleeping dogs rest where they rest, where they don't lie, but tell the truth so far they're barking at a moon they can't even recognize from so far away. Where was I going with this? Ah, that's right: never let someone get the better of you even if that someone is a friend. And don't let love interests get the better of you either, because that happens all the time as well. It happens all the time in relationships in general, but love makes it ten times worse. So treat Aggie like you would be treated to the extent that you can treat her the way you can be treated. Beyond that, treat her like God + the church + Christ himself if it will help speed things along enough for me to rest easy about you, so that I can rest easy as much as you will hopefully rest easy about Gant in time. Because that's all it will take: time, away and forward, away and backward, away and away.

And so must I sail away to London, taking Liza to London and leaving your father with the farm up north. It will be cold and miserable as I adjust to life as some seamstress or other, but it will bring in enough income for me to stay with Liza in an afford-able part of some godforsaken London slum. (I hope this doesn't worry you too much—I know you have enough on your plate as it is! But it is one reason you must stay behind at your school). We'll be visiting your father (and hopefully you too) as soon as July rolls the corner into August and fall begins its gradual ascent into the heavenly sphere reserved for the time of pumpkins and mulberry patches.

Till next time,
Your mother,
Anna

4.

Leo took the exam like it contained his last thoughts on earth, which he thought was a good way to take an exam, a good enough lesson for himself as he got nearer to the completion of his first year at Wensley. Aggie sat next to him during the exam and at-tempted to distract him with paper dolls she'd constructed before she promptly sent them to their deaths against his side very rough-ly. He swatted each one away like they were interrupting his last thoughts on this earth.

They may have interrupted but they didn't achieve much else, for Leo's exam was passing by his mind with flying colors: balloons of memory floated about in his brain space, each one more delicate and able to be popped than the next, him pop-popping each balloon that came his way to get to the next thought that took its place and inflated and eventually was destroyed by the next one that came along.

So it went for an hour and a half, the board filling up with the time demarcations the proctor Mr. Livery was putting up even though there was a rather large grandfather clock at the front end of the room that bonged the hour more dutifully before Mr. Livery—and even let Livery know when to write down the times.

Mr. Livery bumbled something about how these students should recuse themselves like the filthy recusants they were and Leo stopped in the middle of his question, dropped his pencil down, and asked if Livery was for assimilation into the Church of England.

—Not now, son, Livery bellowed. —I'm proctoring an exam… You are all taking this exam… I'm proctoring the exam you are all taking…

—At least we're not papists, mumbled Leo.

—Don't you turn that word against me, replied Livery as he wrote down another time on the board.

—Right, so this will be the time Mr. Leo's exam will end. Note the time, class [nobody looks up] and look at a time when one man's future was cut off. Now this boy will have to take summer classes—hah!

—I had to stay here this summer anyway, said Leo.

—Good, well now you have a reason to.

Leo crumpled up his exam and sent the wad in the direction of Mr. Livery before Livery caught it mid-air and in the same motion threw it in a trash receptacle next to the grandfather clock. —Think on this moment when you want to become high and mighty. You're not there yet, but when you are—maybe—think on this moment. [He put up the chalk as he said the following.] And for the record, I too am a recusant. And it's important to know where you stand—even where *you* stand.

The dorm room Leo had shared with Christian was now half stacks of get-well-soon cards to the dead Christian and half the bunkbed he'd only had half of anyway, so the room was essentially now only one fourth his. The rest belonged to some amalgamation of what the school wanted Christian to be in his passing: a doting boyfriend to Aggie, a diligent student, a loyal family member, etcetera. He maneuvered around the space that had been occupied earlier by Christian's presence every day and found the lack of his roommate unnerving as he finished the semester and moved into summer.

Aggie came crashing into his room, and he asked if she wanted to hear the letter he was writing his mother.

She furrowed her brow before answering that she would, but only if they interspersed it with notes from the class about Christian that were laying in the stack there, and if she could read them aloud.

—I believe that works, began Leo, —but I'd be hard-pressed to want to hear those notes right now. Would you even be ready yourself?

—I won't know until they're read, now will I? [She paused for effect here.] The least we can do is read them and I can step out if need be. Go ahead, read your letter; I'll read these things here, she said finally, taking up a pink-decorated card from the littered stack.

—Fine, said Leo as he brushed his now-bushy hair back and began. —"Dearest Mother-"

—Stop, said Aggie. —It's shit already.

—I haven't even gotten past the address-

—And *I'm* almost asleep. Look! we're both doing something.

—"Dearest Mother, I'm afraid I won't be able to make it home over the summer, as I have pressing business with classes and classmates, and all the go-about around here."

—Go about?

—Yes, said Leo, things are going about, are they not?

—Not around you, Aggie mumbled as Leo was continuing:

—"You know how it is these days, with classes being foreshortened so that summer prep for college can be maintained at a fast enough clip for pupils like myself. [groan from Aggie here] And if the telling of my story won't capture the heart of the nation God save me! for it will be a cold trip towards London if I don't make it into Oxford next year. [second groan] They say that I may be able to get in this year if I study hard enough. I know times have been difficult with the-"

—Okay, my turn, said Aggie, lifting up the pink card into the light the dwindling day afforded the window at that hour. —Dear Leo, this is room 4B. We are terribly sorry for your loss and have not seen you at any of the socials this year. We're collectively not sure if that loss may have impacted you not being at the socials, but I individually (that's me, Caity) was wondering why specifically, as you had promised me an invitation to the formal dance, and I can't be seen alone-" Okay, enough of that one. Next!-

—"difficult with the move and Liza's schooling and frankly bizarre love for literature, but look at all the times the English daytime has shone upon your face—look at every moment you're taking part in, isn't it wonderful?"

—You sound exactly like your mother.

Alright, now I'm pissed too.

—Isn't it wonderful?

—Perhaps. Or perhaps she's infecting your thinking.

—My own mother?

—Your own mother, I think. Yes, that's the same.

—No, I mean how is she infecting my thinking? I don't see it…

—I see it all around you. You think in visions, like her. You extemporaneously gesture towards some greater truth, like her. You encapsulate the unable-to-be-encapsulated with vague notions of right and wrong living, like her but more potently because of your youth. I've seen the way you write letters to her, and the way she writes back is more of the same, more ways to enter a problem that never gets solved, all the while you're hiding things from her and not letting either of you speak truth into each other's lives. It's a bloody epidemic if you ask me.

Leo gripped his papers with a newfound force. —I would appreciate you not speaking so cavalierly about my mother and I's writing habits. It's unbecoming.

—I'll become something greater than your unbecoming. That will be *your* unbecoming.

Yass queen.

—How do you mean?

—I mean you always underestimate me.

—I *meant:* leave my room immediately.

—I'll read one more card before I leave, but yes, I can leave.

—Go ahead, we're all listening, Leo said, gesturing towards Christian's things so grandly that Aggie started tearing up and had some trouble starting to read the card.

—"Dear Christian, we valued your life immensely while it was here. As it is no longer here, some want to disallow your value to continue into the future, want to send you back to the eternal damnation of not knowing your heavenly Father. I am not one of those people; I'll be for you always. I once heard a story about a lively concertgoer who shocked the entire auditorium of chamber orchestra loving acolytes with his rendition of Bach using his armpits. I imagine that's either what you're doing up in heaven, or that that's what you did here—not to extol suicide by any metric, but more to say that it is a flash in the pan, a brief momentary lapse of all one's reason that takes out the 'one' in the equation. [Aggie started crying here.] I wish you could have been here to see the reaction of the auditorium and to continue living both despite and for that reaction, both despite and for your performance, your continued performance into the heart of the minds of the living left behind. With love, Mr. Livery."

Leo dropped his papers when he heard the name, and he began to grab at his arms and ask Aggie more pointedly to leave at once.

—I'll go, said Aggie, —but you need to remember.

—Remember what? asked Leo, hesitantly about to ask her to stay a bit longer.

—No, just to remember. Into memory. That's it.

When Aggie left, she slammed the door, but all Leo heard was the dull sound at the back of his head that reminded him of a Christmas he spent holed up alone back at his family's home, in his room, with books of animals and ancient lore and other things. The jog of his memory exceeded what he was emotionally able to handle and he began to sob uncontrollably at the horror of his roommate's passing and his guilt-ridden complicity in not being able to save him in time. He had no way to unleash all his aggression other than to bottle it up into his studies and occasionally rip up the few letters to Christian and in Christian's memory that he had kept. He did this sporadically for the rest of the night until his forearms got tired from tearing and writing and until he remembered that Aggie wasn't allowed into the room alone with him in the first place.

5.

Dear Growing-Bigger One,

We've been in a bit of a conundrum here in London. Your sister seems keen on riding this new wave of novels into whatever future God grants her, but she seems increasingly unable to attend Mass, something which concerns me to no end, especially as there *are now* designated spaces for Mass—now that we're in the city. I want nothing more than for her to just go to a girl's school and put this business behind her, so she can grow into the woman God wants her to be, but I know at the same time that might not necessarily be what God wants. We've both (her and I) thought of sending her to a nunnery a bit north, especially so that her costs can be taken care of and not jeopardize mine any more than they need to, but a bishop here warned against it, as the Church of England has for some reason a hold of many of the nunneries up north. We can't get away with anything here…

There's a bunch of talk about Napoleon's growing conquests on the continent, among businessmen, church leaders, etcetera. Not that Liza and I pay attention to them, it's more that we're worried England may try its hand at warfare against this exciting new foe and you will inevitably be drafted, especially with your rescuing skills… (Ha!)

To get more to the point, just let Aggie come to you. Tell her everything but only everything that needs to be said to her specifically. Everything else can wait until you two are more consummated in your marriage vows. (If that's the road you decide to take with her!) Otherwise, you'll be down two rivers without any sets of life rafts, and how will you know which river is the one that leads to any sort of happiness? Just take your lumps when you can, and help her take her lumps, and both of you will be lumped together in the hand of the Lord! I don't need to tell you to be kind and gentle, but you should be that too, of course.

We'll be visiting your father at the farm next month. It is an estate riddled with problems, but they are our problems, as the estate is ours as well. We own what we've done and what we've accomplished, and you should too. Lift your chin a bit and the sky looks a little bit clearer—you'll be seeing it then at least.

Till we meet again,
Your loving mother,
Anna

6.

Ailen measured the peat on the moor with a turned-over wheelbarrow. He made markings with charcoal where the new plants could be planted but never moved the wheelbarrow. After doing that, he got sticks to mark the places that were verdant enough to plant crops.

—Oi, what's the wheelbarrow for then? asked a confused Bernard. —Seems to me like you could right just make do with the sticks pokin' out the ground there.

—It's for balance, replied Ailen. —Not balance on one's two feet, but a sort of agricultural even-spreadedness.

After a bit of a pause, Ailen added —so that we know how much to plant, how many seeds to bring in on this wheelbarrow, and what better place to mark it than on the place where the seeds will be carried, ay?

Bernard thought that made sense enough to check on the house, by which his mind meant check on the house for a bit and by which his subconscious desire meant lay around in the common area and smoke a pipe.

But Bernard's pipe smoke made it look like a fire was breaking out, so Ailen leapt inside.

Bernard motioned over to him to take a seat, which Ailen promptly did, flattening out the folds of his mud-streaked apron. —Now, Ailen, began Bernard. —We've known each other for as long as we've been waiting on God's kingdom, which seems to be a while now. … What I'm getting at is that I need to move with my family to London--

—Say no more, interrupted Ailen. —I can be out o' your farm before next evening.

—No no, blushed Bernard. —I was going to say you should run the farm. Was going to say the farm could very well be yours if I decide to follow my family into London.

—My, well I'd be honored. I certainly know the science of it the most out of all the hands here, he said, massaging his knees.

—Yes, said Bernard. —I was thinking the same thing.

—Well, is there anything I need to sign? When should we do it now?

—Anna and Liza will return next month to help me give the land over to your care. And I know you will take good care of it, because I've seen you do it before—that buildup of trust is important, as you know, because we trust you. It's not important because we trust you, but is important by itself, but because of its importance we trust you with it, if that makes sense. Oh dear, I'm not making any sense. I sometimes ramble for a bit—

—You're making sense, said Ailen kindly, with a smile.

7.

Dear Why-Keep-Up-the-Façade-of-Little One,

Liza and I are hoping to see you when we visit our home next month to help sign over the rights to our land to Ailen. You know Ailen, the smart one who goes on and on about the value of peat, etcetera? Well our land is going to him, which you shouldn't be worried about too much, because between you and me it's not very valuable with its bogs and whatnot. That being said, we all hope you won't need that land anyway, you'll be so successful.

Hoping to see you soon,
Your mothering mother,
Anna

8.

The summer months went by as the seasons go by—that is to say, slowly.

What Leo didn't know before he forcibly signed up for summer school was that it consisted of him being locked in his room for two months.

At first he counted tiles on the roof, picturing them as pieces of a different mosaic, one with Greco-Roman undertones, one that could withstand the scrutiny his developing aesthetic mind required. There were women with baskets on their head, large sea monsters that could be destroyed solely with Leo's imagination, and of course a catalogue of various sex acts the imaginary prostitutes in his room could grant him, if he had the required funds.

One of the prostitutes befriended him, and he would ask her various questions about her profession, her struggles, whatever crossed his mind as an appropriate question for a prostitute in that century. Her name was Arla, and she had traveled a long way to get there—from Timbuktu to Westchester, then to the school. She was the first of her family to have a job in an industrial economy, and for this she was proud and Leo shared in that joy for a few minutes.

Arla would run her fingers along the taffeta wallpaper edges next to the door and then peek through the slot where the food was always placed. Although Leo hated this, because whenever the food was sent through the slot, it took the place of Arla's head in his imagination because of the prevalence of his hunger.

But then Arla would stand up again and both the food and her presence would be equally felt, and he would eat the food and be immensely happy. She would talk about her travels, and he would listen. And then she would strip, and he would masturbate himself into a naptime slumber.

With Gant gone, his sexuality had undergone a sort of shift even he wasn't comfortable with. He had been steeling himself for so long to always be on the wrong side of things but then Gant left and made that an entirely moot point. Which is not to say he chose this other route: it chose him in a weird way— he was the one with zero power in this exchange, and he often wished he had more.

Every time after he finished, Arla would stand up, put on her clothes, trace the edges of the windowsill, and jump out of it. This was by far Leo's least favorite part of her visits: she looked so real that every time she leapt out his heart leapt after her. But he eventually trained himself to steel against that too.

The last time she visited he asked her if he was the Antichrist.

She looked blankly at him for a few seconds.

You've done it now bucko.

She eventually let out a large breath and told him that that would be an enormous insult to Jesus.

—How so? asked Leo

—No offense, but if you're what God's up against it would uh not be a very fair fight…

Daaaaammnn.

—Isn't that the point of God though? Never a fair fight because it's the King of the Universe and all that?

—Both your cosmology and your Christology could use some tweaking.

—I've just heard it said that the fight you're talking about wouldn't be fair anyway.

—You're not evil, and all fights worth anything are fair fights.

Then she took a breath – or a ghost-breath – and told Leo that she wasn't comfortable with him calling her a prostitute.

—But that's what you are, stammered Leo.

—Yes, she let out, —but in the future, we will be called *sex workers.*

Leo mouthed the words "sex workers" for a few seconds before deciding that he liked the sound of that. And then he told Arla that he enjoyed it as a term.

—That's great, because I'm not the one thinking it – you are.

—What?

—I am a projection from your imagination. You already knew the term…

Leo decided she was right and they completed their ritual and she jumped out the window again, causing Leo's heart to skip a beat and then fall into the waters of his mind like a skipped pebble.

The tiles proliferated until the only thing left was a white splotch in Leo's mind.

Mr. Livery would come up to the door every morning and evening with food and water, but every time he did he would include a note. The fortieth note read something like this:

A TIME SPENT APART FROM GOD IS NECESSARY FOR THE CORRECT EDUCATION, SO TREAT THIS LIKE YOUR EDUCATION. WE'RE ALL ROOTING FOR YOU AND BELIEVE IN WHAT YOU CAN ACHIEVE.

Leo took the note, put them with the other thirty-nine, and watched the dusk filter through the trees and in through the windowsill, which Arla hadn't leapt out of in over a week now, or maybe well over a week—it was hard for him to tell anymore. There was no reason for him to imagine anything anymore anyway. He just stayed the course of his imagination and his mind followed suit. If there was something to see in the distance, he ignored it; if fruit fell off trees, he paid no mind; if Livery talked to him about theology, he tuned it out.

—Now, boy, Dr. Eaves and I have been discussing the terms of your confinement, and we've both decided you're halfway through it. You're so close to being complete it's almost tantalizing I'm sure, but you shouldn't forget that you're still in our charge and that if you tie your bed sheets into a rope to climb down with, we will whip you for as long as that rope is … Actually, maybe just bring your bed sheets to me, sorry. I would close the window if I were you—if it gets drafty that is.

Leo lifted a heavy sigh out his window, went over to his bed, grabbed the sheets off it, and then siphoned the sheets through the slot in the door and to Mr. Livery, who grabbed them with a fervor so trenchant Leo lost his grip almost immediately.

—Now, boy, this is just a precaution, Livery said before patting his just-fed stomach.

—You two have so many precautions, exclaimed Leo before Livery told him to watch himself and very much before Leo checked his body to make sure a demon hadn't entered it while he was sleeping.

—We need to ask you some questions about Agatha.

—What about her?

—Have you found her to be very influential in your dreams?

—What?

—Has she ever mixed potions into her libations?

—No?

—Does she carry around a medium of some sort, like a broom or a rake?-

—Okay, now that's just uncalled for! She is a very good friend of mine, and we both would know by now if she were a witch.

—Some witches hide their true demonic potential…

—Well she wouldn't hide that from me is what I'm saying.

—Wait. Why wouldn't she hide it from you?

—Because she trusts me implicitly.

—Because you're a satanic force as well?

—No, because I'm her friend.

Livery folded his hands in his lap and rested his head against the door.

Leo went up to the door to speak more clearly with Mr. Livery.

—Mr. Livery, please. If she were a witch you and I both know we wouldn't even be having this discussion. If she were a witch, the cards would be on the table and her hand would be dealt and it would be a deadly hand.

—Recusancy is a strange thing, Leo, said Livery. —I refuse to read the Book of Common Prayer in our teacher meetings—i.e. I don't go to the meetings, and I get castigated for it endlessly. Sometimes I wonder if they think *I'm* a witch.

Leo wasn't about to argue with this man about the semantics of demonic orders (even though he literally couldn't be a witch), but he did find it necessary to say the following:

—I think it's brilliant that you're recusing yourself. If I had a nickel for every time someone didn't have that kind of spine, I'd be— Hey, wait … this is a Catholic school, why on God's green earth would there be a Book of Common Prayer meeting?

—Oh, nobody told you? Livery said. —That's a front. This is a Church of England school. We have big plans for you, he said as he got up from his chair, laughed, and left.

Leo muttered himself to sleep that night.

Dr. Eaves rapped on the door so hard Leo woke with a start, a start that toppled him off the bed and face down on the floor, crushing his morning wood painfully.

Eaves asked if he wanted to see Aggie.

—Sweet God yes, said Leo as he planked the floor and then got to his feet.

—Hallo Leo, said a familiar voice.

Aggie put her eye to the food slot and then winked and put a finger through. Leo grabbed the finger with an entire hand and pulled slightly.

—Owwww, cooed Aggie.

—That's what you get for being a witch, Leo said sarcastically before realizing what he'd said. —No no no, I didn't mean *that* Dr. Eaves, I was just being sarcastic because of Mr. Livery's accusations against Aggie, I didn't mean it, honest.

Dr. Eaves laughed. —We already think she is one. Nothing you can do can change our minds on that one. We just wanted to see if you could mount a defense for your friend.

—What?! shouted Aggie. —I thought I was just visiting…

—And Mr. Livery and I just thought you were a witch. Funny how thoughts work.

—You can't do this, Leo shot back. —When I'm in power, you won't hear the end of it.

—You already know our plan? asked Dr. Eaves, genuinely surprised.

—When I'm pope, I will have you castrated.

—If we make you become pope, you won't have that option.

—Why are you doing this?

—God wants you to suffer for your salvation, we don't. God wins, we don't. Simple as that.

Dr. Eaves grabbed Aggie by the arm and led her away as he screamed a recitation from the Book of Common Prayer down the hall. Leo asked where he was taking Aggie.

—To the Tower of London of course! Eaves screamed back. —She will be our scapegoat!

Blintz was a large boy with a tightly worn crew cut and navy suspenders that went with his always-polished high-top shoes. On his off days he would scour the town near the school looking for books on the Church of England. On his on days he would be a paid bully to the other students of Wensley. Out of all the students, he was the only one who actually knew that Wensley was a Church of England inside job into the highest Catholic ranks. He'd settled a long time ago on not being their Chosen One (he knew it would be Leo as soon as the latter arrived at the school), so he'd made it his mission to get the most out of his transactions with the school, using his fists instead of Gant's precious fountain pens.

The school paid him well enough for him to have his town escapades, and this July he knew the escapades would be his most important, so he attended every artisan meeting or trade agreement or would perhaps even visit a workers' rally. The bullies he'd made "friends" with were not up to his speed, and he enjoyed seeing what the town had to offer him anyway, if anything.

He pressed his lips into teeth so often, so hard, and so thoroughly that blood would creep down the corners of his mouth and onto his chin, creating little divots that weren't quite dimples but couldn't be called anything else very politely. The teachers would nod to him—as they knew his role in the conspiracy—but then would immediately skirt around his menacing figure and go upon their usual walks. This happened even in town.

One day that July of 1808, he met with Dr. Eaves at a local tavern.

—He's in his room still, imprisoned. He doesn't know what's about to happen.

—Good, said Blintz. —Did you hand Aggie off to the London authorities?

—Yes, finally. They've really taken a shine to us recently. We've risen in their ranks so far we may not even need this Catholic façade.

—Don't say that, Blintz said, wiping some blood off his lips. —We need it for the papacy issue; you know that. We need it for the Napoleon issue; you know that as well. It doesn't matter what you believe, what matters is how you act; you should know that better than anyone.

Dr. Eaves smiled; the boy was right of course. Eaves loudly clanked his glass against Blintz's.

Blintz smiled but then switched his expression and whispered, —Your lack of temperance is giving you away. You need to be more careful; you're a public figure in this town.

—What about you, young man?

—It doesn't matter what I do. Nobody's expecting anything from me.

—We have big plans for you.

—Jesus. At least I know what the plans are. More than I can say for Leo.

—You'll see why we chose Leo in due time. Maybe you two should have a chat soon.

—That's a good idea. I'll do just that, said Blintz, downing the rest of the ale and paying and then looking at Dr. Eaves with a strange intensity, hopping off the bar stool, and trotting to the exit.

Leo was bouncing a ball he'd found the day before against the wall opposite from his bed. Now that the bed had no sheets, he could maneuver around it to catch the ball better anyway, and he was taking his new ball out for a spin.

As soon as he'd caught the ball against the wall exactly one time, Leo heard a knock on his bedroom door, the only door, the only way out now. He heard a voice too, a voice he didn't recognize explicitly but somehow knew implicitly; it sounded like the quiet before a death.

Blintz put his bloodied lips through the food slot, and a little blood came trickling down either side of the slot, inching their ways towards the floorboards.

—That's pretty gross, uh … Wait, what's your name?

—Blintz, the bleeding lips replied from inside the food slot. Despite Leo's discomfort, he had to be impressed with the way the lips were still able to perfectly form a name. It wasn't the act of disembodiment that Leo admired, just the way in which it was carried out.

The lips continued. —We've heard you are the Chosen One for Dr. Eaves, for Wensley, for capital-R Religion.

—I see no point in qualifying it.

—You qualify it by being born.

—I don't see how that correlates.

—Your existence was not a guarantee. We're making it one, Dr. Eaves and I.

—What about Mr. Livery?

—Mr. Livery is of no use to us. We will dispose of him when this job is finished.

Leo thought about this for a while, or what seemed to be a while: Livery was one of the kinder teachers here—or at least approximated any sort of ideal of kindness better than the others. So Leo didn't like the idea of him being disposed of, whatever that meant. Although Leo reasoned that if it meant Livery being sent away from the school that would be a fine option, or at least much better than a physical death.

—Leo, we need to have a talk, said the lips. —Ever since you've come to Wensley, you've displayed a keen knack for both a ne'er do well attitude and a certain intelligence, something Religion is lacking at the moment. Sure, we have our executions—we have our claims to vicious fame—but we're losing ground to secularism by the day. The Enlightenment and its revolutions brought in so much ancient learning the scholastics had hidden—one wishes the monks had tried harder!—that there really can be no recovery unless we somehow show the world that us men of Christendom can play by the same rules. Or at least that we own the rules... [The lips take a bit of a break for the tongue to wipe the blood off and scoop it back inside the squashed mouth.] *We* need to show everybody that Religion can play by the same rules Napoleon is playing by, that Christendom will not lose its hold on the populace, no matter how much ground Napoleon gains in his secular conquest and no matter how much our religions differ. In fact, as the next Pope, you will help usher in a new era of religious syncretism, which we can discuss later if you wish.

—How on earth can we discuss this later? laughed Leo. —It's not like I can take your lips with me.

—Actually, said the lips, you can.

And with that, Blintz slid some scissors underneath the door and then pressed his face fully against the door, his nose squashed, so that his lips fully protruded through the food slot.

Leo was aghast and swiped his hand through his brown hair. —I'm not cutting off your lips.

—You must if you want to become pope.

—I'm not cutting off your lips, Leo said more firmly.

—You must if you want to learn what happened to your family.

Leo went pale. —What in God's name did you do?

—I'm not saying if you don't cut.

Leo sighed heavily, bent down, and scooped the scissors up from the floor. He made a comment about Blintz not being able to adequately brace himself for the pain this will cause him.

—I don't feel pain.

—Well that's convenient, said Leo.

Leo broke the scissors into two halves, took one half, and placed it right against the door as he pulled the lips as far as he could with his free hand, eventually moving the door-adjacent scissor-half down the length of the lips, sawing so slowly the blood was pouring onto his face in spurts before eventually sawing faster and faster as he went down the line.

When he was finished, the lips went into formation as if they had never left Blintz's face. Leo could hear Blintz's footsteps fade down the distant hallway as the lips started talking to him.

—We took care of your family.

—What does that mean?

—Your family is dead, Leo.

Leo dropped the lips and started weeping immediately; he didn't need proof to know that what the lips were telling him was the truth.

Goodbye Leo.

He sobbed and said goodbye to Liza, but he knew he couldn't get her to say goodbye to his parents; he knew his parents were already dead and there was no point in getting Liza's last thoughts to be attached to his own at this time. She deserved her own thoughts right now, Leo thought.

9.

Ailen went out the door to greet Anna and Liza, his arms extended like a desperate penitent. Anna rushed into them first, with Liza quickly following, the both of them squished between Ailen's workmen arms so tightly they felt briefly constricted but happy.

—Ailen, Anna said, where on God's earth did you get the idea to run this operation.

Ailen fumbled about for a few seconds before Bernard came up behind him, rubbed his hair, and said, —That'd be my idea now.

—Whatever he says, said Ailen, backing away from Bernard's embrace and in the process breaking free from the embrace of all three.

—I didn't mean to cause anything, said a demurring Ailen.

—Did he do anything Anna? Liza?

—Not a thing, said Anna.

—I should think not, replied Liza.

—Good, then it's settled. What isn't settled is the order of tonight's business. Do we have the ale before or after dinner? Or with dinner? Or a toast during perhaps?

—The last two, shouted Ailen.

—Our God is good, and you sir are correct, said Bernard.

—Dear! Anna said. —When did you become religious?

—Since the both of you left for London of course; it's the only natural thing left for a man of my position and in my predicament to do.

—Well good thing it's no longer your predicament, said Liza, perhaps forcing her hand a little too much, as Bernard and then Anna gave her stern looks.

—No no. I'm still religious now, it's just tempered, as temperance is always good. Fervently religious youngster turns to apathetic adult and that in due time turns to measured religiosity. Maybe someday you'll discover it for yourself, Liza.

Liza spat and said she doubted it before Anna slapped her across the face.

Liza gripped her face and looked at Ailen, who was looking down.

Bernard looked disapprovingly at Anna, who was then ashamed of it all.

Ailen measured his steps back into the house, and everyone else followed, embarrassed to no end that they'd made this man's day worse, as he was the guest of honor.

Ailen opened the door to a waft of stew-fog, and Liza clapped with joy while Anna still looked downcast. Bernard shot to the table, setting it and making sure everything was in place for their supper. As they each sat down at the table, it was not hard to see that everyone was feeling the cumulative effects of the awkward moment earlier. It began its descent like the stew-fog, and, like the stew-fog, dissipated with equal measure and in equal proportion, until everybody at the table eventually just collectively decided to drop it.

—Could you pass the salt? Liza asked Ailen before also asking him about how he feels about the transition of him taking over the land and the other three moving to London.

—It's a weird proposition that, yeah. It is. … I was here thinking to myself that I would retire early maybe and tend the farm I've come to make of my imagination. Now that won't happen, but my mind's never been happier. In fact, it's never been better. [He got the saltshaker back from Liza here.] I can lie down at night and let my mind wander responsibly wherever it wants, it just sitting there with nothing to do unlike the rest of the day of course. And then I think to myself, of course, that another day of work won't do me any ill, wouldn't hurt me beyond how I can be hurt. And then I finally just go to sleep. … It's a good process.

—That's beautiful, Ailen, said Anna, tearing up.

—Not as beautiful as that thunder rolling in the distance, said Bernard, lying back in his chair and almost falling over in the process.

—We're only missing our dear Leo, Liza replied.

—We tried to visit him at Wensley, but they said he was desperately sick and the nurses said it wasn't good for us to see him right now, said Liza before bolting upright, —I know! We'll surprise him on our way to London, maybe take him out on the town, see the big city lights hit the fog just right, down there where the ground is uneven but venerated, every step a journey, every place full of potentiality. That's where I want to go.

—That's where we'll go, shouted Anna.

And with that a cannonball blasted into the wood frame of the house and through to the other side, leaving the opposite side of the house's frame in a series of tatters, only to be broken further by other falling wooded beam tatters.

All four of them ducked under the table until the table too was hit by a cannonball, splitting it in half and tossing both halves to their respective sides of the house. The four of them looked up from the cover of the arms that were shielding their faces from errant shards, and then darted for the storm cellar out back.

Liza went first, and when she came to the outside of the house she stopped in her tracks so hard she almost fell forward. In front of the back of the house—and to all sides—was a cannon stationed with a row of Frenchmen in full military regalia, with bayonets to their sides and stationed, their arms nestling guns to their sides, still.

A man was approaching, and all Liza saw—as the man's largely adorned hat faded slowly into view—were the cannons going off in the direction of the door her parents had just left. She jolted back with the cannon shot and saw the cannonballs surge holes into Anna and Bernard just as a falling wooden plank knocked Ailen unconscious and lying still on the floor. Liza didn't have time to look back at what her parents looked like post-cannonball— because she had completely turned. And just as she could see the man's face come into view, she bolted open the cellar door, entered, and shut it behind her.

Napoleon walked down the hill and regarded the two dead and one unconscious person with a form of contempt and pity that were so close in the mind they intermingled one with the other without becoming a confusing construct. Then he looked at the cellar door, pressed against its locked doors, and motioned for one of the cannons to be rolled down the hill and pointed directly at the cellar doors.

Then he thought better of it and gave the signal to stop the cannon's advance. The artilleryman was confused, and for some reason dropped his weapon. As he was picking it up, he felt a boot on top of his head. Napoleon pressed the man's head into the ground with his boot, letting the peat seep into his sockets and almost until the boot greeted the ground as well.

Napoleon's boot left the side of the man's face and stepped on the ground beside it.

He told the man to get up, letting him know that their time there was done, that there would be no more death that day, that Liza was necessary and that the unconscious man was unimportant.

They left Ailen's unconscious body, the dead Anna and Bernard, and the enclosed Liza unattended for by their world-beating aims.

Liza woke up on the steps of the cellar and then unlocked the doors. She staggered over to her parents first, not because she was injured but because she was in mourning. She clasped her father's hand and kissed a ring he had in his pocket, fitting it on her finger before throwing it down onto his corpse in disgust with herself—before putting it back on her finger and swearing to herself about something she felt in her bones that she could not tell Leo about—swearing about fealty to a revolution that didn't include Napoleon *or* Religion. She kissed her mother's face and closed her mother's eyes with her outstretched palm. Liza took her mother's necklace and made the same commitment as before but it became somehow different. It was now felt deeply within her bones, felt down to a marrow she'd never fully felt before.

She then tripped over the fallen wooden planks on her way to unburying Ailen from his predicament. He was muttering curses in Gaelic until she removed the planks from above his broken legs.

—Are both broken? Liza asked him.

—Let's find out, said Ailen, feigning optimism.

Ailen tried standing but fell down in a heap immediately before sobbing and dragging himself over to Anna and Bernard's corpses. While he wept into the shoulders of Leo and Liza's parents, Liza was tending to his wounds, bandaging them with materials from the cellar. She wound the bandage around the affected area until it was tight and wrapped enough to cut, which she did with scissors the cellar had provided as well. She said he was good as new and he glared at her briefly before laughing heartily—saying that thanks to her he might as well be.

—There is good news, though, said Liza. —Only one of your legs is broken.

—That's the best news I've had all day, replied Ailen.

She fashioned crutches out of the planks on the ground using the scissors. It took all night, but by daybreak she had a good-as-new pair of crutches for Ailen to use on their journey to the carriage station.

It was noon when they reached it, and Ailen hammered on the ticket seller's window with his new crutches. The man appeared briefly before disappearing again and coming round the other side of the booth.

He asked where they were headed and they said Wensley, and he said they could leave immediately; he would just need to wait for the proper coachmen for their journey. They waited an hour before a heavy-set boy with curiously glassy-looking lips ushered them into the coach car. He bit his lips profusely—feeling their glassy exterior—as he introduced himself, and both Liza and Ailen seemed slightly wary of him.

—You'll be there in no time. In fact, you may find that time itself will become nothing in the face of the setting—it will all drift into one blur—and you will find your family member, said the coachmen.

—We hadn't told you about any family members, said Liza, scoffing.

—Are you not Liza Lightbody? asked the humble coachman.

—I am, but how did you know that? asked a scared Liza.

—It's on your ticket, madam.

—Right, but how would you know about Leo?

—My name is Blintz, and I'm a peer of your brother's, or, was at least.

Liza went pale; she hadn't heard Leo's thoughts in so long she could no longer tell if he was alive or not; so Blintz might be right.

—You can't mean...

—Oh he's dead, Blintz said coolly but with the deference of his newly inherited cabbie role.

—Well, take us to him, said Liza promptly.

—Well, about that, said Blintz. —His dying wish was to never see you four—he'd said there'd be four—ever again. I think it would be foolish not to grant it, don't you think?

Liza said that was impossible, doubting the words even as she was saying them.

Ailen asked if they could be let out and that if the boy didn't stop this carriage instantly then he'd resort to violence.

Blintz asked how on earth he would do that from his station in the carriage, and Ailen reached through the fore slot in the carriage to grab the scruff of Blintz's collar and drag him towards the slot, Blintz's breathing cut off by the lack of circulation in his larynx from his collar—his face turned purple and then blue, with his lips remaining the same bluish white. He threw his arms up in the air and flailed them about, letting go of the reins, causing the carriage to crash into the wooded glen the road was adjacent to.

The three of them all got up in a heap. The pacifist Ailen had no rifle to shoot Blintz with. But he didn't have time to fight Blintz anyway, as the latter took one of the two horses and that horse took no time in sprinting away.

—Oh, and, by the way, just a note, you're halfway to London, said Blintz—the two shouted syllables of the city name stretching out the length of a city.

When Blintz was gone, Liza calmed the other horse down for a bit before helping Ailen onto it. She gripped the opposite side of the horse from her side and then hoisted herself onto the creature, all the while holding onto the deadweighted but strangely precarious Ailen.

They talked all the way to London, about how things turn for the worse; about how much they missed Anna and Bernard, about the future and what inheritance means. They pontificated about the stars and whether cosmology meant anything, whether phrenology was really all that it was cracked up to be. They mentioned religion in passing, but gave it no thought. The only thing they thought about was the wind crunching their dirty hair in a breeze they were making, and they also thought about wishing that last clause was true. As it was, they missed their family; Liza couldn't connect with Leo; and both their parents were dead. Liza's mind hardened independent of her will that night, and when they got to London, she'd been thoroughly sent in the opposite direction of monarchies, popes, and orders—a direction that looked like freedom to her and one that Ailen would have been proud of had he known what his companion was thinking, what was brewing in her mind. Liza thought it would have looked like freedom to her parents—and to Leo too—but now that everyone was dead her mind had absolutely nothing to lose in the process.

10.

Leo was let out of his room on the first day of August. The sun shone on him and reflected off the leaves of the surrounding forest and back onto him again. He rubbed his eyes a few times before taking the lips out of his pocket and examining them closely.

—What the hell are you doing? they asked.

—Getting a closer look. Hold still.

Leo noticed they were no longer bloody, as the blood had dried up into a festering wound he would have to treat later. For some reason he felt responsible for these lips—not deathly responsible, just enough to make him reconsider whatever grudge he'd held against their previous bearer.

—I'll take you to them, said the lips.

Leo grabbed a spare horse from the school's stable—the school wouldn't need it—and rode it all day and into the clearing where his parents' graves were marked with two upstanding planks. He sobbed because he couldn't see them, and then he cried because he could just make out their graves. He was seeing everything finally, and the lips, which had been placed on the cellar doors, remained silent and after an hour whistled a Gaelic tune, something Leo felt both cruel and consoling.

Leo asked the lips who did this, and the lips didn't answer because Leo already knew it was Napoleon. If he could have named what next to do he would have done it. As it was he just stood there motionless with the lips in his hands silently whistling a tune that had left Leo's mind a long time ago. There was nothing he could do for his family, except become whatever opposite of Napoleon Dr. Eaves could give him the power to be. To choose power at this juncture didn't seem like a victimed crime—it seemed like justice. And thinking he really couldn't bear what was happening was never an option for him. The only option remaining flittered into the wind with the no-longer-present cannon smoke: to go quietly against his parents' teachings.

Leo wondered how much better it could get than being the Pope and lording it over everyone via a religious coup—leading eventually and hopefully to a real coup against the greatest general the world had seen since Alexander. He thought to himself for one of the first times in his life and it tasted like the freedom of a free thought without any interference from others. The musings he'd had about whether or not his twin sister was safe was in that instant replaced with an insatiable desire to know everything, to be the keeper of whatever knowledge he could muster within himself after amassing. Nobody ever questions the greatest, he thought to himself—and if this was what that took, then how could he join? He would rise in the ranks of the papacy via a Church of England subplot and tower above both realms equally after it was all said and done. He knew the papacy had no scruples in where its papal candidates were selected, as long as they adhered to Catholicism, as it's known far and wide. The family stuff—the lineages, the ceremonious nature of it all, the rings—he knew that was all ancillary to the fact of a matter the church itself held very close to its chest. Other people knew, people like Dr. Eaves, and more people knew now and he was now included in the club. He was just edging towards the precipice of full club inclusion, and all he had to do was jump.

Leo sighed and picked up the lips, putting them next to his ears while he looked at the graves of his parents, watching the day fade as their tissues faded and as his attention span was fading into the deep lullaby pressed against his ear like an early rapture.

The lips purred a bit, solemnly and out of tune.

<u>**Part Three: Papacy (1810–1811)**</u> – a romance

1.

Ailen didn't know why he took it on faith that his godson was deceased, but that evil kid Blintz looked so satisfied at Leo's death that Ailen just assumed it to be true. The road past the hotel Ailen and Liza were staying at briefly—just the night—looked like death in either direction: murky, foggy, clouded with the superstition the world was still trying to rid itself of slowly.

Ailen stopped at a corner just as a carriage was making its way down the adjacent promenade. Opposite him was a park, and he waited for the carriage to pass before making his way across the street and wading in the verdant—but summertime—greenery. The park looked as all parks do right dead in the summer—that is, clinging to some kind of life just at the moment it is losing almost all of it, the parts of its flowery past awash in the sunlight that pierced both its appearance and its foundation. And even though it was night in that moment, it still looked fake how quickly spring turned to June and vice versa.

Two o'clock hit Ailen with the force of a newly renovated cathedral, his sides aching not from the walk but from hunger. Maybe he was the cathedral, thought Ailen. Maybe the upcoming drink would just serve as the lacquer to clean the insides of himself, all the better for him to carry out his mission upon this earth. He wasn't sure what it was, though, so he walked into a bar.

The bar smelled like fresh catches and less-than-fresh people, like food that would enter and leave in the same state and people who would enter and leave your life in the same state. Ailen sat down at the bar, the back of his head almost ringing from the hubbub behind him. After screaming for a good minute at a turned-around bartender, Ailen finally got his attention and yelled at him about the day's current events.

—HAVE YOU HEARD THE ONE ABOUT THE POPE?

—ARE YOU TELLING A JOKE?

—NO, BUT I CAN.

—WHAT DO YOU CALL A POPE WITHOUT A PAPACY?

—NAPOLEON.

—Shite, that was it.

—WHAT?

—I SAID "SHITE, THAT WAS IT."

—I'M GOOD AT THOSE, DO ANOTHER.

—WHAT DO YOU CALL SOMEONE WHO ROBS YOU OF EVERYTHING?

—I HAVE NO IDEA FOR THAT ONE.

—A FINAL REMARK.

The bartender looked at Ailen quizzically before turning around again and before the people making noise behind them slammed money on the counter (one by one) and stumbled out of the door. After they left, Ailen asked the bartender what he thought of Napoleon, and got such a negative response from the other person that Ailen just dropped it then and there, even though the man had guessed his Napoleonic riddle quite accurately.

The military rifles and regalia decorating and lining the walls heightened the nationalist atmosphere of the bar. When there wasn't a bottle, there were guns; and vice versa. All Ailen had to do was point in any direction except the ceiling and the floor, and he would've been pointing at either a bottle or a gun, both of which seemed to be pointing at him regardless of his circumstances anyway. He soon forgot the bartender in his reverie, and didn't hear the following remark.

—It looks like you're alone, the bartender said.

Ailen snapped out of it long enough to register the comment and turn around to face the man for what seemed to be the first time—the first true time certainly, the first physical time perhaps not.

—Excuse me, sir? Ailen shot back.

The man had two adjacent scars on either side of his face, almost meeting at the bottom-side center point of his chin, but neither scar quite making the cut.

—I said it looks like you're alone. Why are you alone?

—We're all alone at birth and death; I'm just trying to cut out the middleman.

—So *you're* the middleman. I've been looking for you.

Ailen sighed. —I guess if you want to put it like that, then I am.

—So what's it like being a Middle Man?

—Just about the same as everything else I suppose.

Ailen looked around the bar for a brief second: it was deserted except for the two of them, one lanky fellow with an uncharacteristically hardened face replete with adjacent scars, and then Ailen himself, short and stocky and farm-built for labor. If this were a hundred years in the future, they would have made a good silent-film comedy duo.

—Did you hear about the pontiff, mate? asked the man.

—What's your name? asked Ailen.

—Ruker, said the man slowly. —The pontiff?

—What about him?

—Did you hear about the assembly?

—It's a fiking religious order, they don't have assemblies.

—God above, sorry, I meant the council, the ouster, the scandal, said Ruker.

—No, Ailen replied. —I've been outta the loop I'm afraid.

Ruker wasted no time. —Apparently, the old Pope has been forced out for kowtowing to Napoleon's rule. Pius VII. He was at his coronation after all.

—That makes no sense, replied Ailen. —Wouldn't Napoleon have a vested interest in keeping Pius on board as a puppet?

Ruker shrugged. —I think Napoleon just thought he was weak. I don't think Napoleon can tolerate the weak.

Ailen plunked some money on the bar counter and got up to walk out, but Ruker pinned his hand down onto the bar before asking if there was anything Ailen needed to confess to.

—I confess I don't really want to have this conversation.

—Why not?

—Because it's going to end badly for you.

Just then Ruker felt a cool metal circle grazing his left pectoral muscle; Ailen held the musket there for a minute before asking

Ruker to let go of his hand—which he did—and before dropping it down to his side again.

—The papacy is just beginning, said Ruker as Ailen opened the door to the Duke's Head and then slammed it behind him, leaving the scarred man to collect the tab and reflect on riddles and pontiffs on his own.

The lobby of the hotel Ailen and Liza were staying in was cold, and leaving for quick intervals made the switch from the heat of outside to the cold of inside almost unbearable. It was a disruption of some sort of body temperature equilibrium, one which Liza found insufferable as she reentered the doors after a short walk to the nearby park.

In the park Liza had seen several foxes, but one stood out. It was a grey animal, almost looking like it'd just been covered by the ash and soot of a nearby factory, the grey sticking to the creature rather than being a natural offshoot or characteristic of the creature itself, like an addendum to a fascinating but ultimately impenetrable book.

Between the copse and grasses of varied hues between green and brown, the grey fox stared at her from a distance of about two yards. The fox shook its hide and the dust and ash and soot fell off in a cloud of motes and particles. Liza felt a shudder and retreated mentally to a bench that was between her and the fox. That the place of retreat should be nearer the strange animal was none of her business, and she treated the incident like one of many, one in a long line of bizarre happenings recently.

So she went and sat over on the bench, plucking wisteria off with one hand and beckoning the creature forward with her other hand. The fox looked back at his fleeing compatriots and then looked back at her before slowly making his way under the human's outstretched hand. Liza removed her hand from his fur; her hand became covered in black, pre-tar soot. She wiped her hand off on her white dress instinctually before realizing what this would mean.

As it turned out, it meant nothing because the soot had fused with the molecules in her hand, siphoning down into her bloodstream and giving her a head rush before she even set her hand upon her dress. When she lifted her hand from the cloth, neither her hand nor her dress bore any trace of filth, ruin, decaying minerals.

The fox heard a cry from one of the other foxes under his charge—one of those not with his markings—and followed the cry into the nearby streets, the fog eventually covering him even after making his markings disappear and his body appear to be nothing more than a waving shroud in the distance.

As soon as the fox's appearance left in the fog-smoke, another one appeared but in the shape of a man. Liza knew before the fog uncovered the man that it was her father, and she waved her arms in anticipation, not of her impending flight to the heavens at the briefly waited for reunion, but to signal to him that she was here (there) and safe.

The scars on the man's face appeared first, as he walked with a significant forward hunch. He muttered to himself about the park not being safe for girls to be out and about in, but he didn't seem to realize that he was the biggest threat she'd faced that night—or would face really, she thought. He shuffled a bit and kicked the copse littering the geometrically aligned park grounds before asking her why she was out on the town this late.

—This is a city, sir, said Liza slowly. —And as far as me being out late, what did you have in mind that it should be such an issue?

—I mean, nothing, I just, I just thought that you would be scared, would have been scared. … Because of my scars.

—Scars don't bother me, and neither does your abhorrent posture, smiled Liza.

—Will you work for me? As a bartender? At the Duke's Head?

Liza reflected for a moment. She needed to support her studies somehow—not financially but for soul reasons, or character, or something amounting to the same thing—and this might be her best bet, or ticket, her best bet on a ticket or ticket on a bet.

They shook hands, and Ruker left Liza alone in the park without saying his name. Liza thought this was a bad sign until Ailen showed up approximately one minute later to reprimand her for being in the park alone.

—Liza, you shouldn't be alone in this part of town.

—Ailen you left me, so why does it matter?

—Because it's dangerous here at night, that's why. You can't go fiking walking around all by yourself; it leads to trouble.

—I got a job, replied Liza.

—Oh God, from who?

—A nice gentleman with parallel scars on his face.

—I forbid it! Ailen said suddenly. —Your parents would not want you hanging out with such riffraff!

Ailen didn't mention that he'd held this gentleman at musket-point, but he didn't think it was important enough to disclose. Either that or he didn't want to risk the embarrassment of revealing that he'd held her new employer at musket-point.

—What will you do about school?

—I'll just not go and work there and get myself ready for Oxford.

Ailen didn't want to immediately give this plan his blessing, so he sat down on a bench and began counting leaves. As soon as he realized the impossibility of this task (three seconds), he began to try to identify the types of plants in the garden. He'd gotten three right and one wrong before Liza interrupted his reverie.

—Wait, have you met this man?

—Who, me? Ailen replied innocently. —I believe I went into his bar, but we didn't talk to each other. From what he was saying to other customers there, I could tell he was informed about current events, though.

He added, with hesitation, —Maybe you should work there after all.

Liza smiled. —I think I will, Ailen. I think I just might.

2.

Leo woke up and saw Adam's finger trying to make contact with God's finger, and like there was a spark or something between the fingers, a light effusing between and then through the distance between. He put his hands on the ground and faced the lacquered wood paneling so crisp he could almost see his reflection in it. He gave up the effort, however, and again fell onto his back looking up at Michelangelo's Sistine Chapel paintings, those hallowed panels he'd somehow never heard of but was experiencing for the first time nonetheless.

His shoulder ached. He grasped at it blindly and felt an extremely large lump, and, fearing a tumorous growth, he screamed aloud at the thought and then at the fear, both of which reverberated from the echoes of his yell inside the chapel.

—It's not a tumor, said the lips.

Leo lifted up his shirt and discovered that Blintz's lips had been fused to the skin on his shoulder, to where it really did look like his shoulder had a talking tumor. The top lip moved along with the bottom lip and gave the ensemble the appearance of someone speaking past his shoulder but lovingly grazing his shoulder at the same time with his bottom lip, like a particularly pernicious confidante.

—How long have you been there? asked Leo.

—What, fused?

—Yes, fused.

—Oh, you know, during the locomotive rides here, connected by carriage, you knocked clean out in a borderline coma from seeing what Napoleon did to your family. It takes a long time to heal from all of that.

—I don't think I'm quite there yet, replied Leo bitterly. —I would appreciate it if you wouldn't bring it up.

—What else am I here for though? the lips smacked back.

—Good question: I have no idea why you're here.

—I'm here to help you *see*, Leo, said the lips.

—But you just talk, replied Leo.

—Ah yes, but right now there's no difference.

—Right now?

—Right. Currently there's someone approaching. Now.

And sure enough, Leo craned his neck backward and saw two familiar legs from a somehow even darker time and a somehow even worse place.

—Hello, dear one, said Dr. Eaves more menacingly than he meant to. Old habits die hard.

Leo looked up at him, but—because Eaves had half of an erection going right now—he just saw the left and right folds of his cardinal's tunic.

—New threads? asked Leo, realizing he was doing it again, what his parents had warned him about.

—Yes, said an Eaves caught off guard, —these are made with the finest threads on the continent. One day you might wear one, he added smiling.

—Is that just, like, your refrain? asked Leo.

—I don't recite poetry, scoffed Eaves.

—We all do, replied Leo. —Some of it is just really bad. If you don't know you're doing it, you must be a pretty bad poet.

—I'm somehow fine with that.

—Is God though?

Eaves smiled. —God knows my limitations.

Leo stood up, looked down at Dr. Eaves' declining erection on the way to his feet, and replied, —Quite.

—Let's get you further into the Vatican City, said Eaves eagerly. —Let's lessen your own limitations.

Leo walked behind Eaves through labyrinthine corridors, each door leading inexorably to the next chamber and inexorably past the next door, until it all became so exhaustive that Leo asked for a rest inside one of the antechambers.

In that particular room were Egyptian statues surrounding a mummy sarcophagus. Leo reached out to touch the hunk of marble beneath the sarcophagus, but Eaves quickly swiped his hand away from it with a look of disgust.

—Have you no shame?

—Isn't that why I'm here?

—You're here to learn shame, not indulge in it.

—Ah, right, so indulging in something now means you don't have it? How does that square up?

—Because the lack leaves you wanting more, like Tantalus and his precious nearby fruits.

Leo went up to the mummy's face, staggering backwards from the look a previous Pope's eyes had given him.

—Ah yes, said Eaves. —Are you in awe of Pius' visage?

—It can't be Pius VII...

—Goodness no, it's his predecessor, Pius VI; he's buried in France but they made a death mask for him here … Look deep into the death mask's eyes and ask yourself how far this man was from an Egyptian ruler.

—I mean, said Leo, —you've made that pretty obvious.

—It was not my doing, young one. It was the doing of Pius VII. You'll meet him soon.

Leo took his finger and ran it along the eyes of the death mask, as if he were trying to shut them out of respect for the dead, for the chain that broke before he got onto the necklace. But then he realized the eyes were permanently open, as it was a death mask, and he sheepishly put his arm to his side as Blintz's lips castigated him for his imbecility.

As they were leaving that antechamber, Leo ran his fingers along the Egyptian gods' skirts like they were lampposts he was keeping track of to find his way home. Eaves looked back, cursed his sacrilege, and muttered to himself if this truly was the one who would save them, and the lips—who heard—hissed back that it was, that his behavior was part and parcel of it, and that he'd best keep his mouth shut if he wanted his doctorate to continue to mean anything.

The next room saw a skinnier man turn around when they entered. At first Leo thought his hunch was due to both the tri-cornered hat (which looked heavy) and the double-cross-medallion necklace (which also looked heavy), but he quickly realized that it was just his natural gait. Pius VII turned swiftly around every which way—while still moving forward—until his swaying form reached the young Leo.

—The young Leo in the flesh, he said. —By the time we see each other again you'll be a cardinal. Then, as I'm sure you've gathered by now, you'll be the pope. Does that sound good?

Leo didn't know what to say.

—I don't know what to say, Leo said as Pius VII's finger rushed up to the lips on his face.

—Shhh, the pope said, —you don't have to say anything.

—I believe the right word for this occasion is forthcoming, said the lips on Leo's shoulder.

—Right, said the pope, nonplussed by the extra speaker —He's the forthcoming pope.

—Everything is forthcoming, the lips replied cryptically.

The pope gestured around the antechamber and his sweeping hand stopped at a Rembrandt painting.

—Did you know Rembrandt was under our thumb?

—No, I didn't, replied an admiring Leo.

—That's because he wasn't, Pope Pius glowered. —Even then we were losing our grip on capital-A "Art", the art that meant something, the art you could look at with your two eyes and envision with your two hands inside a three-dimensional space. Now we have to settle for the occasional genius who happens to believe what we believe, and even those numbers will dwindle eventually, until all that's left is a nothingness art won't even recognize as religion and vice versa.

—I'm sure things will level out, offered Leo.

Pius VII looked at him sadly and said the only thing stopping secularism from taking over the arts too now that education, science, and reason had fallen under its spell was political power, imperialism, and social mores. The pope then predicted all these would give way to secularism as well, would be their own decreasing entities independent from the church.

—Secularism won't kill religion because it can't, because that's not its function, said Leo, realizing he was doing it again. —That will level out too.

Leo continued, —But it doesn't matter if what you're looking for is spiritual connection, not power.

The pope looked at Leo dead in Leo's face before doing a double take and then moving closer to Leo's face until their noses were almost touching.

—This is the kind of blasphemy we're trying to root out, not support. I hope you remember that when you become the pontiff. Because your say will matter more than mine.

Leo squirmed a bit before his second pair of lips spoke up to say that Leo will crush Napoleon to put the reins of power back in the church's hands, or that he will die trying.

—That's easy for you to say, muttered Leo.

—I'm now basically a parasite and you're my host and without you I would die at this point, so it's not easy for me to say. It's actually quite painful if we're being honest.

—I think we can both be honest independently, Leo replied.

Pius scoffed. —You can't be honest without a separation of yourself from your own values, and that is only gotten through religion. I think your friend [here he gestured towards Leo's shoulder] would agree with that.

—I agree only that once we take over … once Leo takes over, he will usher in reforms that would make it impossible to have the papacy go any other way than up. And by "up" I mean whatever will grant religion enough clemency politically to keep it going spiritually, to make everyone believe in a form of control that's further reaching than anyone would care to admit.

—And I think that's a noble goal, Pius VII rejoined, —but I also think we need to be careful what we're sending this young man into. He can't go blindly into the night of spiritual control and make it daybreak, as that is a paradox. We need to make absolutely sure he knows what he's doing.

Pius pointed at the shoulder-lump. —That is why I'm appointing *you* to be this young man's mentor and guide, spiritual and otherwise.

—I thought I already had that title, said both Dr. Eaves and the lump with differing tonalities.

The pope viciously turned around towards Eaves and slapped him clean across the face.

—How dare you question the authority of the papacy!

Eaves reacted unnaturally late to the slap and raised his hand into the air to block the no-longer-there open-faced palm.

—Do popes slap people? asked the lump.

—I didn't think so, replied Leo.

—They're not supposed to, said Eaves finally, massaging the side of his face and overdoing it in the process, hoping against hope that Pius VII would find any space in his heart for pity.

Pius shifted towards Leo before smiling mischievously and asking if he'd had the chance to see his predecessor Pope Pius VI.

—We greeted each other ceremoniously, Leo said, bristling with pride.

The pope peered at Leo's pupils and said that was impossible, unless there was something Leo wasn't telling them.

—I can't speak with the dead, Leo said eventually to both break up the awkward silence and cut him off.

Pius VII laughed and said that by the time they—meaning him and the lump-growth—were done with him, he would be able to. —In fact, by the time we're done with you, you will be able to raise people from the dead.

Leo's jaw dropped very far until he had to bring it back up to express his extreme skepticism regarding the claim.

—No, said the pope, —you won't even come close to that, that was Jesus and we can't replicate that—as much as we've tried. You will, however, be able to be closer to that than anyone else on the earth, so there's that.

Leo found this assertion cold comfort, didn't say that, and instead asked Pius why the papacy didn't reveal its secrets to its populace, the believers.

Pius cricked his neck twice on each side and then replied that not only would they not be able to handle it—that they alone had a special call—but that it would be extremely dangerous for everyone to have those kinds of powers without the proper training. —It would be chaos everywhere, lepers and prostitutes imbued with holy powers so that they can better swindle people and then dig themselves deeper into the pit of despair. Forget it. This is about what happens when someone achieves undue control—they squander it almost immediately. Sure, we disperse power among the holy delegation below the pope as well, but they have to answer to someone. Otherwise, the spirituality will become evenly dispersed among not only the population, but also among all the holy appointees.

—Dispersed yet localized power, said Leo. —Ingenious.

—We didn't come up with it, laughed Pius. —We just brought it out further.

Dr. Eaves asked if he should leave, and, after Pius said that that would be best, Pope Pius VII officially excommunicated Eaves by 1) saying he was in fact excommunicated, and then 2) aggressively pushing Eaves' left shoulder with his hand.

After recovering from the taunt, Eaves said—less evilly than he'd hoped, —I suppose now is a good time to let you know that I'm a plant from the Church of England.

—If you were a plant, you would have even less of a soul, according to Aristotle.

—Zing, said Leo as he was sent a witheringly confused gaze from each dignitary.

The pope continued, —Oh of course, I knew you were a plant, but you've brought us the boy and brought us closer to Napoleon, and you're no longer of any service to me or this city-state, or really of any service to God's kingdom, but I suppose that's for him to decide ultimately.

Guards came in and grabbed Dr. Eaves, who left kicking and screaming, saying the religious wars weren't over, that the pope would get his due, that Leo wasn't fit, etc., all of which Pius shrugged off like an oversized bathrobe.

—Good riddance, whispered Leo.

—Well, he brought you to *us,* said Pius VII.

Leo wasn't sure if he meant "us" as in him and the lump, him and the rest of the religious order, or the lump and the religious order, but his confusion left after Pius patted his lump affectionately: he'd meant the lump—it was a royal we.

3.

Aggie awoke to the feeling of cold stone, and to the feeling of the mud that stood between her face and the stone like the last rampart of an almost-besieged castle. Her arms and legs were chained to the wall, but she was close to the prison grate, so she was mildly satiated by that, in the sort of Stockholm syndrome way of lesser evils that only prisons can provide.

She looked at a rat swirling in the opposite corner of her balmy cell. Its legs twitched around all the places it wanted to go, and it looked so free, and Aggie just wanted to kill it immediately out of envy and spite. It scattered away through the grate, and Aggie watched it scurry off with narrowed eyes and red-hot hatred.

Aggie knew where she was, but that didn't make it any easier, what with London being a stone's throw away and her being stuck in its legendary Tower. For all its legendary status, though, it severely needed some upkeep; it looked as if a procession hadn't so much as set foot in the hallway she could see into, an observation that didn't bode well for the rest of the building. She was glad she got this cell, however, because it would make any visits she'd have much easier.

A thump resounded from down the hallway, followed by some cursing from a familiar voice.

Mr. Livery protruded his portly belly and looked at what he had there: a fifteen-year-old girl. Livery peered into Aggie's cell.

—What's gotten into you? he smiled. —Or, should I say, what have you gotten into?

—I believe I'm in the Tower of London, she replied.

—Yes, I'm afraid you are. Do you know why?

—For supposedly being a witch.

—Are you or have you ever been a witch?

—No, she stammered, but I don't see how that-

—Then why would you be locked in this cell?

—Because they *think* I'm a witch.

Mr. Livery looked dismayed. —Tsk tsk, you should learn your recent history. Our brilliant Parliament passed the Witch-craft Act in 1735, making it officially illegal to claim anyone has magical powers.

—Then why aren't you and Eaves in this prison?

—More asininity, he said as he took his spectacles off and massaged the bridge of his nose. —This prison is no longer operational, but they made an exception for you it seems, because they wanted to make a point to imprison anyone claiming to have magical powers.

—I never said that! Aggie blurted.

—Ah, but Dr. Eaves so graciously did. He let Parliament know about your case while you were *asleep,* and they made an example out of you for the rest of the country—that no one should be able to claim the power of witchcraft.

—What evidence did you both give that I was claiming that?

—Umm… Our word. Which they took. Greedily.

—Yes, but surely a lawyer will be able to help me if I can have visitors.

—You can have all the visitors you want, but Eaves has worked Parliament to where they will never accept an argument from even the strongest attorney in all of Britain.

—Great, I'll put the word out.

—That wasn't what I meant … I don't think you understand what I said.

—I understand that maybe my friends will help me.

—But they don't know you're here…

Aggie thought about this for exactly a minute as Livery stood motionless. She could shout for help, as her cell quite shockingly had a window—barred, but still definitely a window. Maybe her friends would hear her and she wouldn't have to waste away in the Tower until either the end of her days or until they refurbished it and rediscovered her.

—I believe it's in the Parliament's best interest to release me.

—I believe they will ignore you like the plague.

Aggie was quickly beginning to worry the plague would indeed strike her down during her (however long) stay in the ramshackle, disgusting Tower, the soot infecting her lungs, the stones hitting her limbs and body just wrong, the mud caking in layers across her unwashed exterior. And she began to cry very slowly and in such a dignified way that Mr. Livery didn't know what to do, became frightened, looked around desperately for the cause of her tears, and then turned on a heel slowly and left.

4.

It was a Sunday, and Liza was working the Duke's Head's bar after church, when parishioners and members of congregations alike would administer salves to their ailing lives and dispositions. She figured now was as good a time as any to sneak a drink herself; she liked sneaking drinks even though Ruker didn't give two shites about it.

—Making the most of the Lord's Day, I see, Ruker said, sidling behind and around the bartending Liza.

—Aye, leave er alone, she probably gets enough o that from er old man, said Tomothy, a wannabe brawler and actualized alcoholic without the language to describe either of those things.

—Yea, she's jus tryin to wile away the days before eaven, Bentley the charmer chimed in.

—This little lady is not going to heaven, replied Ruker, smiling somehow both professionally and eerily. Liza would be worried about Ruker if the latter weren't so self-involved, and there was so little self to begin with that interacting with him became an exercise in witnessing solipsism firsthand.

Tomothy sneered and then patted Bentley on the back. —Another mark for you, aye?

—She looks fourteen, replied Bentley disdainfully.

—Fifteen, but you were close, said Liza looking up from wiping off some mugs.

—Oi, one more year and you can apply to either Oxford or, y'know, Cambridge, said Tomothy.

—The plan is Oxford, but yes.

—Good luck wi that, said Bentley.

—Why? asked Liza chirpily, —because you could never get in?

Tomothy burst out laughing and began slapping Bentley's back with renewed fervor, as if Bentley had something lodged in his windpipe that Tomothy was helpfully extracting.

When it closed in on closing time, Ruker sidled around the bar and let Tomothy and Bentley know it was five till closing. They took the hint, gathered their stuff (a hat for Bentley and a walking stick for Tomothy), and exited the bar laughing about the last joke of the evening.

—Napoleon is invading Italy, said Ruker gloomily. —Only a matter of time before Pius VII is excommunicated now…

—Who will be pope after him? Napoleon?

—No, that would be impossible, replied Ruker. —And something tells me Napoleon wouldn't want that responsibility anyway, at least not that one.

The girl left the bar and, just as she was opening the door to leave Ruker alone in the establishment, said, —Someone will want that responsibility, I'm sure.

—Girls can't be popes. Women can't either, replied a smirking Ruker.

—I didn't mean me, said Liza, closing the door and walking out into the London night.

The fire-lit city lights glinted off Ailen's lacquered hat, giving it a sheen the daytime rarely afforded, and lending it a mystique Ailen typically cherished. Now, however, he felt a bit miffed that the streets were emptied out and no one was giving him any compliments on it.

He envisioned scenarios of people coming up to him and complimenting his hat, granting it the praise that was its due, before he shooed them off and very politely demurred, saying it was just an old hat from the country, just as he is an old man from the country.

He made it to London Bridge before this fantasy broke down—someone was walking in the opposite direction of him down the bridge, and they didn't say a thing to him about his hat, positive or negative. And it was in that moment that Ailen, now only just getting accustomed to life in the city, realized that no one would ever in a million years compliment his hat—or say anything positive or negative about his hat in the first place. It was also this thought that made him incomparably sad and which made him cross to the edge of the bridge faster than usual.

But as he hit the sidewalk's landing coming off the bridge he noticed a crane lifting its head towards him, as if it knew it would need to look up as soon as Ailen hit the street. The crane gazed at Ailen for half a minute before lifting its head further up towards the night sky, the starlight illuminating its beak and sending wan light in Ailen's direction.

The crane became startled by what Ailen slowly began to recognize were the shrill cries of a girl, seemingly coming from the London Tower, which was a handful of blocks away to the right. He looked up at the crane, and it seemed to be the only motionless thing in the world for some reason in that minute he stared at it, his mind either playing tricks on him *or* not playing tricks on him and at the same time moving slower than usual. He looked in the direction of the flying crane, and only then realized it had in fact flown away.

He stood there motionless for another minute before hightailing it the other way and running as fast as he could across the

Bridge and towards the quarter where he and Liza lived. He tripped over cobblestones the entire way there, bruising his toes quite a bit and making his feet in general very sore. He recrossed the London Bridge coming the other way, but decided against taking a left onto Tooley and heading home, favoring instead going to the Ship Inn, near St. Thomas Hospital, where he figured he could go if the drinking got too serious anyway.

The barkeep at the Ship Inn was a portly lady of about forty-five years of age, something along the lines of someone who typically had Ailen's number, but who understood the number, tolerated it and sometimes even encouraged it to continue. The barkeep took a shine to him, in other words, and it was reciprocated on Ailen's part by his continual patronage.

The inn was better known than Duke's Head Company, which Ruker ran and at which Liza was now working, but part of this was due to it being closer to the Thames and the businessmen who for some reason stumbled into Southwark, probably drunk and fleeing from their places of work south down the London Bridge.

—Aye, back so soon? Junie said.

—Afraid so, Junie, replied Ailen. —I was gonna go down Tooley to see if Liza'd made it back from work yet, but I figured I'd go down the Bridge instead.

—Anything interesting up there? asked Junie as she cleaned a mug.

Ailen scratched his beard. —Nothing much. Saw a lone person walking the other way … and a crane at the end. [Then, as if just remembering,] yeah I did hear a right loud screaming and moaning when I got to the end of the Bridge, from the Tower I think. It was coming from my right at least, pretty sure.

—Yeah, folks in Southwark have been hearin that for a bit now it seems. No protests gone on about it yet, but a few borough officials have sent word to Parliament about it; haven't heard anything back, though.

—It was this unholy racket, said Ailen mournfully. —Not as if someone was imprisoned, that would be too easy for the sound. Was as if the person—girl it sounded like—was trying to leave her body, like her body was just a vessel. That's what I meant by unholy—seemed to desecrate the very notion of the voice if that makes any sense.

—It surely doesn't! Junie chirped back as she handed Ailen a draught of lager. —I'm content not knowing what it is, but then again I don't live right across the river. You both live in Union Yard, yeah? Have you all heard it yet?

—Thankfully, no.

—Well, you'll hear it soon enough. Maybe the wind hasn't carried it over yet.

—The wind's done worse things to this city, said Ailen as he downed his drink.

—Nothing that's as much of a threat to the soul it seems, though.

—What? Of course it has.

Junie thought about it for a second before replying that it probably had before, yes.

—Speaking of the wind, how's your almost-flown Liza doing?

—She's working as a barmaid and studyin for the Oxford exam.

—Well, best of luck with that. What will she be if (excuse me, *when*) she gets in? Seventeen?

—Aye, sixteen or seventeen, depending on when she gets in. She hopes to get in at sixteen, but it may not happen of course and she may have to wait another year. But that happens, it does.

—It's just a right good thing she's not a boy, y'know? She mighta been courted off to war soon were that the case.

Ailen looked disturbed and expressed this to Junie, —Hmmm, why would that be?

—Talk goin round about whether we'll join the fight against Napoleon. He's been right attacking every country on the fiking continent.

—Well, Ailen said a little too nonchalantly as he downed the rest of his drink, —good thing we're not a part of the continent.

Liza left Duke's Head at ten pm, the night air slapping her across the face on her way out the door, little wisps of it getting between what seemed to be even the roots in her hair, resulting in that same hair being blown around and tousled across her face, blocking her vision as she stumbled on the cobblestones outside the pub and fell face forward into the street in front of a carriage.

Ruker jumped through the door and pulled her back just as the horses and then the carriage too disappeared into the night fog, and he smiled, patted her head, went back inside the pub, and closed the door loudly behind him.

The girl flipped around on her heels and took a right and then another right onto New Street on her way to Broad Way to join onto Joiners Street for a sharp left, keeping her path clear from any midnight carriages—although she figured she'd be able to avoid them these next few times, what with the noise of the carriage, which she couldn't hear last time because … because come to think of it, she couldn't hear anything—all she heard was a thin whooshing sound from what sounded like the hollow recesses of her memory. It couldn't be the silence of the city night: there were brawls about, howls to be made, the whole of Southwark trying to make its effort to be heard amidst the bustle of the greater city.

No, this hollowness had a different origin, yet it was still a short-lived one.

As soon as she hit Joiners Street, a scream like a somehow more unleashed banshee hit the very nerves inside her head, making her temples throb, and making her head burst with an unseen but still felt pressure. She looked at the rows of apartments to her left and right to see where the wails were coming from, but she noticed none of the lights were on in the buildings, an odd sight for any stretch of street in this city at this time, regardless of whether it was an apartment block.

She straightened herself against the railing in front of the nearest flat, which happened to be #30, to her left, the railing almost giving way and her almost falling down face-first into a small but well-tended garden.

—Oi, what you think yer doin there, mate?

—I'm so sorry, I'm a bit under the weather right now, and—

—You better get under the weather in a different part of this street or I'll show you a helluva time underneath *this* weather…

Liza let go of the railing and slowly collected herself, taking a deep breath even though the screaming was still piercing the inside of her skull every which way it could. The man finally saw that she was in pain and went back inside grumbling and slamming the door loudly.

She took a left and entered the thickets between the Ship Inn and Joiners, scraping her work clothes something fierce before finishing the trek and flinging open Ship Inn's door to reveal what looked to be some kind of English, moor-stricken version of an American Midwestern soddy wife, making both Ailen and Junie jump out of their skins, and causing the latter to ricochet a glass across the room, which shattered upon impact.

—Missy, said a more-shocked-than-usual Junie, —what have you gotten yourself into?

—Has it been that don around the corner on Joiners, yeah? Ailen let out.

Liza brushed her hair down and tamped it into a more presentable shape.

—Neither it seems, she replied finally, picking out brambles in her hair and tufts attached to her dress. —I was just on my way from Joiners to here and got caught a bit on the way.

—Hmph, said Ailen, —likely story.

—Aye, shot back Liza, —but it's the truth, honest to my word and my word to me heart, my heart.

—Now now, replied a checked Ailen, —what seems to have gotten you there? in that state?

—I heard a vicious round of screaming. Like a dead person come back to life and haunting the streets of London.

—Are you hallucinating, dearie? asked Junie innocently.

—What a fiking question! Liza belted into the air between her and the bar.

—We just need to know where you're at, said Ailen calmly.

—Aye, so it's "we" now, ay? smiled Liza.

Ailen's cheeks turned crimson before Junie shot down any chance Liza had of envisioning pre-matrimonial bliss. —We're not like that. Friends, y'know? You should try it sometime.

Liza, not used to this show of force from Junie, decided to ignore the last comment and proceed, —I heard it as soon as I left Duke's Head—

Ailen leaned over to Junie, —I told her that place was nothing but trouble.

—Anyway, Liza continued, —I walked New Street and onto Broad Way, and started hearing this wailing, like, inside my head, almost over the top of my head at the same time as being inside it, it's hard to explain.

Ailen narrowed his eyes, got up, went towards Liza, and looked deep into her eyes. —So it's only when you're outside, then, I guess?

—It appears that way, said Liza. —Want to try it out?

Ailen looked at Junie, who shrugged. —She's under your care, not mine. I would advise not to do it, but you're the boss in this here situation it seems.

Ailen led Liza outside, and as soon as they'd crossed the threshold of the door into the tavern, she grabbed her head and started screaming almost as loud as the voice inside her head surely must have been, thought Ailen, who guided her back inside.

—What did it sound like? he asked her with baited breath.

—Shrill, loud, like a banshee let loose into the night, only it's in my own head.

—Could you hear anything? Junie asked Ailen, who slowly shook his head.

—Right, well then it's settled, Junie teased. —This little lady is a witch.

—Shhh, said Ailen, —don't say that so loud or they'll lock us all up.

—Did it sound like a girl? asked Junie.

—Yes.

—Well then maybe it was the girl from the Tower I was describing earlier, said Ailen.

—I don' know what else it could be, let out Junie eventually. —It's just that you're both 'earing it at different times and at different locations it seems…

—Do they still hang witches? Liza asked with tears in her eyes. (She was new to the city.)

Ailen laughed and said they hadn't since nearly a century ago and that she wasn't even a witch to begin with.

—Right, but I became one.

—That wasn't [sigh] … that wasn't what I fiking meant.

—You're not a witch, dearie, said a newly concerned Junie, —I'm so sorry to've frightened you; I was only kiddin.

—Well, said Liza, —whatever I am, I have a bloody massive headache right now.

Ailen came to Liza's side, threw his coat around her, and ushered her towards the door, which Liza braced against in fear.

—You're going to have to face this one way or another, he said sadly.

—I'm not going outside again.

Ailen asked Junie if it was alright for her to stay the night at the inn.

—For the hundredth fiking time, Ailen, this isn't an inn, it's a pub; we've been over this.

—Right, said Ailen through his teeth, —so sorry.

Ailen pushed Liza through the doorway until she fell to her knees on the stones below the stoop, and then she grabbed the sides of her head and screamed into the sky above, presumably for help, but not from God.

Ailen grabbed her shoulders and helped her to her feet as he navigated down onto High Street and then took a right onto Tooley. Liza asked why they weren't going to St. Thomas Hospital, and Ailen replied that, because even though he knows she's not a witch, they could put her in jail for impersonating one.

—But I'm in pain! Liza cried.

—They don't care, said Ailen sadly.

It was a long walk down Tooley, so they got a carriage, and, once they were inside, Ailen asked if she was still hearing the screaming.

—No, not anymore, no.

—Have you tried communicating with this voice, telling it something using your mind?

—I have not considered that, no, said a defeated Liza.

—You might want to try it tomorrow night, just to see what ends up happening.

Ailen looked through the carriage window, made sure it was shut all the way, and then told Liza that she might not be a witch, but that she may be a medium.

5.

Gant lay on his back in his Oxford dorm as the sunlight slowly made its way all the way across his face. He swatted at it in vain before realizing that was the permanent state of the sun in the other direction, and he promptly rolled over.

His buddy Ralph, a bunkbed below him, had just woken up and was doing his morning stretches before his track and field practice.

—Hey now, said Gant, still turned over and with the pillow covering his muffled words, —what makes you think you can run so early?

—God has given me the gift of running, and so I must run, Ralph replied cheerily.

—Sounds like God should have his talent back, Gant muttered almost inaudibly.

Ralph laughed. —And what use would God have on two legs?

—The same fucking use he has now, Ralph, replied Gant. —Also, he did at one point, *remember*…

Ralph guffawed all the way to the door, enriched by the thought that he was usurping at least a little bit of God's power.

After Ralph left, Gant took stock of the end of his first year. No new people he was going steady with, and almost a handful of friends; so socially, not terrible. There was the incident back in the Parks with that girl and the stray dog, but he didn't like to think about that much.

(The dog had somehow wandered into one of the colleges, and, after leaving the Law building, made a right and just hightailed it to the nearest park, which so happened to coincide with a date he was having. To impress the girl he'd just met and was rather keen on, he reached down to pet the dog, but it just snarled and used the side of its hide not affixed with a scar to snap back at Gant, who took this as a dangerous omen and one he should heed. So he called things off with the girl the next day, who started crying and said she didn't understand what a dog had to do with anything.) Quite a lot, Margerie, thought Gant; if it was an omen, then quite a lot.

In any case, now that he'd chosen law, he had a more advanced route to the building, instead of just going across St. Giles, and so he probably had to adopt his roommate's running ways, at least for the time being. Law seemed a bit less intense than his previous major, philosophy, and at least this way his intellectual debates could take place in the cold and honest light of political day. At least this way he'd be more honest about his amorality than if he were to continue studying philosophy.

He left his dorm, across from the Classics building and at the direct city center, and walked to a pub near the Classics building, something he did on these moderately lazy Sundays. He didn't get an internship this summer, and he also didn't get a job at the pub he was about to go to, but this did not stop him from going regularly to the pub. He had an inheritance from his dead parents, and he was prepared to use it either to its last straw, or until a year from now when he hopefully had an internship with a bigwig London lawyer.

The pub was crawling with Classics majors who either (uncharacteristically) had gotten extensions on their final projects, or who were just now taking their firsts. He settled down next to Breton, who was understandably very stressed about his forthcoming Latin exam.

—You'll be fine, Breton.

—No, *you'll* be fine, *Gant*. You Balliol boys always are.

—Now now, said Gant magnanimously, —I don't think our great founder had to be publicly beaten by the bishop he absconded with just so that you could make that conclusion.

—You always were a queer one about that legend, Breton said, finally giving up on his studies for the next ten minutes and ordering another round.

—It's an important legend! retorted Gant, —if only because it teaches impressionable minds the trouble they can get in if they have the gall to confront religious authority.

—Since when have you not had that gall?

—Since I was a boy and learned all that God could do for me.

—You mean since you learned what the crucifix was *really* for?

—What, buggery? There are other means for that, Breton.

—Sweet Lord, said Breton, looking down at his glass and whispering conspiratorially, —we've been over this, there's nothing I can do for you in that department.

—Oh, that's fine, said Gant. —It tends to go back and forth nowadays anyway.

—That makes no goddamn sense.

—I suppose it wouldn't to you, but we libertines feel differently, said Gant, folding his hands behind his head and craning his neck back in satisfaction.

—I suppose there's a reason Balliol is an all-boys college, then?

—What, integrity? Gant asked innocently. —Also, *every* college is an all-boys college...

—No, the reason is: so I could finish this Virgil reading.

—What do you have to do?

—Translate the *Eclogues,* sighed Breton.

—Jesus H. Christ, said Gant, leaping up, —please give me your workload.

—You're off for the summer!

—Yeah, but at least I'd be doing something tedious and mind-numbingly simple.

—They're very nuanced, muttered Breton, —and difficult to translate.

—I could translate those in my sleep. Are you doing the *Aeneid* next at least?

—That's all of next year, plus attendant scholarship, plus some Horace thrown in for good measure.

—Thank God above for Horace I suppose, said Gant, laughing.

—What ever happened with you and Margerie? Breton smiled.

—I told you to never speak of that again, glowered Gant a little more than the situation needed.

—What? Not about the park, and about the dog, and about the Law school? ... Skip.

—No, about none of that, replied Gant. —And certainly don't call me by that cursed name.

—I think it fits you quite well, what with Gant being one syllable as well.

Gant put his hands to his head. —They'll never let me hear the end of it.

—They will if you excel in all your Law classes. That'll shut 'em up.

Gant wasn't expecting this level of wisdom from the quasi-nonce Breton, and he found it refreshing. He knew there was a reason he hung around the Classics bar—so that not only could his ego be assuaged and slough off the negative tirades he'd gotten at both his majors, but also so that he could slough off any self-aggrandizement and ego in the first place. It was a curious cycle, and he felt it expire against itself and renew in turn over and over again at this specific bar, and, more often than not, with Breton.

Breton had entered the college without a penny to his name, and, despite not being the brightest bulb on the Oxford university campuses, had somehow made a good enough impression to where neither his lack of funds nor his lack of winning intelligence mattered much anymore to the Oxford powers that be, that were. Something to do with effort and personality, Gant figured.

Gant got up quickly from his barstool as if Breton's word of wisdom had triggered a long-forgotten bit of personal motivation, and, after saying Breton was right and then saying their goodbyes, he made his way down to the Philosophy department down the street, looking at all the university girls in all their May glory. The world was open to Gant, but he didn't know how much of an open-and-shut case his life was until he started law school, which got him believing anew in both determinism and, what amounted to the same for him, politics.

He arrived at the Philosophy building, and was walking so fast that he bumped shoulders with Randeau, the strict Hegelian professor. Gant didn't have the language to call him a strict Hegelian—that line of thought was still being developed (partially by Randeau himself)—but he thought it a fine descriptor nonetheless, as this particular professor was dark, brooding, and exceedingly stern/strict.

—We've … uh … missed you, Gant, stammered the professor.

—Logical fallacy! shouted Gant a little too loudly.

Randeau muttered under his breath, told Gant he was free to sit on a lecture any time he wanted if he still had the inclination, and to exit the building and greet the waning sunlight that hit against the buildings lining St. Giles.

After the door shut, Gant shouted —You're welcome!— at the closed door before going up the stairs towards the lecture hall of Dr. Grisham, who was currently teaching a course on Jeremy Bentham.

—You see, said Grisham as Gant was entering the room, —this Panopticon was developed for the sole purpose of centralizing authority along the lines of the prison rather than the prisoner, while still maintaining the illusion that the prisoners had their own rights. The genius of it is not that they can't see they are pawns but that they are pawns and that the state can name them as such. It is a tool perfectly suited to our times. [Gant was waiting for one of Grisham's famous dialectical turns here.] Yet it is a tool where the power is almost too centralized [there it is], almost too diverted from the locus of its own centralization, too close to being a diffusion of the very thing it represented.

Gant snuck in behind the last person in the lecture hall, closest to the door, hoping against hope that the professor wouldn't see him

—Ah, Grisham said, somehow both getting sterner and lighting up more, —Gant, you decided to join us for today.

—It's not in my major anymore, but I figured—

—You figured what? That you could still walk in here and listen to a lecture?

Gant fiddled with his hair stupidly before standing up and trying his best to make a case for himself.

—You thought wrongly, he said, his tone lowering to an octave Gant didn't recognize from any of his classes. —You are not entitled to the same benefits as those of your fellow students taking Philosophy classes, and, might I add, about to take an exam in a week.

—I never presumed preferential treatment, replied Gant.

—Presumption would take one more mental step than you're taking. You're not even at presumption yet. Perhaps you're at guessing, or assuming, or, maybe even the worst, hoping.

—I think all the steps I take in my mind are preserved right there, in my mind, thank you very much, said Gant with his chest puffed out slightly.

—I think you don't know the first thing about the steps your mind takes.

—I think therefore I am.

—Well congrats, but knowledge doesn't being make; you'll need more than knowledge to sit in on this class. You'll need to attend every session from here until the rest of the increasingly short semester.

—I can do that no problem, said Gant hastily.

—Well, you won't need to, Grisham said before placing his chalk at the bottom of the chalkboard finally. —Because you're expelled from this building from here on out.

Gant felt a shock wave of conflicted emotions surge through his body, including regret, shame, reticence, and even perhaps dishonor. He almost fainted (uncharacteristically), but then decided to steel himself against the wooden doors, open the latch, and draw the heavy doors outward into a hallway he entered with an altered sense of purpose, as he was now fully and forever (probably) a lawyer.

As soon as he got back to his dorm, Ralph was there waiting for him.

—Well, Ralph said when Gant had fully sat on his bed, —Should we get lunch?

—Yeah, let's see if we run into Breton.

—Didn't you just see him?

—Are we not getting fish and chips?

—Are you kidding?

—Mildly.

—How does one mildly kid?

—I do it all the time.

—Well I'm not getting fish and chips, I don't know about you.

—They serve other things there.

—Nothing good, Ralph muttered.

—Well, we'd just be going to see if Breton is there, anyway.

—Fine, let's go then, grumbled Ralph.

They walked down the thoroughfare of High Street until reaching their destination, panting in the balmy air until they reached the inside of the pub. Breton was sitting where he'd been sitting earlier.

—You're back, said Breton from the corner of his mouth.

—You've let the cat out of the bag, Gant smiled back at Breton.

—Oh, Breton replied, —that was nowhere near my intention; I just wanted to make sure your friend knew you were at this den of iniquity earlier, nothing more nothing less.

—Sounds like a good deal less, Gant said as he and Ralph sat down on either side of Breton.

—What is this? asked a curiously newly nervous Breton, —the Spanish Inquisition?

—Yes, said Ralph. —We need to know when your exam is.

—This afternoon, Breton replied. —Why?

—Because we have big plans for you after your exam, laughed Gant.

—Oh no, said Breton. —That sounds less than promising.

—It's the promise of everlasting life, said Gant, —which can be yours later this afternoon.

The three of them finished dinner and then headed up High Street towards Oxford Castle, with Gant at the top of the line looking up at the three-story edifice and motioning up towards it as if to say, —Who wants first dibs?

Ralph and Breton knew what he was intimating, and both of them looked to the floor, as if to say that neither of them were up for this challenge, as easy as they surely would have said it was in theory.

Gant wanted his theory tested independently of them, so he started grabbing at the stones at the bottom, which jutted out in a cross-hatched pattern, making it easy for climbers, something the university would take care of later in that century, after an incident not involving the three of them.

—I wouldn't do that, said Breton.

—I know, smiled Gant, —that's why *I'm* doing it.

—No, Ralph continued in Breton's stead, —I think what he means is it's dangerous. Neither of us (probably) [he looked over at Breton here] give a rat's arse about any institutional reprimanding; it's just about the safety issue.

Gant looked back and then down and sighed, —If nothing happens to us physically, they won't care about it spiritually, one follows the other. If we're safe, they won't care one way or the other, as long as they don't have to explain anything to parents, the state, their God, etcetera.

Ralph and Breton collectively shrugged and then followed Gant up the castle's no-longer-used ramparts until they reached its overlook and began to walk around imperially after catching their breath. Gant waved his arms around his head and twirled in place majestically and then funnily and erratically, so much so that Ralph and Breton both rushed towards him to help in case he fell over, or to prevent him from falling off the tower in the first place.

After Gant was done spinning, Breton looked around the colorful vista in the civil twilight. —Gant, Ralph, could you imagine if all this land was ours?

Gant burst out laughing. —You mean yours?

—Why couldn't we share it? asked Breton so innocently that Gant decided not to ask him if he was being sarcastic.

—I don't think that's ever worked in the past, said Ralph.

—But we're starting a new future, Breton replied.

—Speak for yourself, said Gant. —I just wanna live in a re-christened past, like a past with the knowledge we have now.

Breton scoffed so hard it looked like he'd eaten something bad and it was now coming back with a vengeance. —What about reforms? Policy improvements? Better quality of life?

—Those seem more to do with the mind than anything else, said Gant cynically as he looked up at the sky, at a spot in the sky where the sun was no longer present.

—And what does the mind not have to do with the body? asked Ralph incredulously.

—I don't want to get into a Cartesian fight, here, said Gant backing away slightly, at least in posture, from Ralph, —I meant it only in the sense that I think we often confuse all these corporeal issues with issues our mindsets resolve for themselves as we live in the world anyway.

—I can't tell if you're being a cynical ass or a Berkeley disciple, laughed Ralph.

—You're a philosophy major, said Gant, —so you should know that the most cynical asses are always Berkeley disciples anyway.

—I think we do confirm things with our minds, but that doesn't mean we shouldn't enact things in the real world corporeally, said Breton, causing the other two to look at the Classics major for the first time in a long time, perhaps since they'd met him and he talked their collective ears off about the virtues of a then-underrated David Hume and since that night when they played gin rummy to the tune of the moving-in first years and their hustling, bustling bodies moving furniture to and fro across the cramped Oxford streets, which were closed for the occasion.

—What does it look like when you rule people? said Ralph to the wind.

—It looks unnatural and both parties know it, replied Gant.

—Religion was invented so it looked natural, said Breton after some thought.

—Well, said Ralph, —I'm not sure I agree with that, but you're fine to think that. All that Hume I should think, and his Dialogues of Natural Religion.

—His point wasn't that religion isn't natural, it was that it's a man-made distortion of a harder-to-shake (but probably still dangerous) spirituality, although I'm sure he still thinks spirituality is dangerous itself, I'm not sure; I'd have to read it again to make sure.

—Why don't you just go read some of the fiking classics? asked Ralph almost desperately.

—I only read future classics when it comes to philosophy, smirked Breton.

—What about when it comes to Latin classics? asked Ralph less desperately.

—Pretty sure only past classics when it comes to Latin, laughed Breton.

—I like to read whatever tells my body how to live in the world we live in now, how to become accustomed to the growing split between mind and body in discourse, and how to lead a virtuous life independent of the curse of virtue, either Christian or otherwise, said Gant after a contented pause for all parties involved.

All three of them watched the sun recede beyond the forests in the far distance and imagined themselves to be kings, but only of themselves or, less so, what they could control and, even less so, make better in the world they found themselves in, a world with threatening dictators and ascendant popes, and a world that only they could see the limits and boundaries to, individually.

—Well that must be nice, said Ralph finally.

6.

Because it was obvious Leo – at sixteen – would be the next pope, the cardinal ordination ceremony was brief, to the point, and, other than Leo, only included lay cardinals and secret cardinals. This meant that the College of Cardinals would appoint the next pope largely in secret and in coordination with Pius VII, to avoid the overseeing gaze of Napoleon, who was by this point (1810) trying to end the Peninsular War in Spain despite not having been there—fighting—since 1808. But the great general was at that time focusing more on the Holy See—cutting off the British trade routes to choke the remaining bulwarks in the continent against his rule had already basically happened. And the Fifth Coalition, of Britain and Austria, was destroyed decisively last July, so at that moment it was just a matter of Napoleon not resting on his laurels per se but guarding them with his very life.

Leo chafed against his newfound cassock, the ankle-length garment brushing against his trousers, a fate which the mozzetta never threatened, resting as it did across the elbows and around the torso therein. The square cap, however, was absolutely the worst: the biretta, the new bane of Leo's existence, was red, had a red tuft at the top, and was basically all red, to signify that he as a cardinal would be willing to die for this position—presumably before the pope was killed in his stead, presumably by Napoleon. In any case, Leo had no plans to die, although he couldn't speak for the secret and lay cardinals beside him at that moment.

Pius VII left the inside antechamber and entered into the outside round portico, the train of his garment following him and attended to by a prelate for some godforsaken church in the suburbs of Rome a long ways away from this procession. As soon as the pope stopped walking and then turned around to face the group of about-to-be secret, lay, and Leo cardinals, the prelate/bishop scurried off into the antechamber, out of sight and away from the procession for the rest of the time the procession took to complete.

—Hey Pius! screamed Leo, —I thought I needed to become an Archbishop before this…

All the other almost-cardinals to Leo's left and right looked at Leo like he was a buffoon, or, worse, morally repugnant, and then muttered amongst themselves about why he was picked to be the Chosen One, as everyone there already knew about the upcoming plot anyway. Leo just shrugged his shoulders so violently his mozzetta almost fell off over his head, a feat some of the other almost-cardinals found mildly impressive at the very least.

—We're forgoing all that rigmarole with you, said Pius VII, —because you're—

—Very special, interrupted Leo. —Right.

—Right, said Pius VII, collecting himself ever so slightly, — We're going to start at one end, then go to the other end, and alternate until we get to the middle, or our Leo.

—Not yours, muttered Leo as the first secret cardinal was called up to receive the pope's blessing; there were four secret cardinals to Leo's right and four lay cardinals to his left. These were the last remnants of orthodoxy before Napoleon took over, and everyone knew it. So the ceremony itself became some sort of ritualistic litmus test for how loyal they were to the previous pope as opposed to Napoleon, and Leo couldn't help but laugh to himself because he felt loyal to precisely nobody, not even to himself. He would have excelled in battle, if given the chance.

After the first secret cardinal took his place next to Pius VII, a lay cardinal was called up. His name was Reggie, and Leo appreciated his company more than the other cardinals, secret or otherwise. It was a shame he was a lay cardinal, as Leo thought he would've made a better official one than many of the secret ones, but then again Reggie never had to hide his face in public, so there was that.

Reggie took a couple hesitant steps out of the line of the seven other almost-cardinals, genuflected, and walked up to Pius, almost tripping on the way there and catching himself before he hit the polished-as-a-whistle red and brown tiles below. He looked at his reflection in the glint of the tile and almost didn't recognize himself, but he thought it might be because his biretta had fallen off so he picked it back up, put it back on his head, and retreated forward into the glow of Pius VII's presence.

Leo almost didn't see him at first because the sun was shining so heavily off Pius VII's accouterments, but Napoleon was standing in the window behind the Pope and gazing something fierce into Reggie's eyes, but, because Reggie was so dead-set on Pius, he didn't meet the eminent general's intense gaze. But when Leo saw the figure in the large, rectangular window, he knew the slats weren't deceiving him and that the man who'd murdered his family so coldly a year and a half ago was in the window, not just because he would recognize Napoleon's figure from anywhere based on woodcuts, paintings, drawings, pictures, etcetera, but also because the spiritual bandwidth the general resided on was one Leo coveted and sought to usurp. Leo wanted to be the progenitor and last source of all that Napoleon stood for, to speed things along towards modernity, something he had an inchoate inkling of but approximately zero words to enact or even describe. But he wanted to be that last bastion for the world, so everyone on the planet could finally see something different than they had in millennia, something that couldn't be measured by military or religious success. And he knew the only way to accomplish that was through Napoleon, not despite him: to spite him, not in spite of him.

When Reggie had taken his place to the pope's left, right in front of a Napoleon he didn't see, Pius called the next secret cardinal, who similarly genuflected before the pope read some kind of liturgy Leo didn't recognize and before Napoleon started smiling, closing his eyes, listening to the reading, and looking up past his eyelids, past the roof, and into the sky he probably called his own.

During the process of the next five cardinal ordinations, Napoleon stayed there the whole time, and Leo looked at him during every single ordination, but not only did the general not look over at Leo, he either had his eyes closed in reverie, or his gaze affixed onto Pope Pius VII, who never once looked back either, but always looked ahead, usually directly at Leo even if he was addressing another cardinal.

This dialectical, recursive chain of continual observation ceased when Pius finally called Leo's name. Leo and Napoleon made eye contact for the first time as Napoleon shifted his eyes slowly towards the exact spot Leo was standing in, without looking at him at first, until the reverie finally left the general's look and was replaced by a look of such shining and malevolent hatred that Leo shuddered something fierce, almost causing his mozzetta to fall from his less-than-broad shoulders yet again.

—A chill? Pius asked so innocently that Leo wondered if the pope knew the general had been behind him this entire time. —Never mind the weather, said the pope. —When we're done next year, the weather will mean nothing to you.

—No, said Leo, —I just thought I saw something…

—I hope it wasn't too upsetting, smiled Pius VII.

—It's fine, said Leo eventually, —I'll manage.

Leo genuflected for what seemed like a minute and then looked at his reflection in the tile while he did so, the shade blocking the reflection but only slightly. The sun was on its way down and would soon eclipse with the ceiling of the room adjacent to the portico and all that would be left would be the broad peak of Napoleon's hat as it tilted slightly down and slightly forward like a pointer dog finally landing its mark.

Leo stopped looking at his own face and then his own body, with his own hand over his own heart, and finally turned his eyes upon the Holy See, whose arms were bent forward with the official cardinal regalia, as the ones he had on—the ones everybody'd had on before they approached the standing pope—were not the official ones. He walked up to the pontiff and stood before him, not daring to look beyond at Napoleon's intensity.

Pius said a few things before saying that Leo was a cardinal and helping him to put on the official garments, but Leo was too busy staring at the vacancy where Napoleon's staring form had been. Instead the window led to another window—a window he hadn't seemed to notice before—and, beyond the second window, a garden—beyond the garden, Napoleon's figure walking swiftly away towards a carriage.

After the ceremony, Pius VII came up to Leo and chuckled. —Excited to see the general?

—He murdered my family, said Leo incredulously, —and I'm supposed to just assume a prone position as he murders this papacy and its orders?

—Oh come now, said Pius. —He's really a fine guy. Judge not lest ye be judged and all that.

—I don't think the Sermon on the Mount applies here, and I'm mildly shocked you're invoking it for this cause.

—People have invoked worse things for worse causes.

—Indeed, said Leo bitterly, —but why is the papacy sidling up next to him?

—Because he has political power right now, and we're in the process of losing ours.

—That doesn't mean we should just lie back and expect things to get better.

—Nobody's expecting them to get better, probably not even Napoleon.

—Then what gives him the right to take us over?

—Goodness, laughed Pius VII, —you'd think you were born for this.

—I am born for this, said Leo, puffing his sixteen-year-old chest farther than he probably needed to. —I don't trust that general as far as I can throw 'im.

Leo's newly enraged and betrayed English accent gave Pius a fit of laughter, which eventually subsided but not before the pope was able to tell Leo one last thing, —I should probably tell you this now, he said, —but the way forward isn't in spite of one of you two, it may be in spite of you both: the road to modernity is paved with the bones of those that have come before and the scrolls of those that are coming next.

—You have it too, said Leo, amazed.

—Yes, I do, said Pius. —That's why they call this place the Holy See, he said as he walked away and left Leo alone in the small portico in that enclave between antechambers in Vatican City.

Leo looked past the two windows ahead of him and shuddered so slightly neither his mozzetta nor his biretta fell down onto the tiles below his feet.

7.

Liza received the Oxford entrance exam in the mail on a day where the summer was dwindling and so too was the sunlight on that particular day in that particular season. She brought it back and waved it in front of Ailen, who got excited until he reminded her that she hadn't even gotten in the school yet, or taken the exam yet, or even fiking opened the envelope yet.

—It'll be good news I'm sure, she replied, sticking her tongue out at him.

—It's not news, he sighed. —You know it's just the exam. Also, how can you even get into Oxford; they don't let girls in…

—Maybe they said some nice, encouraging things along with it, Liza offered.

This sent Ailen reeling with laughter and flying backwards towards the small kitchen counter in their crowded apartment. It took him a split second to hit it because of that, however, and he adjusted his position, and his tone, to eventually say that she'll be fine, that she'll pass the exam with flying colors and have a bright Oxford future.

—The Pope made a decree to let higher institutions of learning allow female students—everywhere, apparently. You know what this means, right? Liza asked.

—You're going to take an exam?

—Yes, Liza replied. —And I'll have to quit working for Ruker.

—Let him down easy, laughed Ailen. —Wait. … Who will I get reconnaissance from now?

—Find another informant. Or learn these things by yourself. Or do what you always do and become a recluse who does what he can do very well but only just that.

Ailen was taken aback. —That was hurtful, he said slowly, as if each word was staggering drunk against the next, having a hard time and letting each of the other words know that.

—Ruker will be fine without me, said Liza. —I think he's Bavarian anyway? Or Russian? I can't tell. Maybe go to those places to learn those things? Might help you clear your mind anyway while I study for this exam.

—I hope you get into the school, said a pained Ailen, —but I don't want to set you back. I'll head back to the farmhouse and get everything situated over there so that you can focus on your schoolwork.

—No, Liza cried out, —don't leave because of me; it's not fair. You'll get back, and you'll miss me immediately.

—Of course I will, said Ailen, choking up, —but you need to focus on what's best for you right now, and do everything you can to get into that school and make a life for yourself, and I can't help you with that as much as I once could, as much as I did, as much as I have done.

You'll be fine, I'll be fine, and, most importantly, we'll be fine.

Ailen stepped back and asked her why she was invading his mind like this.

Because you clearly need some direction here. Also I need to practice for the main event.

—What's the main event, said a flabbergasted Ailen.

Liza laughed and said she had no plans to blow up Parliament, she was just going to try to get in touch with Aggie.

—That's a dangerous proposition, said Ailen.

—Why on earth would that be? asked a genuine Liza. —Nobody else has this power; nobody can intercept it I don't think.

—You'd be surprised, Ailen said as he went towards the envelope, which Liza promptly snatched out of his hands.

—I'll be doing that, thank you very much.

She tore off the official seal and then used a letter-opener they had (just for this very occasion) lying around the kitchen to slip it down through the fold in the envelope until it shone alternately bright and dark against the thin surrounding candlelight.

—What does it say, asked Ailen eagerly. —Anything good?

—It's so many questions, said Liza, leaning against a chair.

—I'll leave tomorrow, said Ailen. —And you can't change my mind. You need to focus on this.

—But you help me focus!

—I am a distraction, Ailen said, —and the last thing you need right now is a distraction.

—But how will I live?

—As you always have.

—I meant financially.

Ailen laughed and said that wasn't an issue, that he would send another, very different and altogether more joyous envelope as soon as he finalized the farm buyout.

But Ailen—

But Ailen had left to go to bed that night, his footfall against the creaking boards of their flat interrupting the protestations of Liza, who didn't sleep that night for fear of not waking in time to see Ailen off in the morning.

Liza was asleep slumped over the kitchen table when Ailen left in the morning. He kissed her on the top of the head, tapped lightly against the Oxford exam on the table, and exited the flat into the London morning, the wind hitting him sideways and forcing him to brace himself against a small garden railing in front of the adjacent building.

He had second thoughts as soon as he made it to the train station, his mind racing in front of the stalled train. He placed his hand on a turnstile, and then on the train's railing, before entering a carriage as far away from any people he could see—or who could see him—and weeping for all his life's worth.

Liza woke up and groggily went searching for an Ailen she gradually began to realize was no longer present in the flat. She slammed her fist against the kitchen table, almost knocking the exam off it, until she finally came to the realization that Ailen had left her for good. She knew the ball was now in her court in terms of contact with him, and she didn't want that to be the case. If she'd wanted that to be the case, she would have moved away from him a long time ago—she had the money and means by now.

But if she quit working for Ruker the money would vanish into some kind of financial ether eventually, and she had no intentions of either begging or selling her body to strangers, and so she resolved to quit working regardless, study for the exam, and wait for money from Ailen. Liza figured anything less risky wouldn't fit the situation.

She grabbed the exam, put it in her handbag, and left for Duke's Head after making herself some eggs on a skillet, both of which had been left out by Ailen as his penultimate ritual before leaving her in a dust entirely of his own making.

Liza tried communicating with Ailen via her telepathic powers, but she realized he wasn't a medium and couldn't communicate back to her. Even though it was a lost cause, she decided to say some reassuring things to him regardless. And Ailen did hear them, tucked away in his train car, and even though he didn't respond, Liza could sense that he was retreating further into the carriage's cushions, perhaps with the aroma of coffee trailing outside an open window, perhaps with her voice trailing along the recesses of his mind as he faded off into sleep.

Duke's Head was busier than usual, and all the patrons seemed to either know and not care, or else they knew and were making Ruker's life as difficult as possible by ordering everything on the menu and on tap.

—Ay, love, let out a whirling Ruker, —can you handle the bar right now? That'd be lovely.

—That's fine, said Liza as she put on her Duke's Head apron, —but I need to talk to you at some point.

—Privately? asked a groaning Ruker.

—Of course, laughed Liza, —but it's not bad, I promise. Or at least not bad for me.

—Ah yes, very promising.

—What's all this? burped a patron. —I need my ale, a stout, immediately.

—We only serve stouts, sir, Ruker said, barely looking up, —it is the only ale we carry.

—Are there not varieties then? the belligerent man pressed.

—Infinite, smiled Ruker, —but each worse than the last. You're best sticking with one of the typical stouts. I could see that being best for you.

Just as the man arched his fist back in preparation, Liza, who'd crept up behind him, grabbed his arm and pulled it slightly back and then all the way down, placating him slightly enough for her to say that the man should probably leave.

—I will do that, miss, said the man, cowed, before adding, —but only because of you, not because of that oaf, he said, pointing to Ruker vengefully.

The man plunked out of the heavy doors, and, because he was too drunk to lift them against his weight regularly, he set his girth against the doors instead, and they gladly obliged under his heft.

The bar took two hours to clear out, and when it had Liza approached Ruker with her head down at first but then curiously her head shot up like a cannon towards his gaze. She didn't want to tell him the news at first, approaching him, but as soon as she got to him she realized she wanted nothing more.

—I'll be leaving as soon as I get into Oxford.

—Fike, wait, have you even gotten in yet?

—N-no…

Ruker doubled over laughing, and began to claw at the countertops on his way up to solid breaths. —Oh my goodness. How many jobs have you had? he asked, wiping a tear away from his eye.

—This will be my first.

—Oh Christ, he let out, —don't announce that your tenure at a job is over until you for sure land the other opportunity.

—Good to know, Liza replied blushing. —I'll keep that in mind for the future. But for now I'm leaving. I need to study for my exam anyway.

—Godspeed, said Ruker eventually. —Leave your apron next to the door, and hand me your key now.

—What about tomorrow's work-

—Might as well do it today. I can manage the bar on my own, did for years before you.

—All right, Liza breathed, —but don't write Ailen.

—And where the fike is Ailen?

—He went back to our home.

—Jesus Almighty, where does that place you? asked Ruker, suddenly concerned and oddly parental—which Liza didn't much care for.

—Just a smidge shy of not passing my exam if I don't get out of here quick.

—Alright already, Ruker said with his arms raised. —You can go right now; I'm not stopping you.

Liza raised her apron over her head and then set it on the bar reverently before shaking Ruker's hand firmly and looking him square in the eye.

—It's been a pleasure.

—Likewise, said Ruker as he locked the door behind Liza, who was chipper as she walked down the cobblestone'd street and onto the intersection of two streets, one of which would lead to her typical studying spot.

She rounded Tooley and practically skipped into the Ship Inn. Junie leapt up in surprise before settling back down and then polishing off a glass.

—Just the usual, Junie, said Liza as she let the doors collapse behind her.

Junie did a double take between Liza and the glass she was polishing. —Did you hear the talk going round about this odd fellow by the name of Blintz? Queer fellow, seems like. Downright shabby, odd, and ill-fitting for a human side of any sort of 'umanity equation.

Liza's mind made it halfway through Junie's description before Blintz appeared in her vision in full—in the carriage, riding in front of them, his lips of glass and blood-attenuated face. It was this Liza's mind went back to as Junie waved her hand in front of Liza's face several times before she snapped out of it enough to answer.

—I've heard of 'im, yeah, Liza said eventually.

—They say he got glass lips or somesuch nonsense.

—He does, Liza replied with a glassy stare.

—Ay, Junie said, —and what makes you say that? You seen 'im?

—Ay, said Liza. —Ailen and I met 'im on the way here from our home. He drove the carriage. Glass lips, yeah. And we had an altercation with 'im a bit. And he hightailed it away from us and left us alone to head here—not knowing the way, by ourselves a bit until we made it to the city. I just remember his eyes—like fire they were—and his lips like the ice-cold opposite.

Junie's eyes lit up with sadness and then immediate concern.

—Do you think Blintz would follow Ailen back to your home?

Liza replied that she didn't know where Blintz even was.

—He's been acting for a spell, word on the street is, said Junie.

—Then why would he follow Ailen back? What on earth would he gain from that?

—Does Ailen own the land? asked Junie quietly.

—Y-yes. He owns our land now. It was signed over just before, just before—

Liza broke down into tears as Junie sidled over beside her and quickly brought Liza's head to her breast like she was snuffing out a candle of immediate grief.

—It'll be alright, dearie, Junie cooed. —Just go and see a show at the Globe; they're renovating it now, all because of this new pope.

He'll be there.

Liza shot back from Junie's embrace. —What did you say?

—I uh… I said go to the Globe Theatre, where Blintz might be?

—You didn't say, "He'll be there"?

Junie laughed. —No dearie, where'd you get that idea?

—Nowhere, it's fine, I'm fine. I need to leave now, though.

Liza left a slightly befuddled Junie and entered the foggy London streets mentally screaming, her mind letting itself bend the time and space of its own neurons so that she could know who she was communicating with.

My love, my sweet, laughed Aggie, *it's me. It's always been me.*

You have the gift too?

How else would I be able to initiate this?

Liza stopped in her tracks as a carriage passing by almost hit her and, after watching the cursing, departing coachmen leave down the street, wondered aloud to Aggie why they'd never connected before.

Because we weren't close enough before, replied Aggie.

Where will we be able to communicate best? asked Liza.

Aggie's laughter filled Liza's brainwaves as the former replied that the Globe Theatre would be the best place for Liza to both find Blintz and get in contact with her. *Study in the meantime, though,* advised Aggie.

Thanks, Liza internally laughed before externally laughing, bending over on the street laughing and intermittently talking to herself as the rain hit the back of her bowed head, falling down in rivulets according to how her long hair fell to almost hitting the cobblestones below.

8.

Mr. Livery bumbled into Aggie's view, gradually coming into focus between the bars of her cell.

—I'm afraid, he began but paused for a moment. —I'm afraid I'm the bearer of bad news.

Aggie's heart sank down into a spot just below the barracks of where she was sitting, until she realized that his Bad News perhaps meant Good News—at least for her.

—It seems there is a lawyer able to help you. He has learned of your predicament from the student newspaper of Oxford University, of all places. He seems keen on seeing that you get out of here.

Aggie's mind almost leapt out of its socket, screaming the praises of this unknown man.

—The only catch is he's not *quite* a lawyer yet, laughed Livery. —But I suppose, unfortunately, that he's working on it.

—Quick question, said Aggie.

—Y-yes?

—Do you get off on these visits?

—What *ever* do you mean, blushed Livery.

—I mean, like, sexually? Does it get you randy?

—The thought of you in a cell fills me with nothing but either contempt or deep satisfaction.

—Well then, said Aggie back, —case closed.

—I hope you rot in here, said Mr. Livery between newly clenched teeth.

—Not if this dashing lawyer has anything to say about it…

—I never said he was dashing!

—You didn't need to; I filled in the blank.

Well that won't be the only blank getting filled.

—Oh Christ, what did you say to me? screamed Aggie.

—I didn't say anything, replied a shocked Livery.

—You said that wouldn't be the only blank getting filled, yeah?

—Mother Mary of Jesus Christ himself no.

—Then who is that? she said loudly.

Aggie clutched at her head as Mr. Livery looked on in horror. She started laughing uncontrollably and began to look up into the sky beyond the ceiling of the cramped cell she was in. In the sky she saw a production of *Much Ado About Nothing* being put on and a very handsome man playing Benedick somewhere in Act Two. *Do you feel it yet?* came a thought that was not her own. She looked to the side of the cell to see beyond the vision but could not. She looked to the other side and still found no luck. When she turned back to the cell's front she saw the figure of Mr. Livery bounding away from the cell and down the hall. He was screaming something about witchcraft and the occult and trials and due process, but she couldn't make out exactly what he was yelling. The only thing in her head right now was Shakespeare and someone's narration of it.

Liza was at the Globe Theatre and thinking quite possibly the dirtiest imaginable thoughts of her life with regards to the man playing Benedick in front of her. She was standing up and almost lost her balance when the actor joined the procession, and she lost track of most of his dialogue with Claudio, which seemed important to the play. Her thoughts of fucking him every which way till kingdom come (or till she came) assailed her vision and clouded her judgment so finely that she felt drunk. She had resisted temptation for so long in her life that this first thought of going against her self-assigned regimen made her whole body weak and made her thoughts scream so loudly she thought they were going out of her own head. She tried grabbing her head and singing herself the quietest lullaby, but to no avail.

She was able to resist attracting too much attention to herself, and she took solace in this until a voice entered her head.

Do you see what I see? the voice sang.

Oh God, am I going crazy? Liza thought.

A man, a man, shining in a play, with a bulge as big as the day, with a bulge as big as the dayyy.

Liza started laughing uproariously until the voice continued but more desperately.

Get me out of here, Liza.

Who are you?

Who's the man playing Benedick?

That doesn't matter right now.

That's a lie, but only for you, so I'll let it slide. I'm Aggie of course.

Are you seeing what I'm seeing?

Yes, for now at least.

Keep your eyes focused throughout the play.

Help the lawyer free me from this godforsaken place.

How on earth will I do that? I don't know who he is.

You'll know when the time comes.

Liza stopped hearing Aggie's voice just as a piercing sting ran through her spine and then her head, and she jolted her head up towards the sky, where at first she saw the clouds and then she saw a prison cell filled with mice examining crevices and a hand in front of her face—that wasn't her own—writing a note. The note ended up saying: "Until we meet in person, but it's Act Three now. Lawyer, Benedick not Dogberry."

Liza snapped out of it in time to see the actor who played Dogberry enter the scene. She moved her hand in front of her face, and then pinched herself to make sure she was out of her stupor before she saw the man on the stage. His back was turned when the scene opened, but as soon as he turned around she knew the expression from anywhere: the glass lips, the foibles, the knowing air. He licked his lips and then found her eyes and locked onto them as he recited his lines. Even when he moved about the stage, he kept looking at her like a spotlight was on her. She didn't want this, she didn't want any of this; she wanted the spotlight to be on the actor who played Benedick, like it was whenever he was onstage. (Liza realized by the end of the play that Dogberry and Benedick are never in a scene together.) But no, the spotlight was on her, as this deranged, glass-lipped psychopath made her the reluctant tourist to his Mona Lisa.

She began to start looking down whenever Dogberry was onstage. But as Blintz delivered his last line as Dogberry, he finally seemed to turn his gaze away from Liza's eyes, and made her wonder whether he had met her gaze at all during the course of the entire production.

—I leave an arrant knave with your worship, which I beseech your worship to correct yourself, for the example of others. God keep your worship, I wish your worship well.

God restore you to health. I humbly give you leave to depart, and if a merry meeting may

be wished, God prohibit it. Come, neighbor.

And with that, Blintz was gone—behind the curtained backdrop and into the backstage area, where the actor who played Benedick then entered from for the next scene.

The spotlight was suddenly on the man who played Benedick again, but this time in full force, the force of her gaze summoning everything it took for her not to be lustful until she finally sighed and gave herself the benefit of where the fantasy was going anyway.

By the time Benedick had given his final line and exited, Liza was sighing with relief at the newly finished fantasy, hoping it could come true—except for the fact that the man had gone backstage already and the play was over.

Then, just before everybody filed out, a boy announced who the players were, and singled out the guests who played: Blintz, and the man playing Benedick, Gant.

Blintz said he was delighted to be there, to play such an iconic role.

Gant said he was just honored, as he was just planning on becoming a lawyer, almost was one in fact.

Liza almost fainted.

9.

Liza looked at the Duke's Head window with a brick in her hand.

She needed one last revolutionary act before she gave it up completely.

The wind was at her back, and the moon in front of her and above the bar was glowing.

She was going to Oxford. She would marry that actor/lawyer. She would become herself.

There was no way she could let down Ailen, or ever enact vengeance against him also.

She needed this brick to represent more than she could ever do, and it would, she thought.

I see no way out of my revolutionary bent than to enact it fully and totally in one glorious instance.

Then do what you must, but do it quickly so you don't get caught, Aggie responded in Liza's mind.

Liza threw the brick at the window with all her might, not quite yet shattering it, though.

Liza looked at the cobwebbed cracks in the window, and put her index finger against them.

She pushed slightly and then harder, and the cracks gave way to an avalanche of glass.

Liza retreated away from Duke's Head and towards Junie, studying, and her future.

10.

Leo surveyed the procession that had formed at the steps of the Basilica. He was meant to climb said steps at the very center of them, perpendicular from the procession that had formed. Pius VII was nowhere in sight this time, so Leo figured he really was going to become the next Pope. But something troubled him as he climbed the steps, and that was the fact that Pius VII was, for all he knew, not dead yet. Usually papal succession only happens when the previous pope dies. That was just the way it was, regardless of his special status, and he knew that.

A prelate handed the scepter to the leftmost cardinal, and the miter was handed to the rightmost cardinal. The lines distributed their two items down to the center cardinal, who grabbed them one after the other with a magnanimity Leo thought rehearsed until he realized it was indeed one hundred percent rehearsed—as no doubt he was not around to see Pius VII mitered.

Words were said in Latin, and Leo nodded gravely when one sentence ended and another began. After a while, the head cardinal put the miter on Leo's head so slowly it almost fell off because of where he'd placed it. But he caught himself and then gave a short laugh—to everyone present—and everybody laughed in turn at this injection of humor into the proceedings until gradually a quiet arose again.

Leo then took the scepter and said he would perform his duties to the best of his apostolic abilities, at which some of the other cardinals laughed. But Leo paid them no mind, ridding himself of his cardinal clothes, which a prelate then picked up. As the prelate scurried off towards wherever he scurried off to next, Leo noticed a crowd forming in the distance.

An angry mob had formed outside the gates leading to the Basilica, and the public outcry came swiftly towards where Leo was standing.

They shouted about his height, his age, his stature, his supposed maturity level, until some were blue in the face and some others (mostly men actually) fainted from the shock of seeing so young a pope.

Leo spoke loudly that he didn't wish to set a dangerous precedent, but that he was chosen by God to lead the body of Christ out of this hellhole it was in. Unfortunately for Leo, he used those words verbatim and the crowd became angrier and broke down the gates.

Napoleon grabbed a broadsword from a rack next to the Pope's bocce balls in the grand auditorium that served a recreational purpose for all the Popes immemorial. Pius VII was seated in the center of the room, and he asked how Napoleon had found the room.

—I find the room agreeable, he replied malevolently.

—I trust it meets your accommodations.

—And more, Napoleon said, swinging the broadsword to and fro behind the chair where Pius was sitting.

—Have you come to end the papacy? asked Pius weakly. —You've come too late; I don't even have my miter right now.

—Far from it! laughed Napoleon. —I'm here to save it. You didn't think all that power you wield only stems from the church, did you?

—It comes from God.

—Come now, tisked Napoleon. —Even you don't believe that.

—With my whole heart. Or at least with a full half of a heart.

—Well then, let's make that a full heart, he said, lunging at the pope with his sword in front of him.

Pius VII knew what was coming and fell to the floor and onto his side, still in the chair.

Napoleon cocked his head to the side and then tisked again, lifting the sword high above his head right above Pius' neck. —Do you have any last words that I should hear?

Pius looked ahead of him towards the long antechamber filled with amusements he would never know again, amusements that were now turned sideways, as he was. And it was here that he re- membered a time from his days as a prelate when he caught a falling mozetta and let it wash him of the sin of failing, and he be- gan to long for that to be his legacy even though he knew it never would be at this point.

Napoleon let the sword fall in an arc from high above his head until it sliced through the neck of Pius VII and went between Na- poleon's legs towards the other side of the room. He sighed, picked up Pius' decapitated head by the hair, and walked down the length of the antechamber until he reached a door, sighed, and swung it open with his free hand.

Leo watched as Napoleon went past the heavy open doors and onto the top of the Basilica steps, carrying the severed head of Pius VII in his bloody left hand. The crowd behind Leo began to gasp and then shout even louder until Napoleon reached the edge of the top step and raised Pius' head in the air.

—People of God, Napoleon began. —I am not here to replace your God. I am not here to be your new Pope. I am not here to re-write all the rules of history as they have been written thus far. I am only here to simply say that the old rules for understanding power are over; the way we understand earthly power, even from popes, is over; the way history has been written has been wrong, false, filled with lacunae that leave out the most powerful maneuverings; the God you know of died long ago in a fire of his own making, and one can only assume he will die more finally in the years to come. And all I want to say is that I will be here to replace that power-gap. I will be here to plug the hole of the deficient power structures you thought you knew so much about and which you thought could help you overcome all the evils in this world. And I will become evil. But I will also become you. So godspeed and good luck.

With that, Napoleon slung the head of Pius VII high into the air, lobbing it to where it landed between Leo and the newly stilled crowd, equidistant from both destinations. And he didn't stay longer than that, judging his time there needed to be shortened due to any potentially negative response from the angry crowd that he gathered would be fuming by the end of his speech.

But what surprised Leo at least (Napoleon had left by now) was that the crowd was not only no longer angry, but they were either talking amongst themselves, scratching their heads in disbelief, or yawning at the exhaustion of it all. Their faith didn't seem to be shattered; it just seemed to be staying in place, in a place where Leo never dreamt he would ever return to, and to where few in the crowd ever wanted to return again. The crowd dissipated quickly and sifted out through the broken gates slowly as Leo went over to Pius' severed head.

The lips attached to Leo's shoulder whispered that he should sever off the tongue.

Leo said he wouldn't and then felt his shoulder fill to the brim with pain.

—There's more where that came from if you don't cut out that tongue, said the lips.

Leo relented, got a dagger from the folds of Pius' coat, and slowly sliced Pius' tongue off.

—Now give me that tongue, said the lips.

Leo awkwardly reached up with the hand that was holding the tongue and sifted it into the lips.

—So much better, said the lips. —Now we are Blintz *and* Pius. Call us Pius Blintz.

—You are neither, replied Leo viciously. —You are a bastard-ization.

Leo's shoulder began to ache something vicious until he thought to himself that it wouldn't be that bad having an evil Pope in his shoulder.

—You already did, hissed Pius Blintz.

—But in my shoulder? laughed Leo. —Probably not.

—This is no laughing matter, snapped Pius Blintz.

Leo agreed that it was no laughing matter, looked at Pius' head one more time, and then bent down, shut his eyelids closed, shut his bloody mouth closed, and then nudged it with his right foot.

—Let's see what Napoleon has to say of this papacy, Leo said as he nodded to the cardinals that had just looked up from their fervent prayer huddle and into Leo's burning eyes. Before they all filed down the steps and into the adjacent rooms of the portico, they nodded too.

11.

Breton held a Welcome Home sign while Ralph held a bottle of champagne. Gant's train was late arriving to the station, and they figured they would dip into the champagne early until one of them—it was Breton—suggested they absolutely *needed* to hold off on it till Gant actually got there.

—Alright, sighed Ralph. —But I call first dibs.

—Yes yes, sighed Breton back, —we all know that.

The train pulled into the station, and Gant stepped out looking like a million bucks.

—How was the acting, chap? asked Ralph, pouring the champagne into his glass.

—Oh, replied Gant. —It was acting. What more need be said?

Breton laughed and slapped him on the back as Ralph poured the other two their champagnes.

—How'd you do as Benedick? pressed Ralph.

—I did just about all I could to hold it together seeing so many beautiful women in the audience.

—Did you talk to any after any of the shows? asked Ralph finally.

—Oh, you know, said Gant, —No time. After a show it's just not the first thing on your mind. Also I was there a while you know.

—Really? said a surprised Ralph, —not with all that testosterone pumping in your blood?

—Not even then, said Gant as he picked up his suitcase and led the other two towards the carriage that was waiting for them at the entrance to the station.

On the carriage ride back, Gant thought he saw an audience member he recognized walking around his Oxford haunts—on the very street he lived in fact.

—You can pull over here, he told the coachman.

—We're like two blocks away from the house, said Breton.

—Yes, well I need to stretch my legs anyway, Gant replied shortly as he got out of the carriage, stretched his arms up into the sky, and yawned.

As he was bending backwards, a young girl bumped into him and then excused herself quietly, looking down demurely before looking up and gasping ever so slightly.

Gant looked at Liza and smiled a smile that seemed to be the first smile in a line of smiles he'd smile, one that somehow both preceded and followed other smiles, a dual turn upward his mouth had no control over and which his mind wanted to have no control over.

—Excuse me, said Liza again, blushing.

—No no, said Gant. —The fault was all mine. I was the one at fault. I misstepped. I took a misstep. I erred. I committed the wrong; that was I.

Liza laughed and brushed a long strand of her hair further to the side, gaily commenting that she saw no use in equivocating with these types of things.

As Breton and Ralph looked on with mouths agape, Gant began to talk to Liza.

Breton and Ralph eventually made their way away from the conversation happening between Gant and Liza, and headed back towards their home.

—You played Benedick in the Globe's production of *Much Ado About Nothing!* exclaimed Liza, feigning the realization of this fact that she had held closer to the chest than anything she'd held to it before or since. —You were *fantastic* in it. Absolutely marvelous. What a great character, too! Much better than that *Dogberry* fellow, she laughed.

—Yeah, isn't Dogberry such a cad? laughed Gant back.

—He absolutely is. And his outfit and hair? Stuff that. I know he's supposed to be lower class in the play, but the way they portrayed him seemed to be a bit masochistic towards the actor.

Liza blanched before asking how working with that actor was.

—Oh Blintz? said Gant nonchalantly. —He's an arsehole. Pure arse. If there were any way to make a person more of an arse than was humanly possible, God gave that quality to Blintz.

Liza felt strangely reassured by this and asked Gant why he was in Oxford now. As a tourist? she asked.

Gant laughed and said he studied law here, that he was about to become a lawyer and that the whole Globe thing was a lark they just happened to let him get away with.

—Why (and how) on God's green earth did you do that? Why would you interrupt your studies like that? How'd they let you even act in it? Do you have experience with that? Was it hard to land that part?

—Fiking Christ, laughed Gant. —So many questions.

—Well I'm not leaving this block until you answer all of them, smiled Liza mischievously.

—What was the first? asked Gant, laughing either despite himself or actually because of himself.

—Why did you do that?

—For fun.

—How did you do that?

—Saw a flyer posted on the Oxford University community notice board.

—Why would you interrupt your studies like that?

—My studies quickly began to bore me, and I needed an outlet for what I was learning anyway.

—How'd they even let you act in it?

—I tried out a few months ago, and they posted back that I received the part. Apparently they were impressed with my raw theatrical stamina, whatever that means, Gant laughed.

—Do you have any experience acting?

—I played Dogberry in a children's version of the same play as a child. That's about it.

—Was it hard to land that part?

—I will put my cards on the table and say that the hand that I was given was a good hand, but wholly supplied by fate, thus making my audition among the scariest experiences of my life, but also among the most rewarding.

—I think that was the last question, smiled Liza.

—If you have more, let me know and you can join me for a drink later.

—I have so many more. Where and what time?

—Eagle and Child. Seven o'clock tonight.

—I'll be there, said Liza, as she departed, only realizing she didn't reveal why *she* was at Oxford just as she turned the corner into another street and towards her own flat. She figured finally that everything would work itself out in time, and that she was excited for her first date since she got to Oxford—and it was with the mysterious actor who played Benedick—no longer mysterious, no longer urgently pressed onto her by the telepathic matchmaker Aggie, no longer someone she couldn't know just by figuring out who they were.

Gant arrived at The Eagle and Child early, half an hour early in fact. He found the wait so nauseating that his anxiety began to take a hold of his thoughts. He began to think she wouldn't show up, that she was scared off by how much they each knew about each other, that he had spoken too much when they met, that he hadn't let her speak about herself enough, that he'd hogged the stage time of their discussion, so to speak, filtering everything inextricably through his view as they stood in the center of the intersection having a five minute conversation.

To make matters worse, Gant wasn't seated in the pub's miniscule back room (he hated that back room), but was instead seated at the bar directly in front of the doors, where he would hear her footfall and know it was her, a footfall he wasn't hearing, which continued to make him even more nervous than he had been when he'd gotten there.

Gant heard the same light footfall that he'd heard as Liza left, and immediately knew it was her walking into the pub. She sat down on the stool next to him and laughed her way into a free drink from the bartender, which she refused to not pay for in any case.

—Did you find it without a problem? asked Gant, immediately regretting it.

Liza looked at him slanted and said she'd been around the block for a few weeks now.

—Ah yes, said Gant. —I forgot. Classes already started here. What do you study again?

—Literature, laughed Liza. —I wasn't aware we'd been over that.

—We didn't, sighed Gant. —I'm sorry; this is going horribly.

—No, said Liza, —what's going horribly for me are my damned classes.

Gant was going to say something like "Already?," but decided not to out of courtesy.

Liza filled the pause in the conversation with saying that she'd just arrived from London a few weeks ago—she'd passed the entrance exam and was looking to get her Firsts here.

—Wow, said Gant. —That's a task and a half. I should know; I've been trying to for years now. It's slow going, but I think this year is the year.

—To Gant's year, said Liza, raising the pint of ale that had just been set in front of her.

—To my year, Gant smiled back as they both downed half a pint, both of them surprising themselves anew.

—What will you do once you get your First, are certified, and become a lawyer? asked Liza, hoping for the right answer despite already knowing what he would say somehow.

—I'm going to free the last remaining soul in the Tower of London, said Gant proudly. —A young girl trapped in there for no reason other than a fear of superstition, if that makes any sense.

—Not quite, Liza lied.

—Well, since the Witchcraft Act passed in Parliament, people who've claimed to be mediums, in touch with spirits, of the occult, ministers of Satan, you name it, have been hunted down and tried in courts for being in direct violation of the act. It makes no sense. Leave people be, even if they claim to have superstitious powers, or supernatural powers or what have you. I'm trying to change the amount of people being tried for that asinine provision in the act, and this is the most high-profile way to do it, I think.

Liza thought that Gant's plan checked out, but needed to make sure they were on the same page. —Who's trapped in the Tower? Is she the only one trapped there?

—Aggie James. She's the only one.

—Are you taking it to the courts, then?

—That's the plan, Gant said as he downed another mouthful.

—When will you be certified?

—After this year.

—You've got some time to plan, then, yeah?

—Yeah, Gant said wistfully, —that's the plan.

—Can I help? Liza asked, surprising herself.

Gant looked at her and thought of all the times he'd left his own questions unanswered, and began the process of asking them anew in the presence of this person he was slowly beginning to trust. —Ay, he said, —that's also the plan.

Liza brought two pints of ale to the booth where Gant and her were now sitting, making sure not to spill any on either of their hands.

—I brought you the best, Liza said.

—Nothin' but that, I s'pose, yeah? said Gant, wearing his accent on his sleeve more than he usually does. Liza thought to herself that this was good—this vulnerability.

—I just can't crack it, Gant said. —How am I s'posed to have a judge hear this trial? The very foundation of it is absolute lunacy.

—Just do what you can do, said Liza evenly, —and they will eventually see the necessity for it. Maybe make a speech about it to Parliament, get the feelers out there for a trial, get interest up.

—That's brilliant! said Gant, a little too loudly. —They'll jump through the roof to try this case; I just know it. Judges will line up left and right. And then what's more, we'll win.

Liza smiled and tried to make the smallest talk possible amidst his near outburst, however positive. She wanted to be the counterbalance for him, a role she was quickly beginning to think underneath her, for good reason. She was on the verge of realizing that she could never be the counterbalance to such a force as Gant, and that it would be detrimental to *her* to be the counterbalance to anybody—when Blintz walked into the Eagle and Child suddenly, trailed by whatever ill will he left in his wake.

Blintz ordered a round of drinks for himself and then smiled close to the direction of where Liza and Gant were sitting.

—Honey, said Liza, —that's your old acting partner, Blintz. Do introduce me.

Liza could hardly believe she had just said that, but somehow she felt it would be fine with Gant at her side. What harm could Blintz do to her now anyway? His days of evil seemed to be past— he was an actor now.

Gant walked up to the glass-lipped gentleman at the bar, and then waved for Liza to join him.

—Liza, Gant began, —this is Blintz, the famed Shakespearean actor known for his comedic roles, for playing the clown.

And then Blintz's glass lips did something Liza didn't think was possible: they somehow frowned. Blintz started, —I have never played a comedic role in my life, he said.

—Wow, dedication to his roles! laughed Gant, not realizing Blintz's sincerity, such that Liza looked over at him as if to ask if Gant was serious. But they then both knew it was Blintz who was serious.

—Every character Shakespeare writes is serious in his or her own way, Blintz eventually said weakly.

—Blintz, said Gant, apparently trying to match Blintz's weak tone, —this is Liza, a student at Oxford, studying English.

As Blintz smiled and said he was charmed to meet her and grabbed and extended her hand to his glass lips, the carriage ride faded into view, as did her survival of Napoleon's attack on her home. As her hand confronted Blintz's cool, glassy lips—which almost protruded out to meet her despite being glass and stationary—she felt the cool of the lips and the cool resign and world-weariness of Blintz himself, as if that was being transferred into her thoughts like her and Aggie—but without either party having to think. She breathed in sharply and then let out a cough. Good, she thought to herself, her body was rejecting the parasite—she would be no host to Blintz's machinations, in whatever form or fashion they arose.

—Dear, said Liza suddenly. —I do believe we should go. We're going to be late for the theatre.

—Oh, said Blintz excitedly, —what play?

Liza immediately regretted her mistake. —It's the local university players. They do try their best, really.

She didn't regret that, though.

—I must be off as well, said Blintz to break a silence that seemed oddly attenuated with his complete and utter judgment of the concept of a "university players" theatre.

As Blintz walked out the door, Liza mouthed a swear—one that Gant laughed about for so long that it was only until they got in the carriage and moved towards their destination (the playhouse) that he stopped and then looked solemnly ahead of him.

—Quite, he let out eventually.

—As you can see by the diagram on the board, our plaintiff is surely lying. She is not telling the truth. She is a fibber, as it were, as it was, as it is, stammered Gant as he stood in front of those responsible for certifying him a lawyer. A Parliamentary delegation was seated behind them, among them the finest Tories and Whigs the world had ever seen—apparently—up until that point. Gant tried to shift his focus away from their anxious faces and began to look straight ahead of him, at an imaginary point of light directly in front of the door that he hoped to walk out of with his certification in hand.

—Yes, said one of the delegates, —quite. But how on earth could you prove that without the substantial evidence?

—There is no evidence when we speak of witchcraft and magic, which is why it was allowed to be perniciously followed tooth and nail until people lost both of those things through rigorous torture methods. It is finally time to transcribe the words of those possessed into the language of human speech so that they can be fully understood and evaluated.

—And how do you propose we do that? gasped a Whig.

—We must try to prove their innocence through other grounds. Such as insanity, which we can safeguard and study carefully so that these things don't happen except under extreme watch, extreme lock and key.

The gentleman who'd asked the first question asked a second, to the tune of wondering why anyone would want to follow the insane down the paths they've carved out for themselves.

—Because there are no witches, sir, not anymore. There never were any to begin with. It's been a lie fed to us by Catholics immemorial. And also undiscerning Protestants, Puritans, those who left us long ago anyway, perhaps to hunt witches on different soil.

—Without concrete proof either way, how can you reach a verdict one way or the other?

—We all reach verdicts one way or the other without evidence, said a shocked Gant. —You know that, surely?

The gentleman smiled and said he knew it well, but that it seemed uncharacteristic for a young lawyer to put human needs above the law.

—Where else would the laws go to when they had a bad day? Gant quipped.

—Excuse me?

—What I meant is that, why use a system not built for human use on the humans who created it and who operate it on other humans?

—So that they can be fairly tried! yelled out the same Whig from before.

—And I'm finally tried of this interrogation, said the gentleman. —Congratulations, you've passed the exam. Receive this diploma, and wear your appointment with pride.

Gant stood up and approached the director of Oxford's law program.

—I've been appointed somewhere? asked a flabbergasted Gant.

Gant shook the man's hand vigorously.

—Yes, as a matter of fact, smiled the gentleman as he let go of Gant's hand. —You'll be appointed to a court near the Tower. To be the defense for the girl there I believe.

—I'm honored, sir, Gant replied, coming dangerously close to bowing before the director.

Everyone else besides Gant, the director, and Liza had left the room by now.

—Don't be honored, he said as he left Liza and Gant alone in the room. —Just do well.

After the doors slammed behind him, Liza turned to Gant and grabbed his two hands with her two hands. —Can you believe this? she exclaimed.

—No, Gant said, almost sadly, trying to bury that emotion beneath the joy two held hands affords.

—I can, Liza continued. —You've been working so hard for this, and now is your chance to show the world that you can become your own Benedick.

Gant replied that he couldn't become Benedick even if he tried. He'd tried for years to be the kind of person that looked back on his earlier days with correction and empathy, not complacence and sympathy. He said he thought he'd accomplished that, and Liza readily agreed.

You hear that, Aggie? You're not going to rot in a cell forever.

Liza! Have you been practicing? asked Aggie.

Only for the opportunity to tell you that we're coming for you.

Who's we?

Me and the handsome lawyer. He's a lawyer now, thought Liza as her chest swelled with pride.

Congratulations. I'm sure you're as ecstatic as I am.

Let's not get too ecstatic, thought Liza. *Don't want any more trials, now, do we?*

I've been tried beyond human comprehension already, so one trial is enough for me.

Liza closed the thought loop at that, and resolved to return to it later when her and Gant could afford to live past the London they'd known, to arrive at a London they would come to know. To return to the thought whenever the inclination to look over her shoulder arose.

Gant and Liza's wedding was an elopement, but that did not mean that they spared any expense. Birthed in what he deemed "financial blessings," Gant made sure the church in the moors above London where they spoke their vows was adorned with the finest materials money could buy for the age they lived in, for the ages they were. The fountains all had stems floating helplessly in the eddies they were comprised by; the flowers outside the church were all either Irish purple tulips or English white tulips, with one lone black tulip hanging down so that it almost parted the bride and groom walking into the church. Inside, the church was practically littered with white flowers of all shapes and sizes: white tulips as they entered, white irises as they walked down the aisle, white roses strewn all around the church's knave—except for two conspicuously flowerless spots where the bride and groom were to stand.

And the stained glass, too, was covered by sheets of the finest linen, to where the sunlight of the fading day entered almost every stitch and gave symmetrical unity to the yellow flecks lining the insides of the white roses' petals, which almost always nearly folded outwards to let the three onlookers gaze at their ever so slightly variegated beauty.

—I'd like to recite a hymn, said the priest finally.

—What? asked a shocked Gant under his breath. —You can't be serious.

—"Oh for a thousand tongues to sing
  My dear Redeemer's praise.
  The glories of my God and king,
  The triumphs of his grace!

  My gracious Master and my God,
  Assist me to proclaim,
  To spread through all the earth abroad
  The honors of Thy name!

  Jesus! The name that charms our fears,
  That bids our sorrows cease;
  'Tis music in the sinner's ears
  'Tis life and health and peace."

—Now, the priest continued. —We are gathered here amidst the earth, and the fruits of the earth, and all that can see using the gifts God has given them, to bring us life and for us to cherish that life forever and ever. And we know, as these flowers all know, that the coming of the day of the resurrection of the body and of life eternal with Jesus Christ our risen Lord and Savior is at hand. They know because their fault lines match ours—they burn, wither, grope, fiend, die, reach out for nourishment, and receive nothing in return. We know that to be like them is to be adored among our Lord in heaven, who looks upon His creations with the ferocity of a roving jungle predator. And we know that, even if we become assailed by the furtherance of the Evil One in the natural order, that Our Lord will save us and redeem us, and that the lines running through our petals are the source of Him above and not just nature below. Therefore, we should give abundantly towards this earth that God has blessed us with, and feel the ground beneath our feet as if it were sacred, always. Gant, repeat after me: I promise to cherish and respect you with all my heart from here forward.

Gant sighed, as the vows he wrote suddenly didn't match the priest's high pitch so far. But still he began, —I promise to cherish and respect you with all my heart from here forward.

—Now, Liza. Do you take this man to be your lawfully wedded husband, cherishing him in sickness and in health, in good or bad times, etcetera? [It was at the last word that the priest raised his eyebrow a bit before shrugging and continuing.]

—I do, Liza said as she put the thought, *You bet your arse I do* into Gant's head.

Gant thought to himself, *You bet your arse I do,* before quickly brushing it to the side and looking at all the white roses lining their feet, the circles joining in tandems where some rosebuds poked out through the arms of another rose—or another rosebud poked out from between two other competing rosebuds. He thought it all very beautiful, and he thought it all very much in line with the way Liza and he conducted themselves always—iconoclasts, against the world, missioning out into the uncharted social territory of Victorian England with only the two of them to show for it, and leading the way all that besides.

It was in accordance with this that—after the priest pronounced them man and wife, and after they kissed—that each ran to one side of the church and started ripping down the linens that'd been covering the stain glass windows, until eventually the room became bathed in red, blue, and yellow light that cast an enlightening countenance upon the various flowers in attendance, and even dotted the priest with the outlined figure of an apostle.

They laughed as they exited the light-speckled church interior, counting the steps aloud before descending them, Gant whistling for the coachman who was off further in the field doing God only knows what. Liza got in the carriage and started quickly undressing—even before the door was closed—so that Gant had to speed into the carriage arms first, smiling the entire way there.

<u>**Part Four: Reign (1812)**</u> – an adventure

1.

Ailen watched the sheep graze on a nearby hill from the confines of the same house Napoleon had obliterated a few years ago. Repaired by now, it had the sheen of something covering over something else but not completely being separate from either in definition. Its newly white-bricked exterior only served to heighten its initial purpose as a wooden house, much like a shack but sturdier; much like a house, but homier. And this new outline it adopted after Napoleon shed its old one away from it forever only made Ailen look around as if he's missing something, sometimes even touching the brick whenever he decided to pace around the confines of the hut like a glorified, housekept racehorse.

But when he looked away from the fireplace and onto the sheep that flocked around a ways away, outside, he began to be reminded of the benefits of shepherding, even from afar. He sighed and then saw a hat crest the hill—a small hat for a small person—until the hunched-over man was almost fully visible coming down through the boggy moor, dodging the small space of land inhabitable for the sheep, rounding the edge of the pen, and heading towards the house, his face covered by what appeared to be a very thick scarf.

Ailen leant his musket beside the door and opened it when the stranger got close enough to talk to. The stranger didn't seem to mince words, but they remained muffled by the scarf to such an extent that Ailen could barely catch any of the scant words he actually said.

—D' 'ou 'ave bi' 'f 'pper?

—Excuse me? Ailen asked after a moment.

The stranger mimed putting a spoon up to his scarf.

—Oh, of course! exclaimed Ailen, leading the stranger in and slamming the door with the musket still beside it. —I'm sorry; I can just barely understand you behind that scarf. Well, there's no need to have that scarf on still. Here, lemme get it for ya-"

Ailen reached for the stranger's scarf but the latter swatted Ailen's hand away and then turned his head to the side slightly. He went over to the coat rack, looked at the musket, turned again to the coat rack, put his coat up—revealing an immaculately polished suit, complete with frills—and finally went to the table to sit down, leaving a stunned Ailen massaging his swatted hand slightly and going into the kitchen to (quickly) pour some soup for him and the man.

The man sat in his seat, still scarfed and still peering out from its folds to stare ahead of him, which—due to Ailen's darting form—meant his encased eyes sometimes locked onto Ailen, who at first caught his breath when he left the kitchen to witness the stare, but who then decided to just serve the stranger anyway. He placed a bowl of lentil soup and a spoon in front of the man, and the man grabbed the spoon, dipped it into the soup gradually, and then brought it up to his scarf. Ailen sat agape at how the man was able to successfully guide the spoon into the folds of his scarf and navigate it in and out of his mouth without losing any soup in the process.

—How d'you do that? asked a flabbergasted Ailen.

The man shrugged.

—Well you, sir, said Ailen, somewhat drunkenly, —are a fiking *art*ist. 'At's what you are. Yeah, an artist.

Either it was Ailen's imagination or the sides of the scarf on his face moved slightly towards the sides of the man's face, as if he was smiling and the scarf was just naturally and dutifully guarding it. —But do take off the scarf and hat, Ailen let out eventually, after staring for a bit, —I feel like an unwelcome host, if you can imagine it!

The man shook his head several times before Ailen stopped asking, took his bowl, and went into the kitchen again. He cleaned off the bowls and put them on a rack to dry, when he heard the stranger get up out of his chair and walk towards the door. Out of the corner of his eye, he saw the stranger take off his hat and scarf, place them on the coat rack, lick his glass lips, and make a move towards the gun beside the door.

Ailen grabbed the heaviest and longest knife, whipped around, and threw the knife past the kitchen door frame and into the front door so far the handle almost became lodged in the door as well— right between Blintz's outstretched arm and the musket. Blintz smiled and finished grabbing the gun, which he turned around and pointed directly at Ailen, walking up to the man and then placing the circular muzzle on his lower chest, pointing it at the portion of his torso where everything was equidistant except the legs, until Ailen was between the muzzle of the gun Blintz now held and a window behind him.

Blintz smiled and, while Ailen was in the middle of saying that someone oughta clean the shit off his glassy smirk, Blintz shot him until his newly unrecognizable body blasted out the window and landed between him and the pen of sheep, who looked up for a minute to make sure everything was okay before eventually return-ing to the portion of grass allotted to them. Blintz walked up to the pen and unlatched it, expecting the sheep to leave. But they stayed put in the pen, never daring to leave the confines they'd been given until one of the other sheep took the first step.

But Blintz never saw the first sheep take that first step, as he was busy rifling through papers on Ailen's desk until he found the deed to the land that Ailen had signed only a year ago. As he put the sheet of paper up to the light and cocked his head towards the paper, chin up, his glass lips shone the fading sunlight directly at the sheet of parchment, illuminating a hidden message.

LEO HAS ALWAYS OWNED THE LAND.

It was in Ailen's handwriting, and Blintz had no choice but to believe it as true, and to try to deliver the message to the new Pope himself. How the new pope would treat the news of his home Blintz had no way of knowing, and, whether it was good or bad didn't depend on him at all; it would depend on how it was deliv-ered. And Blintz would make sure it would be delivered as effec-tively as humanly possible; he owed it to the papacy.

When Blintz's horse had trotted down the final streets leading up to the district of Rome inside the newly-minted Kingdom of Italy—under Napoleon's rule—Blintz hopped off and went through St. Pacrazio's Gate and down the street to St. Peter's in Montorio, a local parish church that divided its time between kowtowing to a worried middle class and kowtowing to the rising Napoleonic tide rising up around the city, two elements which were soon to be joined at the hip until the general invaded Russia.

—Hello, said Blintz, —I'm looking for-

But the guard didn't speak any English, and indicated this by shaking his head fervently. Blintz was allowed to pass through the gates of the parish and came across a clearing in the building, a garden with paths of slowly lessening concentric circles looped around each other until they reached a point at which a stand stood. In the stand, a puppet show was occurring, which caught Blintz off guard, as puppet shows were 1) more typical in Florence than Rome, and 2) not typical in a church or place of worship. Blintz decided not to report it and to just go up to it and see what the deal was in any case.

—You are going to witness a parable of great import, began the voice behind the curtain, hammily. Two dolls on strings were lowered just in front of a curtain that would move slightly forward every time the puppet-master exhaled in his feverish talk.

—There once was a powerful ruler, the marionette said as the puppet-master moved it up and down. —And all this ruler wanted was power. He didn't care about money per se, or women, or whatever any other trade would be able to procure for him; he just wanted power.

—But, shook the other doll, —this meant he had to forego some of the things that had made him special before he pursued power. [The doll here looked at the other doll and then turned to the side with its hands over its eyes.]

—It became clear to the ruler that he not only needed to gain power, but he needed to take someone else's power as well, said the other doll, who began to be chased around the small stage by the power-mad doll.

—This other leader, though he is not sane, is not as power-mad as I am, said the power-mad doll. —Therefore, I will take his power to cover over my own sins, and I will use his righteousness to my advantage. There will be nobody against me as soon as I usurp his power and then make the economy better.

The "sane" doll then began to be savagely beaten by the power-mad doll (who was wearing a suspiciously Napoleonic hat), until the puppet-master dropped the puppet's handle onto the marionette, which the power-mad doll began to hover and dance a jig over like the madman he was purported to be.

—This is now not only my land, but will soon be my people, my kin. They will join forces with me on this quest towards a superseding power of great significance, one that goes beyond the power of Popes or cardinals or kings even. No, this will be a full partnership between a sister republic and I. But who is this?

A more ostensibly working-class puppet entered stage left and began to ask the Napoleonic figure question after question.

—Who will maintain our crops?

—Why, you all will, laughed the power-mad puppet.

—Who will restore our economy, since it's been in shambles, tied to the papacy as it was?

—Why, I will of course. It's already happening my good boy.

—Who is to blame for all the ills afflicting the peasantry?

—Why, the pope and his cronies, of course, replied the power-mad puppet again.

—If heaven is real, then why does suffering exist?

—What?

—If heaven is real, then why does suffering exist?

—No I heard the question, I'm just not sure I understand the premise of it…

—'Tis a religious question, sir. A question of religion it is.

—No, I got that, laughed the puppet. —I just think the answer is for a different question than the one you're asking.

—Please explain, o eminent one, said the peasant-puppet, a little too dangerously sarcastic, thought Blintz, who became worried for the puppet he was now rooting for, the peasant-puppet.

—I mean, I think that's a square question for a round peg answer. Get back to me when you no longer believe in God's eminent domain; then I'll be able to answer your question in a satisfactory manner. You no longer believe in the papacy, why believe in God—why not just cut out the middleman?

—I'm not sure what God has to do with the papacy, except historically, said the other puppet eventually. —A person's spirituality should be their own, not a Pope's.

—I agree completely, laughed the Napoleonic puppet.

—Last question: why are you a puppet too? By which I mean how are you a puppet?

—What?

—Do you not see the strings you're attached to?

—I do.

—Then are you a puppet, just like the Pope was, just like we all are?

—Oh God.

—No, not to God. Maybe to something else, but not to God, according to you.

—No I just meant that if God isn't controlling us, who is? Other people?

—You're the puppet, look up and ask the puppet-master, if you dare.

—Will he even talk to me? asked the Napoleonic puppet, biting his nails.

—If it's not fate, God, other people, it has to be someone or something. Maybe try to grab the strings we're attached to by yourself and move yourself along.

[The Napoleonic puppet attempts this, but is unsuccessful.]

—Well then, it seems you're in a bit of a dilemma, said the peasant-puppet. —You've given up so much just to be where you are, yet your life hangs in the balance between the opposing whims of the story and the puppet-master. How tragic to be where you are and not see the strings or the puppet-master!

—I can see both if I look hard enough, protested the Napoleonic puppet.

—You can't see either because all you see is me, yourself, and the distance between us that the puppet-master allows for. You need to get to a spot where you can see only yourself.

—How does that happen? asked the Napoleonic puppet.

But as soon as the one puppet said that, his puppet was launched towards Blintz until the puppet landed squarely on Blintz's lap, an effort that Blintz thought would have required the puppet-master's hand to leave where it was, but strangely it didn't—the master's hand never left the part above the curtain behind the frills that disguised it.

Blintz looked at the Napoleonic puppet in his lap, then looked at the blank stage (except for the other puppet that was standing and staring creepily ahead still), and finally threw the puppet with all his might into the stage at the puppet master. The other puppet fell down and a thunk was heard from behind the curtain.

—Eat your own creation, you halfwit, said Blintz eventually after spitting at the stage, spittle that began to evaporate in the hot Roman sun as Blintz walked out of the parish church and into the street again.

One of the sheep hesitantly took the first steps outside of the gate, at first looking around it nervously and then at Ailen lying down between the pen and the house, and then walking towards the prostrate Ailen.

Ailen awoke to the aural sensation of happily bleating sheep, as well as the textural sensation of a tongue licking his face. He opened his eyes, grunted, squinted, and then saw the first sheep who had escaped, licking his face incessantly. He reached out in front of his face in a vain effort to rid his cheek of the sheep's shockingly wet tongue, and then eventually gave up and lay there for a minute more to try to get his breathing to slow down so that the shrapnel could (unfortunately) find some time to settle in.

He put his elbows behind him to vaguely sit up and assess the situation. He looked down at his belly; it was ripped to shreds. Not knowing what to do other than drag himself to the house, he ended up doing just that, then looking above him at the cupboards.

He found the cupboard he was looking for and struggled to get up on his own two feet, eventually having to settle for a heavy lean against the counter below the cupboard. He painfully reached up and grabbed some herbs and then a cloth from the counter.

After removing his shirt with difficulty, he put the herbs all over his stomach and then wound the cloth around his belly and torso—horizontally and then diagonally around his shoulder. He knew it was no good, that he would die eventually, but he figured this would do the trick long enough to tell the others what to expect when they came to see him eventually. In the meantime, he had enough victuals to ration out and enough herbs and cloth to prolong what had now become both a life sentence and race against the clock, with the prison the earth and the time just the time. He did have the benefit of Blintz thinking he was dead—and possibly reporting that to others, which was even better.

He looked outside and watched the sheep who'd licked his face wander back in the direction of the other sheep, remarking how some things never change and then feeling extremely foolish for voicing that thought aloud, even just to his own ears.

After putting his shirt back on, he realized it was backwards. After rearranging his shirt until it was pointed the right way (always north), he went over to the bedroom, closed the door, tossed several books onto the bed, and plopped down. He was leafing through some hack press' Visitor's Guide to Rome when he leapt up, realizing he hadn't seen the deed to the house where it was sitting on the dining room table. He jumped up and stumbled/ran into the dining room, where he found that the deed had in fact been stolen and where he also found a note from Blintz, which read:

"Dearest Ailen,

While you will never read this, I am providing it for you on the off chance that you survive. Because you will not survive, my conscience gets to the do the double duty of both knowing that I provided you with extremely valuable information regarding those you care about <u>and</u> knowing that I helped you recuperate, however that happens and whenever it happens. You should know that I met your lovely goddaughter, Liza, as well as her paramour (husband now? – there's a bit of a rumor going around that they eloped). You should also know that I am tracking them down, as they are on their way to Rome as I write this I believe (on good, old-fashioned Victorian sources, you know). I'm tired of going to bat for the Catholic Church and all its cover-ups, and I've even become tired of the Church of England (which has now become the ultimate Catholic cover-up). No, my allegiance now resides with that great, eminent general, and I have been writing him, and I expect an answer on whether I should assassinate your Liza (and her husband Gant) from Napoleon himself when I arrive at the post office in London (a very close walk from the post office – how convenient!). In any case, I'll let you know when they're dead, as I know you can't go anywhere. The Church of England has lost a soldier, but what they've lost as a soldier, Napoleon has gained in a son of sorts. (Not an actual son, mind you; one of them presides over a district in his new Kingdom of Italy, in fact.) No, I am now a foot-soldier for the oncoming tides of a new world order so pre-saged in meaning and power it will make everyone's heads spin.

Apologies for the whiplash,

Blintz, Esq."

Ailen looked at the sheet of parchment and held it up to the light. Nothing was revealed.

2.

Leo flopped out of his very high, very well decorated bed, near-ly knocking his head on the bed frame and (in actuality) scaring his attendants half to death.

—Pope Leo, said one of them, —you're going to ruin your appearance before your daily briefing.

—I don't *have* an appearance before the briefing, replied Leo coolly. —I would say you wouldn't be able to understand this, but you of all people should understand this.

—Quite, the prelate replied, —I'll just fetch the briefing, then.

—Make sure to read it aloud, said Leo as he settled into a chair two feet from where he'd plopped.

—Oh, of course sir. That goes without saying.

—Ah yes, I forgot, Leo let out drily.

The other attendant returned to the room bearing a sheet of parchment, which Leo saw and commented on—something along the lines of "there's a war going on!" but he didn't have the language quite fully formed in his mind yet, so he held off on saying it.

—Do you want me to begin? asked the attendant holding it, dubiously.

—Absolutely, Leo replied.

—News from Africa, sir?

—Get to Britain first.

—Right away. "There have been some preliminary reports from the British Parliament that a witch resides in the only operable cell in the Tower. The reports are preliminary because of the designation of this individual—Aggie James is her name—as a witch; some want to proclaim her that and keep her in the cell, others want to say she is pretending to be a witch (and that she should stay in the cell), and still others think she is a witch naturally and want her to be able to leave the cell. The consensus, however, seems to be that those in Parliament, as well as the gentry and the laypeople, believe she is not a witch and that she should never have been incarcerated in the first place. And, what's more, they think it's ridiculous that an at first very useful law prohibiting the practice of putting witches on trial has now put a person professing to be a witch in a cell while a trial swirls around her. The obvious question for you, then, should be whether you try to influence the British Parliament through a declaration, or rather if you speak to the Queen about it. Either way, the Witchcraft Act requires a trial to settle it—rather strangely—and so we must uphold the Parliamentary precedence. These are the options remaining to you: either a declaration, a meeting with the Queen, or wait and see how the trial bears out. Their finest lawyer is on the case, a lawyer named Gant Freeman—"

—Read the last sentence again please.

—Their finest lawyer is on the case, a lawyer named Gant Freeman. As you know—

—Stop! Where was he educated?

—I don't know that, sir. I would have to ask somebody.

—That's fine. I know it's him.

Leo's expression went farther than out of his window in the Vatican, and traveled back to his childhood at Wensley. What he saw was taunting and everything almost having a rose tint to it whenever Gant was around him; he remembered the outline of Gant's young figure gliding as he was playing, and wistfully remembered watching him play, with all his angles working in tandem. Leo suddenly had the intense desire to see what Gant looked like now, after so many years.

—Bring the lawyer here, then, Leo said at last.

—He must be all the way in England, surely.

—Well, find out. Thank you.

—Yes, hissed Blintz Pius from Leo's shoulder, —bring the lawyer here.

—Sir, your shoulder, said the servant, —It spoke.

Leo grabbed a loose bed sheet and tied it around the shoulder with Pius Blintz on it, as a muffled cry emanated from his shoulder.

—There, said Leo, —That about does it.

As the two prelates looked at each other with concern, Leo got up from the chair and looked out his bedroom window onto the porticos of the Vatican City below him, out into St. Peter's Square, out at the Obelisk that marked its center inextricably. It looked like the squares where he played at Wensley, and he was about to thank God for this fact, before mentally crossing himself away from any sort of religion to speak of—he wasn't about to get superstitious just because of his new stature as the pontiff. He customarily shook the servant's hand, took the parchment briefing, and let both of them exit for him to make his statement alone.

He sighed and dipped his fountain pen in the ink on the dresser he'd sat down at. He needed this statement to reach people where they were at; how they were struggling and what they were struggling with was the bedrock foundation from which to craft the statement of consolation in these trying times, for Italy, France, England, and the world at large. He had so many followers, had so many subjects now, and he couldn't begin to think of someone less suited to the task than himself. But then he thought about it a bit longer, pen between him and the paper, some ink dripping onto the paper already, and began to think there was possibly nobody *more* qualified than him to write this statement. So he began.

"Brothers and Sisters in Christ,

Do not mistake any of your recent trials for spiritual warfare. It is surely not. Angels and demons have no interest in what we do on this earth; they are busy doing whatever it is angels and demons do that we humans are just not privy to. Also don't mistake recent struggles you've had for crimes against you perpetrated by other people. It is the system people have now constructed that will be what you are struggling against. We are setting up so many systems to hold people down, that I would not blame anybody for thinking the papacy was one of them, but I will ask instead that you think of me (and this office) as a kind of mentorship, where I lead and you follow, where I show the way and you take it. I am not forcing you to do anything, and if I have any say in how this office itself is run in the future, there will be less force used against people who don't fit the mold or are less politically advantageous—they are the truly forgotten: forgotten by the systems we've been setting up, even as you read this missive. I am trying to lead you out of the dark, but I only have a candle, and it is a weak one. It is up to you to take care of your own candle, such that it shines brighter and brighter every day. You shouldn't need someone to tell you all this, and maybe eventually you'll grow out of it, out of this office, out of the church, maybe even out of Christianity as it is commonly practiced. And this is okay to me, because how good is any organization of people if it collapses after losing a few members? Not very good, I assure you. Instead, you will find whatever you are looking for in the world Napoleon is setting up for you, and perhaps he will set up systems that reform themselves gradually towards a utopia. I'm not so sure. But for my part I will reform systems such that they become able to reform themselves—myself—so that I can stand before a people free to serve not me, not the systems, but God himself. May the everlasting waters of God's mercy flow upon all of you, and God's peace towards you all wherever you are.

His Holiness, Pope Leo"

Leo stood up, sighed, lifted the parchment, and went to deliver it to one of his prelates.

One afternoon a few months later, a prelate came up to Leo as he was sitting down to read.

—A boy has been sent for, courtesy of the archbishop of Sicily, the prelate began.

—Thanks, but I have no need for street urchins, Leo replied sharply. —It's 1812. More important things are happening, like war with Britain.

—Not even ones who perform special *tasks*? the boy pressed.

Leo sat upright in his chair. —How old is he? Leo asked quickly.

—Fifteen is what the boy said. He's run into some hard times, and needs our—err, your—help, o Holiest. He just needed forty soldi to get through the week. He promises to be good, winked the prelate, at which Leo shuddered something fierce.

—I'm sure he does. And I'm sure he will be good. The charcuterie board is ready, yes? Then send him in.

The boy rushed out of the room, and within five seconds a thin, tanned young man of what appeared to be sixteen stood in front of the seated Leo.

—I didn't order you; you know that, Leo began before the young man cut him off.

—I know, the youth said, —but the archbishop said you'd been staring out windows, and he thinks he knows what that means.

—I'm not sure which is worse, laughed Leo, —the fact that that's a horrific assumption to make, or the fact that he was one hundred percent right.

—Should I disrobe, Your Highness, err … Your Holiness?

—You think we're going to fuck?

—Da che pulpit viene la predica!

Leo laughed uproariously. —The same pulpit that's going to refuse you. I want to know about you—what makes you tick?

—What makes me tick, Your Holiness?

—What do you get off on?

—Well, Your Holiness, I usually am on top…

—Well undoubtedly: you're servicing bishops and archbishops.

It was the young man's turn to laugh and his smile radiated almost out of the windows of Leo's buffet room.

—Please, said Leo after both had laughed for half a minute, —please eat. There's plenty for both of us, if not for a whole town, unfortunately.

Without saying anything, the young man tore into the food on the board, eating the chicken legs and occasionally dipping them in the caviar, something Leo found innovative and made a mental note to do in the future.

—I realize the meal is a little bit more than just charcuterie, laughed Leo.

—Oh, said the young man with food in his mouth. —I'm sure I'll get over it.

—Why do you do this? asked Leo.

—Do what? said the young man.

—What's your name, if you don't mind me asking?

—Paolo, said the young man.

—Paolo, why do you sneak around and seek the first lay you can get, the first lay that pays?

—I think of it as work, sir, Paolo replied.

—But why does it have to be work for you? asked Leo. —Don't get me wrong; it's fine that it's work, and I'm eighteen and know the deal. But don't you long to make a more lasting impression upon those you love and who love you in return? Don't you want a smack of officialdom to the whole thing? Don't you want it to be thought of as a normal, human interaction rather than something done in shadows you constantly have to create meanings for? In short, don't you want your fucks to be official?

—I'm not sure I understand you, sir, said Paolo. —All my fucks are official, official business, often with important personages such as yourself. It doesn't get more official than that I think…

—Yes, but people with similar predilections as yourself may want to be free to express themselves as they wish without the threat of political intervention, not to mention societal intervention, or religious intervention.

Leo thought briefly of Arla and her statements (or his statements, really) about "sex work" – if they were true statements – and he had no reason to doubt them – then that means that, in the future, sex work would be either taboo or normalized (both?)

because the underlying sex acts outside of societal constrictions such as marriage would be normalized as well, i.e. there would be a stigma but that would be it. And although Leo wasn't sure how he felt about the practice, he had to admit that its future independent of societal norms sounded better.

Leo finally got up out of his seat at the table. —It just seems like we have *such* an opportunity to rid the world of this problem once and for all, the problem of thinking it's a crime or even a harmless perversion. If we can eliminate all that from the top down, how much better would the world be? Think of it: from the highest-ranking member of the Catholic Church, a rigorous defense of men who love other men—think of all the good that could do? People would swarm the streets, they would—

—I don't think there are that many of us- It's us, right?

—It's us, reassured Leo. —And I beg to differ. You should see how many of the pontiffs of the past, and the prelates of the present, and the bishops and archbishops of the future need to get fucked right up the arse!-

Leo cut himself short.

—You're *British?* laughed Paolo.

—I can have you hung for telling anyone, Leo shot back.

—What? stammered a shocked Paolo.

—I can have you hung on a whim, why not for that?

—What happened to your previous idealism? Paolo let out.

—It doesn't operate under the assumption that people know I'm from Britain.

—What happened to all that gobbledygook about letting us roam the streets free?

Leo sighed. —How old are you really?

—Sir? Paolo stammered. —I'm fifteen, like I said to the archbishop and then the prelate.

—How old are you, in all seriousness. I won't judge.

—Sixteen, the boy blushed.

Leo massaged the bridge of his nose and sighed heavily. —Why did you feel the need to say you were younger? Leo asked.

—All the previous Popes have preferred younger boys, everyone in the order has.

Leo put his hands under the side of the table, and was about to flip it over sideways before he took a deep breath and, as he was letting it out, let Paolo know that that would no longer happen as long as he was Pope. —That perversion is all about power, the way those in *power* abuse power.

—Well then, laughed Paolo, —you'd have to make an edict saying they'd be allowed to have sex, within the order at the very least. Not that any of it needs to be public, just needs to be written into whatever rules the Catholic Church follows for their elected officials.

—I can do that, said Leo. —We can make that happen.

Paolo let out a laugh. —Ah yes, have fun getting excommunicated.

—I'm the Pope, Leo protested.

—And even Popes have to follow the rules, said Paolo.

—I can rewrite the rules, though.

—You need backing for the rules.

—Let's stage a miracle, then, said Leo, smiling.

—Let's work on the miracle right in front of us. Then let's focus on the other one, said Paolo, suddenly assertive and walking towards Leo.

Leo's eighteen-year-old body rang with the promise of another sixteen-year-old boy to spend the night with, and his heart clanged a melody that he was about to write down before Paolo kissed him on the lips from the side of the table. Then he forgot it.

Leo stretched his arms as he sat in his divan chair awaiting his daily briefing.

A prelate approached him and delivered him the missive, which read, simply:

"O Holy Father,

As we briefed you last week, the wife of Gant Freeman has been ascertained. Liza Lightbody is her name. We know your surname is Lightbody, but surely she is of no relation to Your Eminence, so we didn't look into that at all. Instead, we learned that the newly christened Liza Freeman and her husband, the aforementioned lawyer of the case involving Aggie James, Gant Freeman. We have learned that the lawyer and the plaintiff both went to school with you, and are hoping you can lend a personal touch to this matter. Gant and Liza are currently honeymooning in Rome as you read this, and we at the various dioceses would appreciate it if you sought them out and persuaded Gant (surely not her too!) of avoiding this case and letting his former classmate rot in a cell in the Tower of London until tourists dig her up later. She has been making a mockery of all that we hold dear; namely, that the supernatural realm exists and we are the first and foremost recourse towards flushing it out if it is at all demonic. We have no reason to believe this Aggie character is demonic; she is simply a nuisance. And, as we have treated nuisances in the not-too-distant past, so too will we treat this one. I trust your full cooperation in this matter. As always, we are at your beck and call should you need to consult us on anything."

The prelate stopped reading, and Leo sat up fully on the divan, wondering at how his Gant and his Liza had met and how they'd fallen in love. He didn't go too far into the daydream before feeling nauseous and going to the window to get some fresh air.

—Sir, asked the prelate, —should I be going?

—Yes, said Leo after a pause, —I think that would be best.

The prelate slunk out of Leo's bedchamber and closed the door on his way out, leaving Leo alone to think to himself about how his estranged twin sister and his former lover were now married to each other, till death do they part. It seemed strange to admit to himself that he thought less of it than he would have initially guessed; it was simply an unfortunate occurrence to add to his list of unfortunate occurrences, a list that held the dubious title of the longest list in his life, right next to the list of all the times he'd pondered upon the list.

He knew what he wanted to say for his statement to his people, and he knew how he wanted to say it, why he wanted to say it, and where and when the Great Event he would speak of in it would take place. He went to his desk, dipped his pen in the ink chamber and began.

"Brothers and Sisters in Christ,

Do not let people take away from you what makes you special. Don't let the naysayers hold court in the house of your personhood. Allow yourself the freedom to know what to do and then do it to the best of your abilities. If that includes things some people would declare perversions (i.e. consensual sexual congress with age-appropriate members of the same sex), then so be it. If anyone knows how to do what you want to do better than you do, test them on it and then learn from them if they do. Otherwise, follow your heart as it guides you into the newfound territories of the world, into places of the world not even explored by those who forbid them. Even if the people forbidding them have their own perversions of a similar nature, they will not be living as freely. And this freedom is what I seek to establish when the Great Event arrives. When it arrives, you will know. When it happens, you will know. Until then, wait and be gracious with one another, as there is no firmly grounded scriptural precedence for justifying same-sex love, but there will be I assure you. It will be coming soon. I have a few things I need to take care of in the meantime. One of these involves a lengthy court case about to take place between England's Parliament and a young woman who I will not name who's being put on trial for pretending to be a witch. Now, I will be investigating whether her supernatural powers are indeed God-given, but in the meantime I urge there to be no rioting in the streets of London and all through England. And be sure to treat the Church of England, there, with the same graciousness I described above. (Even if they are currently to some degree your oppressors, which I have no qualms saying, as it's true, surely.) All will be revealed, but while waiting for the revelation, use love as a cure-all for whatever ails your temperaments, your personhoods, and your communities. May the everlasting waters of God's mercy flow upon all of you, and God's peace towards you all wherever you are.

His Holiness, Pope Leo"

Leo yelled for the prelate, who jumped up behind him and gave him a start.

—Jesus, kid, you scared the almighty hell outta me.

The prelate got a shocked look in his eyes, the shock waves in his body from which he was cleverly suppressing.

—Ah hell, said Leo. —Here, take a lira.

The prelate was very enamored with the coin, tossed it around to himself, and then dashed away past Leo's bedchamber doors, down the hall, down some stairs, and into a square in Vatican City that Leo could look through his windows and see clearly, running through St. Peter's Square like a madman.

Leo laughed at the young boy's excited running, and then settled down again onto his divan after dancing a jig himself. He reflected on the statement he'd written and about how he'd lost nothing in the process.

3.

Gant and Liza were doing what any British tourist would do upon confronting the politically confusing and dense metropolis of Rome: they visited the Roman Forum ruins and the Coliseum.

—Honey, said Gant. —Have you seen this yet? This is the Agripola, this is where they would buy and sell produce!

—Yes yes, very nice dear, Liza replied as she looked around her, where in every direction was a ruin, thinly trailing her view wherever she turned. Every location she looked seemed to conspire against the view she'd had of the ruins—what she'd read about somewhere in a book, or what she'd been told by hearsay. Now she could only use her eyes, and they were letting her down severely.

—Just try to imagine what it must have been like, exclaimed Gant proudly, puffing up his chest and sucking in the air in equal measure. —To think that Roman Emperors once walked these lanes.

—Two things about that, said Liza quickly. —One, they no doubt did zero walking, and two, they could hardly have been called lanes with how busy it must have been after every harvest.

Gant grumbled to himself, as she was right. —But, even so, think about what happened here, all the commerce and the debates.

—I think that they never distinguished the two should tell you all you need to know, replied Liza sharply.

—Because they were in such close proximity, you mean? Gant asked. —I beg to differ; I think it was precisely *because* of their close proximity that they were able to see the ebb and flow of debate and its practices as a natural offshoot of their entire beings, entire beings they thought were at least partially comprised of the ebb and flow of debate. How cool is that? To have a culture so in tune with what it thinks and says, to have a culture where the two are synonymous in the syncretic unity of a democratic process.

—Are you thinking of the Greeks, dear? asked Liza faux innocently.

—No, said Gant, —I am thinking of the Romans. They may have been decadent, but my God did they get some things right.

—The debates during wine and cheese? Liza teased.

—Yes, laughed Gant, acquiescing to her jibe, —the debates during wine and cheese. Perhaps even *between* wine and cheese: have a little wine, then a debate happens, then you have a little cheese. Seems like a great afternoon to me; I don't know about you.

They laughed and talked for a bit before deciding to go to the Coliseum.

When they got there, a line had formed of tourists. Most were British.

—Hallo, said one gentleman they were just behind in the line. —Whereabouts do you two hail from?

—London, replied Liza before Gant could speak.

—London, aye? said the man. —Same for us. My wife and I that is. [He motioned to his wife to join the conversation.] She's always been hounding me to bring her to Rome to see all the sites it has to offer.

—What was the starting bid? let out Gant, with Liza looking over in embarrassment at him briefly.

—I say. Bid?

—Just a bit of a laugh: you said the sites were on offer, as if they were up for auction.

—Ah yes, laughed the man. —Good show. Although I imagine one of our countrymen could snag a couple of these sites while the picking's good. [He nudged Gant's arm here.]

—Just count me out of that auction. That's far too much money than I'd be willing to drop down.

—Dear, said Liza quickly, —I'm not sure you even *have* that much money.

The other couple laughed and looked at each other fondly before the other gentleman spoke and said, —Have you 'eard the news about the Pope, yeah?

—Goodness, no, said Liza. —Inform us, please.

—Apparently, based on the statement he just put out, said the man. —It uh … it implies that someone will not be excommunicated for engaging in sodomy or other similar interactions between members of the same sex. Quite a communiqué – I do wonder how much trouble this Pope will get in, but he says there will be a miracle backing it up, from him. So I'm keeping my eyes peeled. It's one of the reasons I came to Rome in the first place; see how this all reveals itself. In any case, it makes me right glad that I'm with the Church of England. I can't even imagine what British Catholics are going through right now. Pope Leo has some very strange ideas, indeed.

And it was then that Gant got a far-off look in his eyes, and his knees went weak.

—Do you need to lie down, dear? asked Liza.

—No, dear, replied Gant. —I'll be fine. Was just reminiscing on old times a bit.

—Good times? asked Liza mischievously.

—Yeah, said Gant sadly. —Good times.

—Well, we'll leave you to it, said the other gentleman. —It was very nice to meet you both.

—Yes, very nice, said the gentleman's wife.

—Nice to meet the both of you as well, said Liza, before turning to Gant, who said what amounted to the same, just with slightly different words.

Gant and Liza walked through the Coliseum, marveling at the chambers below, walking down the center of the building—in the eye of the Roman storm—and looking down into where they would have kept the lions and people in preparation for their duels. It reminded Gant of looking down from the sky somehow, with each individual blade of grass and the different motes representing the people, all inside buildings that'd had their roofs blown off of them so that Gant could look inside. The fact that the chambers had once just housed bored lions and nervous men only heightened the disconnect Gant felt between himself and the little segments of earth he was looking at. And it was this facet of looking down from the center of the Coliseum that unnerved him the most, not what used to take place there. Because what used to take place there was forgotten about as soon as he lifted his head up towards the stadium above, and the architectural marvel it truly was: the rows upon rows, and the colonnades outside that he'd witnessed before entering the former stadium. He sighed and looked over at Liza, who was marveling at the ground-level spectacle of it all, and he started to lose confidence in the commonplace assertion that tomorrow wouldn't be better. That was the rejoinder he'd lived with ever since Wensley even, and he no longer wanted to believe it; not for Liza's sake, but just for his own. He knew that they needed to talk to Leo, but how they would manage that was beyond him. Gant did remember the Leo from Wensley always going on about how he was the Chosen One: could he have become the Pope in this little of a time? Gant thought it possible, but only barely.

—Honey, said Liza as she looked with concern at a motionless Gant, —are you coming?

—Yes dear, Gant replied, as he caught up with Liza and they exited the Coliseum and made their way down the street, laughing and gawking at the line of tourists that had formed by then.

Blintz pulled a Napoleon-hatted puppet out of his pocket, and tossed it up to himself several times before squaring up his line of sight with the departing Liza and Gant, the Napoleon puppet falling on his view of their figures as they walked down the street.

Leo sat contemplating whether to issue a papal bull about all that he'd been thinking about, but decided to hold off until whatever miracle he'd conjure up could happen in front of the laity. He hated that he had to answer to this group, like they served as a kind of check on what he could or couldn't do while he was in his papal office; it was humiliating. He wanted his intellect to roam free, to soar on the wings of its own making rather than have to bow down to fictitious dogma all the time. In short, Leo felt trapped, more than he did at Wensley. At least there he could be an iconoclast, a rebel, an outlier. Here, he had no choice but to play by the rules until he could change the rulebook; he needed to conform to what the Pope should be in this trying time.

To that end, he decided to pay a visit to his constituents. Perhaps, his thinking went, the miracle could happen then. But now, he could only schedule a time to address the city. So he sat back down on his divan and counted the tiles on the floor until one of his prelates showed up randomly.

—Hallo, said Leo, —what's this?

The prelate was carrying a missive, which he handed to Leo, who read the following:

"Your Holiness,

We have become concerned with your actions lately, and would like you to explain yourself in front of the archbishops and nearby bishops. We trust that you have everything under control, but to make sure you do we would like to schedule a visit for two weeks from now. We are anxiously awaiting whatever "miracle" you can bring to the table.

Archbishop of Florence, The Most Reverend Torno Acchio"

Leo sighed and handed the missive back to the prelate.

—You don't want to keep it, Your Holiness?

—And do what with it; pray tell? Look at it before bedtime? Get out of my sight.

After the prelate had left Leo's sight, he had a change of heart and yelled for him again.

The prelate appeared again, this time without any missive.

—I need to meet with someone, Leo said eventually.

—Who, O Most High?

—Fellow named Blintz. I don't think he has a surname, but his given name should be more than enough to go on. Find him, capture him, and bring him to me immediately.

—A crowd will gather, sir, stammered the prelate.

—Did I fiking stutter?

—Right away, Your Holiness, said the prelate, as he left quickly before his answer could be construed to him saying that the Pope stuttered right away.

Leo had felt the lips on his shoulder move as soon as he'd said the name Blintz. Now, after the prelate left, he started shuddering so hard he was afraid the cloth he was gagging Pius Blintz with would come undone. But it didn't.

Blintz had followed Liza and Gant to the inn they were staying at, overlooking both the Sisto Bridge and the Tever River and reminding Blintz of his run-in with the puppet-master right across that bridge and river. At first he camped out in the underbrush at the outside lawn of the inn, the one facing the river, but then, after realizing how terrible of a hiding and surveillance spot that was, decided to move to the other side of the inn and just see when they entered and exited it.

The first morning of his surveillance, Gant and Liza left early to grab a bite to eat, and he leapt up from his perch and followed them into a café. They each ordered ham sandwiches and, a new discovery for Blintz—as worldly as he was—coffee. Apparently, based on their reactions, it was good coffee, so he ordered one too. Everybody was ordering coffee, even—oddly—some young prelates from the Vatican City down the street.

As soon as the waiter handed him the coffee and he put the drink to his glass lips, it almost conducted towards his face and sent shock waves down his nervous system and towards his brain stem and vertebrae, reflecting down towards his extremities and eventually causing him to shake and spill the coffee all over the floor to create a commotion in the small café.

It took a minute for Liza and Gant to recognize that the withering man in front of them – a wisp of his former rotund self – was the loquaciously evil Blintz, but realize it they did.

Liza and Gant turned around and gasped, repeatedly yelling out the name Blintz and pointing at his protesting form, until the three young prelates went over to Blintz and forced him into a headlock and then bound him with a rope one of the prelates had in his pockets for some reason.

—Don't bind him, said Liza. —That's inhumane.

—He had a musket, said the prelate who'd had the rope, —and he was planning on murdering both of you.

—Well, in that case, said Liza, waving her hands.

—Does the Pope want to see him? pressed Gant.

—Yes, as a matter of fact, said another prelate. —The current Pope, His Holiness Pope Leo, wants him brought in.

—Wait a minute, said Liza suddenly, turning to Gant. —Is that our Leo?

Gant nodded gravely and then asked if they could see him as well.

—His Holiness said nothing about seeing the two of you, or, at least, hasn't in quite some time. We'll let him know you sent for him.

—What power do we have to send for *him?* said Gant before Liza nudged him severely.

—That sounds wonderful, said Liza. —Do let us know what you come up with. Here's the address of the inn we're staying at, she said as she asked for a sheet of paper from the café, wrote it down, and gave it to the prelate who'd had the rope.

—We'll send for you when you're needed, said the prelate eventually before the three of them dragged the kicking and screaming Blintz out of the café.

—When we're *needed,* said Gant with wonder as soon as they'd left. —Can you imagine that?

—I'm trying not to, said Liza.

4.

Leo untied the cloth gag from around his shoulder and let Pius Blintz speak to Blintz, who had just been dragged into his bed-chamber and dropped onto the floor roughly.

—Look who we have here, said Pius Blintz.

—Who's side are you on? pleaded Blintz.

—I'm on the side of history, said Pius Blintz, before sticking out his tongue at Blintz and sending a line of drool down Leo's arm, which he quickly wiped off with shock and disgust.

—Weird how the side of history switches so often, laughed Blintz ruefully.

—You're still loyal to the Church of England, then, we pre-sume? taunted Pius Blintz.

—That is Pius' tongue, is it not? It sounds like his voice anyway. [Leo nodded.] Ha! So you've just turncoated based on who you're attached to... Classic Pius Blintz, said Blintz.

—This debate is truly moronic, said Leo in a (surprisingly meek) effort to break it up, —and I won't stand for morons in my presence.

—That's reassuring, said Blintz.

—Now, Blintz, said Leo, beginning to walk around the glass-lipped man slowly, —what brings you to Rome?

—I'm carrying out my duty for the Church back home, said Blintz, —the one you turned your back on.

—And what duty would that be?

Blintz sighed. —Eliminating anything that could cause Napoleon to lose his future kingdom.

—Wait, said a confused Leo, —then what was that about the Church of England?

—I've come to realize that the Church back home stands to gain nothing without Napoleon's reign and everything with his reign. While it's assuaged my growing crisis of faith, it has left the gap open for eliminating the possibilities that might overthrow Napoleon's coming reign, i.e. you and the way you're leading the Catholic Church right now.

—You read my statement? asked Leo, trying in vain to hide his satisfaction.

—Who didn't? laughed Blintz. —It was shocking and beautiful. I would say you should write more, but I believe it's Napoleon's place to set in motion those kinds of things.

—What kinds of things?

—Modernity, said Blintz, —the coming age of enlightenment that will be bigger than the original iterations. It will be the most total, and you cannot be the person attached to it, coming as you do from a position of spiritual power. It must come from the top but in a non-spiritual manner, from a layperson who happened to become a world-ranking general, who happened to build an empire with his bare hands and command everything from then on out.

—I think you'll find that the secular worldview-starting empires you build will be as bad if not worse than the religious ones of the past.

—I somehow doubt that, said Blintz.

—The Church will rule once more, shouted Pius Blintz before Leo punched his own shoulder.

—What he means, said Leo, —is that the Church will reform itself until a secular power of the sort that builds worldviews will be unnecessary.

—But societies and countries will develop to where there will need to be another source, said Blintz desperately.

—Not after the miracle, smirked Leo. —Then everybody will know.

—The miracle of your presence, or what?

—Close, said Leo. —You'll see when it hits. It will be big news, news that will spread near and far and reach the farthest corners of the globe; even the as-yet-undiscovered portions will hear about it. Not in their own languages, but they will hear about it.

Before Blintz was able to say that makes no sense, Leo punched him in the face with a right cross. Blintz fell onto his hands, and spat out blood.

—What are the current impediments to your plan to keep Napoleon in power? asked Leo.

—Certainly not your laity, laughed Blintz. —They love him to death. He's helping with the economy and whatnot.

—I was *trying* to murder your twin sister and her husband, said Blintz as he plucked out a tooth.

—Knowing Gant, he'll get into enough trouble that that won't be necessary, said Leo ruefully.

—That's odd, said Blintz. —I followed them around Rome for days and I never once got that impression.

—Well maybe we have different impressions, said Leo between his teeth.

—What's yours? asked Blintz as he finally finished plucking his tooth, —an impression of his dick? You'd like to get an impression of that, eh? Maybe make a little sketch for a natural botany observation, yeah?

Leo wasn't expecting this assault, and his eyes welled up beyond his control.

—Oh sure, said Blintz, —everybody in England knows about you and that boy, or should I say "man" now?

—Say what you want, Leo replied, —but that's an experience that will stay with me.

—Does it still stay with you? asked Blintz with an evil grin. —That itch?

—If you're implying I've done what other church officials in the cloth have done, you are way off base. I've never even done that with someone younger than me—always older or my age, in fact.

—Nice to know the sample size of one has grown by at least one, laughed Blintz.

After he reminisced on Paolo for a bit, Leo asked Blintz what he'd done recently, or rather, who he'd done.

Blintz laughed and replied that it was no one of significance.

—Young girls, though, yes? said Leo as he lowered his eyes.

—What does it matter? said Blintz. —I'm done with religion.

—But there is that part of you that regrets what you've done to those girls, what you've taken away from them, even independent of the "your body as a temple" stuff.

Blintz started weeping uncontrollably and saying that he was very bad indeed.

—I am not into that, said Leo as he took off the garments covering his torso. —But you know what being Pope *has* made me into?

—What's that? asked a Blintz desperate to hear a good answer.

—Love, smiled Leo as he opened his arms wide for the glass-lipped Napoleon sycophant.

Blintz blubbered out something like "thank you," except so long and drawn-out Leo wanted to cut it short, so he kept his arms wide open to hug Blintz.

As soon as Blintz entered the hug, and after Leo closed the hug with his hands, Leo put his right hand at the back of Blintz's head, pressed it as hard as he could into his shoulder—the one with Pius Blintz's mouth attached—and then told Pius Blintz to chomp away.

And as Blintz screamed bloody murder, his eyes were being eaten by Pius Blintz—all the latter's wise words going to shit as the stuff that made up Blintz's eyes now became mush and slid down Leo's arm.

Leo finally let go of Blintz, after which Pius Blintz spat out the viscera and groaned with disgust.

—I thought you'd enjoy that meal, said Leo.

—I'm blind! shouted Blintz.

—That tasted horrible, spat out Pius Blintz.

—How does it feel to eat out your sight? laughed Leo. —Don't worry; we'll get you some glass eyes shortly.

—Where will I go? asked Blintz. —How will I live? *Where* will I live?

—We were thinking Siberia, over near Russia, you know?

—I'll be done for, gasped Blintz. —That's a death sentence.

—More time to think, said Leo, —which I suppose for you means death.

Blintz started sobbing until his glass lips shone brightly.

—Also, by the way, said Leo, —you're excommunicated. So, you know, if I win, it's lights out for real on both you and your *vision.*

A new railroad was being built along all of Siberia, on special request/loan from the Pope, and Blintz held onto that train's railing for dear life as he got off—helped by no one.

His glass eyes and glass lips made him have a fish-like face, one that warded off any potential human connection. So, naturally, he asked around for a bar where he could stay, i.e. one that had an inn attached to it.

He was in (some) luck, as an inn and bar had a vacancy in a town near the Tom River, fittingly named Tomsk, Blintz thought.

He hobbled up to the bar after the barkeep helped him to a stool. He waved the barkeep away, then had second thoughts and tipped the barkeep exactly one kopek. The barkeep knew this was a fortune for the exile, so he cherished it—holding it up to the light, polishing it, etc.—before pocketing it decisively and skipping away.

The bartender asked what Blintz wanted to drink.

—Whatever you have, breathed out Blintz.

—Well, we have two types of ale, regular and extra strength. [He put his hand to the side of his mouth.] The extra strength stuff is illegal.

—I'll take the extra strength, thanks, replied Blintz, putting his head into his arms on the bar.

—What brings you here? asked the bartender foolishly (but happily).

—Exile.

—We have a lot of folks around here the products of exile, yes, said the bartender. —And you won't believe how many exiles the Trans-Siberian will carry on its way here when it's fully completed. I'm sure you saw it on the way here, yeah?

—I can't see.

—But maybe you weren't looking.

—No, I literally can't see. Anything.

The bartender hunched over and squinted to look into Blintz's glass eyes before waving his arms in front of them to make sure.

—You're not kidding, said the bartender.

—Don't know why anyone would kid about that, replied Blintz coolly.

—Some people are cruel, especially around here. You'll find that out.

—I'm living in an eternal hell, said Blintz stupidly.

—I'm sure you don't know what hell is. Being blind in this place will make you realize what it is; I'm sure.

—Hell is other people, said Blintz as if it were a prophecy, but sounding even dumber than before in the process.

—Now now, said the bartender. —I would say that's no way to talk, but honestly it is a way to talk if you want to die. If you *don't* want to die, I suggest you start making some friends quick. Or else this tundra will eat you alive.

—I can't leave this bar. Do you have a room?

—I … we … no. Who told you that?

—Somebody at the station.

—Well they were wrong, said the bartender.

—Ah yes, first time needing another person and it all goes to shite.

—You need a room?

—Yes, said Blintz with as puppy-dog a face as his fishface could muster.

—Fuck, fine, said the bartender as he called to the barmaid. —Yes, hi, do we have a room available permanently?

—Well, once the Pope makes the edict after the miracle, several rooms will open up.

—The Eastern Orthodox Church is changing its views on homosexuality as well? gasped Blintz.

—Well, of course, said the barmaid, looking at Blintz like he was an absolute moron, —they don't want to get left behind.

—Nobody does, said Blintz as he spit out the extra-strength ale he'd been given. —This is terrible by the way.

—Yeah, nobody likes it. Shoulda told you that to begin with. Sorry.

—It's fine, said Blintz, wiping his mouth off. —Do you have a room available or not?

The bartender looked at the barmaid who nodded and then said, —Yes, we happen to have exactly one room available, rent-free. We'll try to feed you, but you need to get a job to cover the food, sorry.

—That's fine, said Blintz, who wanted to cry but was afraid his glass eyes would fall out,

—I'll manage. I just need to get back on my two feet, which, thankfully, I still have. Those aren't glass yet.

Blintz began to laugh loudly, and the bartender was very glad Blintz was blind, as he was looking around awkwardly during his entire laughing fit, which lasted about a minute straight. He was also glad the barmaid, who'd just left his presence, wasn't around to see that either.

The next day, Blintz woke up and fell off his bed and into a cheap, woolly carpet that made him have a sneezing fit. He recovered himself and hobbled out of his room, asking the bartender (who he'd heard yawn) where he could find a solid job.

—I'll get you together with a local man here sells newspapers. You'll need to learn Russian.

—I know Russian; we've been speaking Russian this entire time. I'm fluent, Jesus Christ.

—All right, laughed the bartender. —Just checking. That is the one qualification after all.

The bartender was glad that Blintz didn't see his wink, as it had been extremely cheesy and embarrassing. But Blintz did notice there was no food on the table for him.

—What happened to the food? asked Blintz.

—That was an arrival/welcoming meal, replied the bartender. —You're on your own from here on out. But I'll contact the friend who distributes the newspapers, yeah? We'll have you on the cold cold streets plopping newspapers down in front of people's doors in no time.

—What types of newspapers? asked Blintz idiotically.

—Oh, you know, said the bartender. —Propaganda.

—Well then it's good I can't see anything.

The bartender laughed so hard he dropped a mug and it crashed onto the floor and broke into a million little pieces. He shouted at Blintz that he should, under no circumstances, walk towards his voice; that Blintz shouldn't come near him.

—I heard that, said Blintz, licking his glass lips and wondering why life's blessings were always the most difficult things in life. Then he mentally flagellated himself for the thought, which managed to assuage both his ego and his intellect at the same time, leaving him happy and free to think about the job ahead of him.

The next day, with Blintz not having eaten in forty-eight hours and therefore fairly starving, the newspaperman assigned Blintz with the task of delivering newspapers by shaking Blintz's hand. Blintz got to delivering newspapers right away, having been told that he should walk three paces and throw, three paces and throw. And so he followed that dictum until the very end of the street, and the change in elevation would let him know when a street ended and when it began. That and his walking cane, as well as strangers' kindness; his neighbors along the four streets he was in charge of delivering newspapers to would stand outside their doors and shake their fists at Blintz' departing figure.

Even so, Blintz continued his work unabated, earning a kopek a day, which was an exceedingly good pay rate, especially considering Tomsk would become a booming epicenter of the growing Siberian economy. So by the time old age crept up to the craven fishfaced madman, he was blindingly wealthy and enjoying this new world he hadn't helped create but didn't help hinder either.

Leo began to feel extremely constrained by his Vatican City haunt, and began to plot ways of escaping it. The window was far too high, so that was not an option, not even using his (admittedly fairly long) bed sheets. And murdering a prelate and stealing his clothes seemed a bit too drastic, but was more doable, so he began to think he was making progress in his thinking at least.

He finally seized upon what he thought to be the best excuse (and a historically underutilized one, Leo thought): exercise amidst fresh air.

He called in a prelate, relayed the message, and then sat there waiting for a response.

The prelate looked embarrassed, and then looked very seriously into Leo's eyes before saying, as if he was announcing a death, that Leo could leave and go for a run anytime he wanted to, it just needed to be in Vatican City.

—Well that leaves me with barely any options, said an exasperated Leo.

—There's a courtyard outside, Your Holiness, offered the prelate.

—Thank you, said Leo with a groan, —I'll do that. … We should expand the gardens by the way…

Leo left his bedroom, went down the stairs, and entered the courtroom, looking up at the window he'd spent so much time reflecting out of and finally deciding that this was where he needed to be after such reflection: running in the fresh air.

As he was running, the same prelate came up to him again.

—Oh my God what is it? said Leo.

—There's a missive for you, Your Holiness.

—Let me see it.

The letter contained information regarding the inn Gant and Liza were staying in, as well as when they were leaving and what sites they planned on seeing for the remainder of their time in city. Besides being just generally curious as to how his prelates gathered the last bit of information, Leo began to picture Gant and Liza engaging in sexual congress. And this made him want to rip up the letter, eat it, and shit out what's left. He decided that it was too raw for him to see either of them, and that his master plan would have to wait a bit. After all, Napoleon's battles were stalling at this point, and he figured he could bide some time while he regained his composure and became less nauseous at the very thought of even being in both of their presences.

He called to the prelate and told him to put the missive on the desk in his bedchamber, for safekeeping. The prelate nodded sharply and ran off across the courtyard and up the stairs to the bedroom. Leo sighed and looked across the courtyard at a single white rose amidst the red ones; there at one end of the courtyard, strategically placed for him to notice it.

He let go of his thoughts and followed the flower to whatever entranced land of placid nature it lived in. He walked up to it, but it didn't feel like he was walking. It felt like he was floating.

Reaching out to touch the white rose, he cupped it with one hand, then the other, then both and dipped his head until his nose crested the edge of the petals and dove into them. He breathed in deeply, smelled of the earth and its gifts, and then finally held his head back up and looked at the rose with amazement. It had little lines of black seeping up the folds of its petals, starting at the base of the bud and ending at the edges of each individual petal. He marveled that there were no divots where these lines were, only a translucent gray that complimented the white of the rose severely. It was as if something was telling him it was going to be okay, whatever way the world went, Napoleon or him. That the earth would be okay at least, and that was all that mattered in the end.

Leo agreed with the flower and left the courtyard happy and grateful.

5.

The latest batch of herbs on Ailen's wounds was only causing him to become gangrenous. He figured he only had a couple of days left to live at this rate, and a knock at the door seemed to confirm that.

He hobbled over to the door, opened it, and smiled widely at seeing Liza and (he presumed) Gant in front of him and looking with concern at his wounds.

—Oh these? laughed Ailen. —They're nothing. You should see my back!

Gant laughed slightly, but Liza's nudge silenced it even quicker. Gant cleared his throat and asked if there was anything they could do.

—I'd doubt it, said Ailen. —I'd give it a couple of days at the most.

Liza let out a cry of emotional pain that sounded much more painful than what Ailen was currently enduring. Ailen hugged Liza tightly and then invited Gant to join the hug. —You're Gant I'm presuming.

—You presume correctly, said Gant. —Have you heard about me?

—Only through the person who did this, that Blintz fellow.

—Oh, you won't have any trouble with him anymore, said Liza. —We saw some church officials apprehend him when we were in Rome. I'm sure he's injured worse than you and excommunicated to a place where nothing grows. That's my hope at least.

—What did he do to you? Gant asked with genuine and deep concern.

—Put a musket muzzle to my chest, and then shot me point-blank, said Ailen, half ruefully and half (oddly) filled with pride.

—Fike, exclaimed Gant, —how did you survive?

—You're telling me. … I have no idea, honestly.

—How have you stayed alive? said Liza.

—A combination of herbs and soil, winked Ailen. —Family recipe.

—Is that why you've got gangrene, now, though? asked Gant, somewhat unable to read the small room.

—I suppose some of the soil wasn't as pure as I'd hoped, said Ailen graciously.

—What news do you have? Gant asked. —We might not have that much time.

—Yes, said Ailen as if he'd forgotten and as he trailed off into the dining room, with them trailing his lead. —Blintz stole the deed to the land, and he must have read that Leo would inherit the land, so he swore to kill you both for the sake of Napoleon's coming kingdom, as opposed to Leo's, who's the Pope now, yes?

—Yes, said Liza slowly, —Leo is the Pope now.

Liza didn't believe the words that had just left her mouth, but Ailen nodded regardless.

—We need both of you healthy and ready to talk to Leo as soon as possible, said Ailen with a prolonged, heavy, and painful single breath. —Here's his note. Go as soon as possible to Leo and speak with him.

Liza looked at Gant, who sighed and then told Ailen that they had other business, in London.

—What possible business could you have that's more important than meeting with a brother and friend of you both now?

—Well, began Liza, —there is a young woman wrongfully being locked up in the Tower. Gant and I are going to free her first.

—Well then I hope that Leo took care of Blintz once and for all, said Ailen. —Now the three of you need to keep a close watch of whatever Napoleon does, even while defending that girl. Do whatever you need to do to free the girl—which seems to be important to the both of you for the time being—and then meet with Leo.

Gant had been reading Blintz's note and suddenly blurted out, —Wait. Why does Blintz align himself with Napoleon if he still proclaims to be with the Church of England, however obliquely?

—He seems to be operating under the assumption that the Church of England will benefit most from Napoleon's rule, as opposed to Pope Leo's, err... our Leo's. —He's probably not far off on that, said Gant, as he watched a rain start to build outside the cottage. —So Leo owns all the land, eh?

—Yes, said Ailen. —Well, now the Catholic Church does, to be more specific. But with the way he's been leading in his papacy, I guess it is just his.

Gant began to look around at the godfather of Leo's possessions, strewn about: maps, boards, drawings, plottings, outlines, books upon books upon books, some unopened, some opened to a specific page, but most just marked somewhere in the middle. Gant was proud of the family he'd inherited, that had inherited him, and that he got to inherit equally with them. His eyes became wide after opening a cupboard and seeing a staggering array of different soils all catalogued, with notes specific to each about what would grow best with which type of soil, and what to expect when those things did grow from the soil—how to take care of the plant. He closed the cupboard and mouthed "wow" at Liza, who smiled, blushed, and turned her face to the floor, her shyness in this instance shocking even herself. But how else was she to respond to this immediate and unabashed stroke of gratitude in the one she'd given her life to? She hugged Gant tightly, and he looked at Ailen with a blush of his own, one that Ailen smiled at with a smile somehow broader than he'd ever smiled before, which is exactly what he thought as Liza left the hug of Gant and began her quest towards Ailen, whom she hugged just as tightly but differently, taking it as a form of penance for the time she spent away from him and how she could never have helped him fend off Blintz and prevent his tragic demise, which she still somehow felt responsible for. And Ailen, knowing she was thinking this instinctually, hugged her back and tried to match the tightness of her grasp with his own.

As soon as Ailen left the hug, he took a deep breath and exhaled for a concerning amount of time. And, indeed, that was the way that Ailen died: not because of a hug, but after one.

Aggie could see Mr. Livery's bumbling form being followed by two new people – Gant and Liza! Aggie screamed with delight so loudly that Mr. Livery put his hand over his heart, then crossed himself, then blushed fiercely.

—What was that? laughed Aggie. —I thought you weren't recusant, Mr. Livery… Frankly, I'm shocked. I expected better from a diligent, Church of England man…

Mr. Livery grunted and less than obligingly stepped to the side to let Gant and Liza have the full view of the cell, brushing shoulders with Gant intentionally on the way around. Gant brushed his shoulder off as Mr. Livery's footsteps were heard somehow both stutter-step and elephantine as he walked down the hallway away from the cell.

Liza almost started crying when she looked at the sight of Aggie's squalid living conditions, not to mention her state: frazzled, near starving, and damn near a hazard to herself even despite the state of the cell she was living in. —I just can't take it, exclaimed Liza, burying her head into Gant's shoulder.

—Aggie, said Gant slowly, —we're here to help you.

—I believe you, Aggie returned, matching the slow pace with which he spoke, —but I don't exactly know how that's going to come about.

—I'm not sure if you've heard from someone, maybe Livery, Gant began, —but I'm the lawyer who's been assigned to your case. I will be addressing Parliament this afternoon, and any information I can glean from you would help expedite the court proceedings. Anything at all is much appreciated, and will hopefully be able to help you escape this absolute squalor you find yourself in.

—There's not much to say, said Aggie. —Being a woman, I am apparently not allowed to explain myself and must have others do the talking for me. Not that I mind you representing me in court – I just wish I had a voice.

—Then let me be your voice, said Gant a little too gallantly. —What I mean is, let me speak through you, or let yourself speak through me. I can be your medium kind of – if you let me. Let me know what to say to them today, and I'll say it.

This assertion made Aggie smile from ear to ear, and then made her hold the smile and look at Liza, who smiled back knowingly. —I am a medium, said Aggie.

—What? gasped Gant. —You can't be. M-my entire case rests on the fact that you have zero supernatural powers. Not one or two, but zero. You can't really be a medium; that would destroy this case.

—I am one, though, said Aggie confidently. —I'll show you. Have Liza whisper something in your ear. She'll relay what it is to me, and then I'll say it aloud.

—This would sound fun if my entire defense didn't rest on proving a game of telephone wrong.

The word will be apricot, thought Liza into Aggie's mind.

Liza leant over to whisper the word "apricot" into Gant's ear.

—Okay, Aggie, said Gant hesitantly, —what was it?

—The word was apricot, said Aggie proudly.

—That's not fair, do another, stammered Gant.

The word will be phrenology, thought Liza into Aggie's mind.

Liza leant over to whisper the word "phrenology" into Gant's ear.

—I'm ready, said a not-ready Gant.

—The word was phrenology, said Aggie proudly.

Gant stammered, then cursed, then started pacing in front of the cell's entrance, in front of the metal grate dividing him from this apparently supernatural being.

Then Gant stopped. The thought *Remember the times we had at Wensley?* popped into his head, and he wondered if the thought was sent by Leo until he looked into the cell and saw Aggie smiling at him. He began to see the two of them together for a brief time after Mr. Livery's class, her against a stone cornice, and him thrusting into her quickly so as not to be caught. Remember how easy it was? he thought, against his will. *I'm sure she's better* [Aggie looked over at Liza here], *but do you remember how the threat of being caught lit us up from our very insides. Well, that is how I feel constantly – searching myself for the answer to a question that never materializes. It's gone into the ether between what I desire and how I desire, maybe even between what I desire and how I operate. This is your opportunity to speak on my behalf; not for me, but for everyone who feels othered by the powers that exist in this world. Otherwise, that meeting at the cornice meant nothing. Otherwise we meant nothing; otherwise you and Liza mean nothing. Do you see what I mean?*

Gant looked at Aggie, straight in her luminous eyes. —Yes, I understand you completely.

—Understand what? asked Liza. —What's going on?

Then Liza began to think things against her will as well. *I just planted thoughts inside your husband's head, not to make him go insane or to confuse him, but to enlighten and persuade him. For the former I used logic, for the latter I unfortunately had to use a memory of Gant and I engaging in sexual congress, in order to completely destabilize his defenses.* Aggie looked at Liza and continued, *What did you think would happen when you married someone who everyone at Wensley knew, in the Biblical sense? Did you think you would walk away without a scar? No, I already know you didn't think that – I can tell you're in this game for the scars that it brings. That's good; that means Gant has met his match. I'm happy for you both, but right now, I need to focus my attention on Gant, who will hopefully be able to free me from this asininity. In the meantime, cling onto the thoughts I've given you now and cherish them.*

—Jesus H. Christ, Gant, said an exasperated Liza. —Who didn't you fuck at Wensley?

Gant blushed and – at least half to change the subject – asked Aggie how he was supposed to get what she was thinking in order to prepare for the trial.

—Wait, said Liza, —you can transmit thoughts from miles away, yeah? You've definitely done that to me.

While Gant was feeling strangely jealous and confused about it, Aggie replied that she could not only do that, but she could now put the thoughts so completely into Gant's mind that he will think they are completely his.

Gant stood up to the podium and adjusted his leaflets, which until that point had been scattered across the top of the quasi-lectern in disarray. He cleared his throat and asked that everybody be seated.

This part's easy, said Aggie's voice in his head. *Just convince them that they are here for an important purpose, that their cause will be noble and their righteousness duly measured and just, etc. etc.*

—Gentlemen, Gant began. —I stand before you because of the wrongful accusation of Aggie James as a self-proclaimed medium and even, God above forbid, a healer.

The crowd murmured its response in triple-tone mumbles that coursed throughout the chamber like a slowly rising tide.

Now say you believe that what they have in front of them is a miscarriage of justice of the highest order. Make no bones about how unjust my treatment here has been, how poorly I've been handled by Mr. Livery and the other guards, how squalid my conditions are.

—And it is not as if what we have before us is a menial sin. No, a grave sin has cast a shadow upon all of England, and it comes bearing the name of this Parliament – the entire body, with the sinned against being a young woman named Aggie James. She has survived amidst horrific conditions, absolute and utter squalor, menial food to eat, and the most ghastly treatment from a man of the Church of England named Mr. Livery, as well as sundry other guards present at the Tower facility, as it maintains that one cell for the one operation just so this body can make a show of a poor, innocent young girl who possesses no supernatural powers, except that of a caring heart.

The congress of well-dressed men coughed and then scattered their grunts and small claps across the entire body like a ripple.

Make them believe that I can do nothing supernatural. This part's important; provide examples if need be.

—And I have seen the accused even today, Gant professed. —And she can no more lift a finger against any supernatural force than Mr. Livery can lift a finger against anyone, including himself. [Upright laughter from the crowd this time.] And I can assure you that she harbors no ill will to her fellow man – she has even taken the liberty to not press charges against anyone in a countersuit, including the eminent Mr. Livery himself. No, she has chosen instead to write down her hardships in a book, the publisher for which is still being sought out but will no doubt be found soon. And her book will be picked up and become a runaway bestseller, bringing some much-needed attention to this legislating body's egregious oversight.

Strike at their pathos.

—Gentlemen, said Gant gravely, —would any of you be willing to put your daughter or daughters in those conditions, to say nothing of your son or sons? I should think not! Because the fight we have before us is either to be remembered as a barbaric relic of the past or a trailblazing light into the future. I know which side I would want to be on. Do we want to be remembered for the way we handled ourselves as a young girl lives like a dog in the world's most infamous holding cell, or do we want to be remembered for having fought against this injustice with all our might?

Strike at their logos.

—And it is not morally right to hold her there, either. It sets a dangerous precedent for future cases. Say in a year or two there is someone who claims to possess either angelic or demonic forces, that they say they have those forces at their beck and call; that they can call them up on a whim to decide the fates of somebody or even of several people. No, we should *house* those people, just not in a cell of horrific magnitude. Instead, we should let them live the remainders of their demon-possessed or angel-possessed lives in the safety and comfort of familiar surroundings, what they know best in other words. Now, we are all a logical, sensible bunch; that's why we're here. Then why does a young woman rot in a cell while we reap the benefits of keeping recusant Catholics at bay?

Strike at their ethos.

—Which is not to say her release would engender another religious war or some such nonsense. No, people have long ago given up the hope of returning to the days of such barbarism. Instead, we have logic and religion aiding each other in perfect harmony. What more could anybody want from an ever-progressing nation independent of the Pope, independent of a full monarchy, independent of us going insane at the slightest mention of something outside of the normal. No, this is England, boys; we didn't just invent the normal. We coined it *and* the outside edges of it. This legislative body is the last bastions between a peasantry and growing middle class on the brink of a revolt (and needing a religious reason therein) and the rising tide of Enlightenment ideals finally hitting our shores. Don't *pretend* you weren't listening when someone made that inappropriate joke, or when someone confessed their love to another person in public. You were absolutely listening, and loving every minute of it, savoring every second that enabled you to feel like you were better. Well, boys, we are better, and it's time we showed that to the world stage and let this poor woman go.

Perfection, thought Aggie, sending the thought into Gant's mind and making him smile widely in the process. The Parliamentary delegates stood up and cheered so voraciously that even some of the Whigs became red in the face with passion.

6.

Leo exited his bedchambers and fumbled his way down the stairs in his official garments, tripping over them because he'd barely used them so far in his tenure.

When he got to the courtyard outside, he saw the Archbishop of Florence and the Archbishop of Sicily sitting together very nervously. Perhaps too nervously for their own good, thought Leo.

—Your Holiness, said the Archbishop of Florence.

—O Most High, said the Archbishop of Sicily.

—Please, said Leo wrily, —just call me Leo.

The two archbishops had a hearty laugh at this for approximately half a minute and then (eerily simultaneously) stopped mid-laugh to look sullen again.

—There are very important matters to discuss, said Florence.

—Yes, said Sicily, —matters of the utmost importance.

—What we mean, said Florence, —is that some of your choices for your statements have been questionable at the very best, and downright retrograde at the very worst. We're afraid it's the very worst side of this unfortunate equation.

—Yes, interrupted Sicily, —and I'm afraid- … We both are terrified you will issue a papal bull about your extraordinarily radical viewpoints, which would spell the end of the Catholic Church.

—The end? laughed Leo. —Don't you think that's being a bit dramatic? I thought that was Napoleon's shtick…

Florence looked at Sicily. —That's what we're trying to say, Your Holiness. You are jeopardizing the world position the Catholic Church holds. We know you hail from a country where our brothers and sisters are still oppressed, but that is not so everywhere. There's a certain *je ne sais quoi a*bout our church, and you will not only bastardize the church away from any kind of doctrinal existence, you will also alienate the very members of our Church we are trying to amass – recent converts, of which there are an increasing number-

—What he means, sir, interrupted Sicily again, —is that because you're continuing to issue these radical statements, the Church is beginning to lose its foothold of not only converts but the laity itself, our brothers and sisters in Christ-

This time it was Florence's turn to interrupt. —And that is exactly what Napoleon wants – a weakened Catholic Church. He's already forced us into essentially a position of indentured servitude. Now you are making sure that his reign will continue. The laity is already positively predisposed to that fucking general because of what good he's done to the economy, minting new coins and boosting the economy almost twofold.

—Twofold of what? asked Leo with a grin.

—Twofold as in we can either be under Napoleon's boot because of your idiocy, or we can change course and stay the strong rock that our laity leans upon.

—That's not twofold, laughed Leo. —That's just double.

—And we're doubly asking you to please stop putting out such shit in your statements. Not only is it unbecoming of the office you hold, but in essence it is destroying the very doctrinal foundation we as a Church, as an organization, as a body, as a unit, as a whole, as a whole comprised of parts, as whatever term you call something that's so established in the world order that it's inextricable from human existence, ... hold dear.

Florence was red in the face and had to take a breather while Sicily picked up the pace.

—We're merely trying to get you to see the error of your ways, repent, and do the penance of issuing statements reversing your previous statements, so that we can rest easily and not be worried our entire religion will be wiped off the face of the earth.

Leo frowned and guided the two unwilling archbishops to the flowers at the other end of the courtyard.

—What's this? asked Sicily.

—A garden in a courtyard, replied an entranced Leo. —You see, boys, this is a gift from God. It will not be here forever – it is only here for a finite amount of time. And in the time given it, I trust you will say that it has done its job to the best of its ability; it has served its purpose so ably that *we* are able to look at it every day and marvel at its simultaneously simple and complex design.

—The garden? asked a stupefied Florence. —But I planted those myself.

—No, the white flower with specks along it in a trail from the petals to the stem.

—Ah, replied Florence.

—This flower does not choose what it is afflicted with in our opinion; it just exists and that's that, nothing doing. But if we hold that opinion – our thoughts castigating it for being differently hued and then thinking that's not a presupposition we're bringing into the equation – then we will miss both the simplicity and complexity of the organism, not to mention the beauty of it. This opinion is wrong twofold: it's wrong because it assumes the flecks on the flower are a categorical reason for castigating it, and it's wrong because it's not afflicted in the first place. It's just existing.

—I don't know what you're telling us, admitted Sicily.

—Gentlemen, said Leo carefully, —some men (and some women) can't control whom they love, and it's not a question of increasing the societal barriers against it, because it is a natural overflow of human sexuality. It is instead a trial of us continually removing our presuppositions regarding the love itself and the societal implications of it. It's not the fault of the men or women, it is a fault of the society that places categorical imperatives on their actions, thus stifling their will to act, thus stifling their human instinct and, eventually, their will to live. I'm not trying to destroy the Catholic Church; I'm merely trying to save people who carry the unnecessary shame of having their natural inclinations either discovered or hidden irreparably, with the threat of real, physical violence haunting their every movement all the while. I'm merely asking for you to try to understand the situation as you understand other situations, using your vast intellects and hearts on this matter of grave importance.

The archbishops gasped loudly, declared Leo a heretic, and went off to try to get the Pope himself excommunicated. Leo shrugged and looked again at the flower; it looked close to wilting.

7.

Liza and Gant appeared in front of Aggie's cell without the intervention of Mr. Livery this time. When Aggie mentioned this, Liza smiled and said he was no longer even partially in charge of the Tower's operations, that he was now wiling away his time in exile in a flat in the east-most part of London.

—That's good at least, said Aggie. —So am I getting out?

—Not yet, Gant replied. —But getting rid of Livery is of course the first step.

—How many more steps are there? asked Aggie, trying to hide both her anger and her disappointment.

—We have convinced Parliament to allow you to leave, but the Catholic Church here is afraid of another religious war breaking out if you leave, as most of the non-recusant Catholics here are very much in favor of you staying put.

—What does that mean? Aggie groaned.

Liza looked at Gant and then at Aggie. —That we have the support of every corner and every facet of British life, except for the non-recusant Catholics.

—Jesus, said Aggie, —how many non-recusant Catholics can there be? I find it hard to believe there are more than a few.

—That's the thing, said Gant. —There *are* only a few non-recusant Catholics, with recusant Catholics comprising the majority of the laity here. But Parliament doesn't want to be the source for a religious war on their end.

—And I'm asking how they can be that source if a vast majority of the Catholics are in line with the Protestants in this instance.

Gant looked at Liza and then again at Aggie. —Parliament is worried about secret Catholics.

—They're worried about your safety, said Liza quickly. —Nobody wants another Gunpowder Plot, even with a building practically nobody wants anymore.

—This is unbelievable. If there was even a shred of evidence for such a plot – which I'm sure there's not – then it would be dealt with swiftly and I'd be out of here. But there is no plot, and Parliament just doesn't want to upset the status quo.

—No, said Gant, —that's not right. If anything the status quo is in your favor. You're the first long-term prisoner in the Tower in over half a century, and almost the entire population is in favor of letting your roam free.

—Then what's the hold up?

Gant sighed. —Parliament wants to make sure *everybody* is in favor of letting you roam free before they do, assuaging the secret Catholics somehow.

—And I'm letting you know that that won't happen ever, said Aggie. —There can be no assuaging that group, who are either complacent living their lie, or are seething and will be angry at literally anything under the sun.

—We know, said Liza. —But we're out of options right now. The only thing that could break the impasse is a meeting with somebody in the Catholic order, and that doesn't seem forthcoming at this point.

—Didn't you two go to Rome recently? asked Aggie. —Use a connection there to meet somebody. Use anything! just get me the fike out of here.

Leo got up from his bedchamber's divan and went down to the courtyard.

A group of prelates were walking around at the other end.

Leo began to think about the situation with Aggie in the Tower prison – how she was near starving – and thought back to how instrumental she was in helping him get over the death of his roommate Christian, how she talked to him endlessly about suicide not being the best course of action for anybody ever, and how if he ever felt that way it takes a great deal but mostly sometimes just taking stock of something good – anything good – and he would remember that advice for the rest of his life he thought. He sometimes even found himself with her voice in his head, telling him to get on with his life independent of his thoughts, which come and go, and independent of others' actions, which he can't control. And it was this presence of mind that he sought to return to whenever a bad or unnatural thing occurred in his life – something that he had a hard time getting over – and it was also this voice that reminded him that he was pure inherently, and worthy of love.

Leo called over to the prelates, asking one of them to come forward. The middle one bounded over and asked what the matter was.

—Oh nothing's the matter, said Leo. —I just struck upon an idea and wanted to let my friends Liza and Gant know about it. Please send a prelate to London to carry the message that I've summoned them for a meeting with the pontiff. You can even go if you want.

The prelate looked ecstatic at first and then with the blink of an eye turned crestfallen. —But Your Holiness, that would be impossible.

—And why is that?

—It's a stupid reason, blushed the prelate.

—If it's a reason for this matter, it's not stupid I assure you.

—I can't go because I wouldn't be able to wear my traditional garb…

Leo initially began to think that was indeed the dumbest fucking reason he'd ever heard for not going to London, but then he realized that this young boy merely wanted to be a good Christian in his eyes, and that those eyes had been developed over time to include traditional garb.

Leo sighed slightly. —God doesn't give a flying fike what you wear.

The prelate looked up at Leo excitedly and was about to leave before asking why Leo was sending for them in the first place.

—To free our mutual friend, Aggie James, from her imprisonment in the Tower.

—Your Holiness?

—Yes? said a slightly exasperated Leo.

—Is that such a good idea?

—How do you mean?

—Is it a good idea to meddle in the country's affairs like that?

Leo was shocked. —I think in this instance it is, yes.

—But what if it upsets the natural religious order in England? asked the prelate innocently. —It's very precarious over there right now.

—I'm not trying to upset anything. I'm merely trying to save my childhood friend.

—You need to put out a statement before I go, said the prelate quickly. —Or, as I go. That way, the move will make sense to everyone. Mention the friend from childhood angle, that's good.

—Jesus, said Leo, —shouldn't it be done unofficially, as quietly as possible?

—It's the Tower, Your Holiness, said the prelate. —Everybody knows about the girl trapped in the Tower. Apparently, it's a point of discussion over there, a severe point of discussion in fact.

—How in God's name do you know all this? asked Leo.

—You didn't know that prelates get briefings too?

Leo pictured this young boy sighing about the coming day and drinking coffee while grumblingly reading his daily briefing, and began to laugh heartily.

—What is it sir? asked the prelate, slightly hurt.

—Oh, nothing, laughed Leo, —just had a funny thought. I'll get the statement to you this afternoon; swing by the bedchamber at two o'clock.

After the prelate nodded vigorously and left Leo's presence, Leo bounded up to his bedchamber to write the statement.

"Dear Brothers and Sisters in Christ,

I am calling for the freedom of Aggie James. She should be released from the Tower of London immediately, and I am calling on my laity in England to quit spreading both misinformation and malice, about her or the situation, around the city. Aggie was instrumental in me not committing suicide because of shame over who I was and what had happened to me, and I trust anyone who has met her and had the luck to befriend her would say the same thing. She engaged in solidarity with me regarding sexuality, when I fell desperately in love with a boy who didn't deserve my love. This may come as a shock to you, but we have so sequestered the homosexual impulse towards dark corners where they are not allowed to flourish healthily as they would if they were in the light. And in terms of her helping me avoid the tragedy of suicide – that was how. I was too overwhelmed by love for the boy that I considered it the ultimate tragedy not to have it reciprocated. Now I see that, even though what I engaged in was natural, I was too consumed with it, maybe even because I too still thought it was unnatural. But Aggie taught me that not only was what I wanted natural – that it should in fact be finalized, or, to be more crass, consummated. And so my appeal to you, my followers, is to be gracious and loving with those in times of trial, even if their times of trial are different from yours or conflict with your viewpoints. Even then, struggles are struggles and should be preserved from harsh treatments that exacerbate them and harm the person further; because that could cause suicide sometimes – a culture eating its own children through negligence. So I urge all of you to love with the fire and ferocity of Christ – a fire that cleanses rather than destroys.

Pope Leo"

He called for a prelate, and the same one bounded up the stairs and into his bedchamber.

—This is my statement, said Leo. —Now please go to London. Wear whatever you want.

The prelate read it over and over the course of reading it his smile turned into a frown.

—I don't understand, Your Holiness, he said eventually.

—What don't you understand? sighed Leo.

—What does homosexuality have to do with any of this?

—What?

—Seems like you're just constantly making this about you.

—I'm trying to help.

—Most people don't want the help.

—But some really need it.

—Even some of *them* don't want the help.

—So it should just be ignored, then?

—No, laughed the prelate. —It's just you're trying to square a round hole. There is absolutely zero groundswell for this massive of a societal change.

—Would a miracle change that?

—Yes, but even then it would have to spread like wildfire.

—That's fine, said Leo. —I can manage that.

—Are you planning a miracle? asked the very doubtful prelate.

—No, I'm not, said Leo. —Every day is a miracle. … Send out the statement in England, and keep a copy to hand to Liza and Gant. Thank you.

—Sure thing, said the prelate, —but I'm telling you – most people are happy just to have their perversions.

—Well, I'm trying to make them not perversions…

—But some still would be, yes?

—Well, yeah, laughed Leo. —The unhealthy ones.

—I guess that makes sense, nodded the prelate. —I'll deliver this right away.

—Thank you, said Leo through clenched teeth.

Leo walked down into the courtyard again and smelled the flowers. They smelled like the fresh side of a spring day.

Liza, Aggie, and Gant were in the middle of their deliberations when a young boy dressed all in red – with a tassel tied around his waist – ran down the hallway towards Aggie's cell, finally stopping to gasp for air and asking whether this was Aggie.

—Ay, said Gant. —This is Aggie. Why?

The prelate handed Gant a missive from Leo.

"Dearest Liza and Gant,

I write to inform you that I am throwing my back into this case, so that Aggie can roam free again. Expect action to be taken on this soon, not because of me, but only because I was the last remaining piece to make that happen. Regardless, I want all three of you to visit me as soon as Aggie is released, which will be immediately forthcoming. Sending love to you three.

Pope Leo"

Following this short notice was Leo's longer statement, which – after Gant read the first note aloud – Liza wanted to read, seeing as she did that there was more to the letter.

Gant looked at the statement, then over at Liza, then at the statement again, then over at Liza again, and said it probably was best she probably didn't.

Liza snatched it from Gant's hand, read it, and then looked up at Gant with wide eyes.

—He never told me about any of this, she gasped.

—He was probably too young to tell it, Gant replied, nearly blushing.

—This is a side of my brother I've never seen, said Liza.

—Then it's a side you can bring up to him privately when we meet him.

—What is it? asked Aggie breathlessly.

—Pope Leo has requested a visit with the three of us, said Gant to her, happily.

—Leo's a Pope now, said Aggie, smiling and then laughing uproariously.

—What did he say? Aggie asked.

Gant handed her the note and then stood back from the cell.

As Aggie was reading it, twin tears started to form, one in each eye, until she had to move the note away from her face out of fear it would be irreparably soiled.

—You're a prelate, I presume, said Gant to the prelate who'd been standing there the whole time.

—Yes sir, said the prelate.

—What can you tell us about Leo as he is now? asked Gant.

—Well sir, smiled the prelate, —he certainly knows how to make the rest of the clergy run circles around themselves trying to figure out how to respond to each of his maneuvers.

—That sounds about right, said Gant.

—That's our boy! said Liza proudly.

—Checks out, said Aggie eventually.

—And he's been trying to initiate reforms of the order that state the clergy can have intercourse if they so wish, in an effort to curb the increasing spread of pedophilia within our ranks.

—And has that met with any resistance? asked Gant.

—Not from the prelates, sir, said the prelate, laughing slightly and sadly, —but some of the cardinals, bishops, and archbishops are incensed, my guess is because they can no longer do what they're accustomed to doing with impunity, sir.

—That also sounds about right, said Gant. —People in such positions of absolute power rarely give that power up, much less away.

—How did I not know this about Leo? asked Aggie.

—What, him being the Pope now? asked Liza. —You've been in a cell the entire two years he's been the Pope. The bigger question is how did I not know my twin brother was homosexual.

—No, said Gant. —I don't think he's homosexual. He's just engaged in it in the past. Nothing more, nothing less.

Aggie looked over at Gant knowingly, but resisting a smile for Liza's sake.

—But even so, said Liza, looking around helplessly. —Who was that boy this note talks about? Aggie, do you know?

—Yes, said Aggie slowly, —I know.

As Liza was still looking pleadingly at Aggie, Gant looked over at her too and shook his head.

—Then who is it? asked Liza.

—I forget, said Aggie.

—No, said Liza, —no, you don't. You just don't want to tell me.

—Fine, then I just don't want to tell you. It's better if you don't know.

The prelate asked quickly if he should go, and they all stared at him until he did leave.

—I need to know, said Liza slowly after half a minute.

—It was me, said Gant.

—What?! said Liza.

—I was the boy he was in love with at Wensley, said Gant.

—Why did you never tell me this? asked Liza.

—I thought it would ruin what he have, said Gant, —that you'd doubt what we – that is, you and me – actually have, that you'd think what me and Leo *almost* did would negate what we *have* done.

—So you're saying you and Leo never actually did anything? said Liza.

—I'm telling you that me and Leo never actually did anything, clarified Gant.

—That's not what Leo told me, said Aggie, looking at her nails.

—Then Leo lied, sighed Gant.

—So you two never consummated it? asked Liza.

—How do you mean? asked Gant, nervous.

—What do you think I mean? said Liza, exasperated. —I mean then you and him never committed sodomy?

—First of all, said Gant, —it's not something to "commit." Second of all, no, we didn't.

—What are we defining as sodomy? asked Aggie quickly.

—Anything that doesn't fall under the category of what Leo and I actually *did,* said Gant.

—So it was never consummated in any way? asked Liza, for some reason wanting clear clarification on this matter.

—No, said Gant finally (and somewhat sadly, Aggie and Liza thought). —We kissed and that was the extent of it.

—But you were young then, said Liza. —Do you think if you'd been older that it would have been?

Gant looked at the ground, not happy with this interrogation. —Yes, he said slowly.

—It's not a big deal, said Aggie to Liza. —This happens to kids in boarding schools all the time, and then they have to keep it secret, etcetera. If anything, it's kind of a Godsend they weren't old enough to truly consummate it and live in shame the rest of their times there…

Liza nodded sadly. —You're right, she said.

The three of them looked around alternately awkwardly, reflectively, and sadly.

—Do you feel that way anymore? asked Liza, bordering on tears.

—Feel what way? asked Gant, feigning innocence.

—Towards boys, err… men now? Liza clarified.

—No, said Gant. —I honestly don't anymore. And a part of me wishes I did, if only to be on the front lines of the battle against current society and religion and politics that your brother seems to be on. But most of me is just glad that that part of my life is over and done with.

Liza looked reassured but had one final question. —Do you still feel that way about him?

—Who, your brother?

—Yes.

—No, said Gant. —I haven't thought about him at all until all this Pope business to tell the truth.

—Aggie? said Liza suddenly, —is he telling the truth.

Aggie looked at both of them like "don't make me do this," but Liza's look was persistent enough to where Aggie replied, —Yes, he is.

Gant looked at Aggie appreciatively.

No problem, thought Aggie into Gant's mind, *a part of me doubts she wanted to hear that you still think of Leo and that a part of your mental space is not devoted to her still.*

Gant looked through Aggie's cell window, saw the Globe from across the Thames, and was at peace for as long as it took him to look.

8.

When Gant's gaze returned to the cell, a portly man appeared in his periphery, walking down the hallway towards Aggie's confinement.

—Mr. Livery, said Aggie more happily than usual. —What brings you here?

Mr. Livery adjusted his garments. —I'm here to set you free, young lady.

—And why would that be? smiled Aggie back.

—I'm not such a bad Catholic that I don't take the Pope's orders and run with them, grumbled Livery.

Before Gant could say that didn't sound right, Mr. Livery pushed Gant and Liza to the side and got busy unlocking the key to Aggie's cell.

Aggie quickly glided up to the bars and put her hand onto Livery's hands. —Thank you, she said in a tone that made everybody in the room question the statement's sincerity.

—Don't mention it, hissed Livery. —I should say before you go, he said as Aggie began to hug Liza and then Gant fiercely, — that the matter is still not resolved totally. It is in terms of your imprisonment, but not in terms of how you will live right now. I would flee the country if I were you. Not everybody is as amenable to the Pope's wishes as I am.

—Way ahead of you, said Gant. —We're headed to Rome.

—Godspeed, said Livery, bolting the cell behind him and then exiting down the hallway.

—Godspeed.

—Godspeed to you too! shouted Gant, but he wasn't sure Livery had heard it before the door closed and the three found themselves in the hallway alone.

—Shall we? asked Gant, near giddiness.

—Oh, said Aggie as the three exited the hallway, —we shall.

When they were outside the Tower, Gant looked at the London skyline against the Thames again. It was approaching dark, and they would probably miss any boat if they got dinner. Liza looked up at Gant's concerned face and immediately understood.

—We don't need dinner, Gant, said Liza. —We just need a boat.

—I can't be seen in this city, not in this way at least, said Aggie quickly.

—We'll get you a scarf, said Gant. —To cover your face, avoid detection.

—Everybody knows who I am, protested Aggie. —I'll be singled out!

—Here, said Gant, removing his shawl and giving it to Aggie, as she quickly fastened it around her face up to her eyes.

The three of them approached the Thames, where the wharf was littered with small boats, some with oars and some without. As they were looking for a boat with oars, they saw a schooner approach them from upriver.

—Oy, said the man on the schooner, —are ye' lost?

—Yes, said Gant. —Hopelessly in fact.

—Please help us! screamed Liza up to the man.

—We've got a saying for yer kind around 'ere, we do, the man said.

—And what is that? asked Gant, doubtful the saying would be helpful.

—Lost! the man screamed back at them, after which he fell into a fit of laughter. —Do ya know where yer goin?

—Kingdom of France, said Gant under his breath.

—What was that? asked the man.

—The Kingdom of France! yelled Gant at the top of his lungs.

While Gant was blushing the man caught wind of where they were going and nodded gravely.

—That there is a treacherous journey, at least for the end of it, said the man.

—Can you get us there? asked Gant loudly.

—Aye, I can, said the man as he pointed at Aggie, —but not with *her*.

—Jesus Christ, muttered Gant under his breath. —She's with us. She's just cold and wearing a scarf.

—Why are ye going to the Kingdom of France?

—Crossing it to get to Rome to visit with Pope Leo.

—Why would that be? the man asked with narrowed eyes.

—My mother was excommunicated when I was little, Gant said. —I'm just a devout Catholic man trying to reverse that.

Aggie and Liza looked over at Gant as if to say "is that all you've got?" and then looked at each other as if to repeat that sentiment.

—Aye, said the man, beginning to lower the gangplank to the schooner onto the dock. —I know the feeling, me mum 'as a bit o' the gout, yeah? We've been tryin t' get 'er to see reason, but she doesn't. She 'as cursed the church 'cause they could do nothin' for 'er, and ended up excommunicated in the process. Bloody terrible.

The three of them walked up the gangway and onto the deck of the schooner after the man helped them up.

—An' what's yer names, yeah?

—I'm Gant, and this is Liza and Aggie. What's yours?

—Frederick, said the man, —but you can call me Fred if y' please.

—Thanks Fred, said Gant – all of a sudden very measured, — and when would we be able to land in the Kingdom of France?

—Fike me, said the man, —There's no way we're docking there. Are y' kidding? There's a war goin on, didn't y' know?

Gant nodded and said that was fine, as long as they could be within swimming distance and as long as there was food on the ship.

Liza and Aggie looked at Gant and were about to perform a joint protest, until they looked at each other and decided to hold off and wait for the answer to the two questions.

—Swim, mate? laughed Fred. —We have rowboats attached to the side, yeah? Or y' didn't see those?

Liza and Aggie breathed a collective sigh of relief.

—What about food? said Gant quickly.

—Aye, that too, said the man.

After all three of them breathed a sigh of collective relief, the man began to unfurl the schooner's sails.

When they arrived near the coast of Boulogne, France, the three thanked Fred profusely and carefully placed themselves within a rowboat that Fred then lowered into the Channel's waters. When the rowboat plunked into the sea, Fred looked at the three of them with admiration and goodwill, or so it seemed to Gant.

—Safe travels, yeah? Fred said as they were rowing away.

—We'll certainly try! Aggie shouted back, which made Liza giggle.

Fred nodded and went up past the foremast and towards the wheel to steer the ship away.

When they got to the coast of Boulogne, the three of them rigged the rowboat to a dock, got out of the rowboat, and tried to find a tram. They found one that took them to the train station, where the three booked a train – a whole car! – to Rome.

When the train passed by Paris, Gant couldn't stop looking out the window at all the displays of Napoleonic fervor – even in the outskirts, even in the countryside. People proudly displayed French flags, and had a newfound sense of what that meant for them and their nation; some of the doorways of the country houses had "liberté, égalité, fraternité" painted on them, presumably by the vast pro-Napoleon, but still revolutionary forces in the city and presumably just from those who felt it more severely than others, especially in the country. But Gant continued to find it odd to find those painted doorways cropping up – why castigate them for something they're already doing? And why use a Biblical trope to do it?

Liza never once looked out the window; Aggie looked occasionally.

Gant would update them constantly on what was happening, especially once they got to the capital, where he frankly just wouldn't shut up, as the three were cramped inside the tram.

—Okay, said Gant. —So apparently support for Napoleon has been growing here in France, and there are a lot of new people here, many of whom are loyal to him. And now we're passing the Arc de Triomphe, newly erected by Napoleon himself to symbolize military glory, but interestingly much of what's engraved in it has to do with memorializing those who died in the French Revolution and not just those who died in these Napoleonic Wars.

—Make it stop, groaned Aggie.

—It's extremely reminiscent of Ancient Roman design and architecture, very Neoclassical, said Gant proudly. —And I think it wears it well.

—Very nice, dear, said Liza finally.

—And we're now on one of the most famous streets in Paris, the *Axe historique.*

—Oh God it's starting again, said Aggie.

—This street passes the Louvre and the newly constructed civilian bridge the Pont des Arts.

—Dear, said Liza slowly, —why don't you go to the deck to see all this? It seems very exciting for you, and maybe you'll get the best view of it all from there.

Gant grumbled and went to the very back of the tram while the other two sighed with relief.

The train ride from Paris to Rome took five days.

On the first day, Gant was happy as a clam, sitting and reading, reading and eating chocolate croissants, eating chocolate croissants and drinking hot cocoa. Aggie and Liza, meanwhile, became very glad as they moved away from anything of significance and moved into the countryside of eastern France. And, after they consulted the map, a plan was made to try to get Gant to be asleep as they passed the next relatively big cities, Lyons (in France) and Turin (in Piedmont). They only prayed that the train didn't pass Florence on their way to Rome.

They guessed that Day 2 would see them pass Lyons, and with Day 3 Turin would arrive, so they planned accordingly, with Liza trying to get him to bed very late on Day 1 by talking incessantly, serving him coffee, and borderline faking hysteria and various hypochondriac ills that made no sense on a train (except for claustrophobia, which made no sense in their luxury suite and which neither of them vocalized anyway). Day 4 would be Florence maybe, but Aggie had a plan for that.

On Day 2, Liza kept waking Gant up because of her "ills," and Gant would gruffly sit up for half a second each time and then roughly fall back onto the carriage seat. He would mumble in his sleep next and Liza would wait five more minutes before waking him up again.

Aggie found her way to the train's conductor, who listened to her explanation to not stop in Florence with a reserve typical for his station. He nodded sagely, and then asked *why* she wanted to not stop in Florence.

—Well, sir, said Aggie, —it's just we have a very important meeting with the Pope, and it absolutely cannot wait. We must be there as soon as possible.

—Young lady, said the conductor, —Napoleon abolished the papacy. How could you not know that? There is no acting Pope right now.

—What do you mean? asked an incredulous Aggie. —He sent for us. Officially no less.

—I mean what I said. There hasn't been a Pope since he exiled Pius VII.

—No, said Aggie. —There's an acting Pope, and he'll meet with us shortly.

—And I'm telling you that for all intents and purposes the office of the papacy no longer exists, and won't unless for some godforsaken reason Napoleon is defeated. He's abolished the office in general – all its political power and trappings.

—Well, said Aggie, —all the same, skip Florence so that we can meet with the *symbolic* Pope.

—That I can do, replied the conductor happily. —Already done.

Aggie thanked him and then left the front carriage and headed towards her cabin.

When she got there, she stifled a laugh at Liza waking Gant up for the umpteenth time.

—Liza, said Aggie sarcastically, —now that's not very nice.

—You can laugh if you want. Might help me do my job better.

Aggie started laughing heartily until Gant woke up again, sat up of a sudden, grunted, and fell back against the cushion, asleep once more.

They arrived in Rome and filed out of the train: Gant then Liza then Aggie, the last of whom looked back at the conductor whose smile seemed to get bigger as she looked back at him. They made eye contact and he nodded and Aggie shuddered violently and sped up to catch Gant and Liza.

The three went through People Gate and down a cross street until they got to the Tever River, where they rowed down to St. Angelo's Castle. Gant wanted a tour of the castle, but Liza literally kicked him in the shins until he forgot about the castle visit. They went down the street until they got to St. Peter's Palace, whereupon a prelate – very strangely the same one who'd delivered the missive about the meeting – met them at the entrance to the palace, told them to keep their shoes on (but to wipe them off strenuously), and guided them through the palace yard towards Valio's Palace, where Pope Leo had been living in hiding for almost three years.

As they approached, an Italian boy (looked seventeen, thought Gant) was leaving the palace at that exact moment, departing from it into the courtyard Leo was so familiar with.

—Hello Paolo, said the prelate officiously.

—Ciao, said Paolo quickly before leaving the prelate and the three friends, to walk down the length of the courtyard.

The prelate called after Paolo, shouting to ask whether Leo was in Belvedere, but Paolo didn't hear the prelate.

Then the prelate – who still wasn't wearing proper attire – shouted Paolo's name so loudly that the latter turned around in a huff.

—Who is that? whispered Liza, in wonder.

—Oh him? said the prelate nonchalantly. —That's just Paolo. Friend of Leo's.

Aggie smiled knowingly at Liza, who didn't return the smile.

—Paolo! shouted the prelate again, more forcefully this time.

Paolo sighed and turned around, making his way towards the three friends and prelate.

—Yes? Paolo asked as soon as he had backtracked far enough to within a couple feet's distance.

The prelate smiled, —Tell them about your *friendship* with Leo…

—It's not a friendship, said Paolo bluntly. —We're fucking.

Aggie laughed, Liza looked down, and Gant looked forward angrily.

Gant shot back, —He's the Pope, how can you do that?

—I think probably because this pope has made sure the groundwork for *official* fucks has been laid, sneered Paolo.

At that moment, Gant had a fantasy about beating the living pulp out of Paolo, of resorting to his schoolboy days just for a moment – but he severely suppressed it and just grunted.

—Is Leo going to confront Napoleon? asked Aggie suddenly.

—Yes, said Paolo slowly.

—Where? Aggie pressed.

—Where else? Where the art is… that's all he told me, Paolo said as he turned to leave.

<u>**Part Five: Pacify (1813)**</u> – a drama

1.

The three entered the doors to the Basilica and saw Leo slumped in Mary's arms, apparently not breathing.

But before they could all simultaneously gasp, Leo jumped down and greeted them, saying he was having a bit of a lark, hopefully not at their expense.

Liza breathed out, Gant smiled knowingly, and Aggie let out a high-pitched laugh.

—What's new? Leo laughed back.

—So many things, said Gant. —First, I think you should –

—So you and my sister are married? asked Leo, suppressing a glare but not very well – especially not for himself.

—Ay, said Gant slowly. —We are.

—I love him, said Liza sharply.

—I'm sure you do, replied Leo, his tone bordering on sadness but only Gant caught it.

—What we have is real, clarified Gant to nobody's question but his own unspoken one.

—I never doubted that, said Leo. —The only thing I doubt more frequently is whether our love was.

Gant blushed fiercely and put his head down until Leo extended his scepter and lifted Gant's chin up using its tip.

—Shush now, said Leo.

—I didn't say anything, said Gant.

—Your blush speaks volumes, replied Leo as he retracted the scepter and put it by his side again.

—He's embarrassed because you're being a heel, said Liza. — Just like old times.

—I've got the world under my heel almost, Leo laughed. —What use does my boot have for the side of Gant's face now?

—Hey, said Gant to both Liza and Leo, —I can speak for myself.

—And how strange that then nothing comes out, said Leo.

—No, said Gant. —Nothing comes out that you specifically want to hear, because most of my words are in service of devotion to your twin sister. And if that's too much for you to hear, then I feel bad for you.

Leo smiled at Gant. —Thanks. That's all I needed. You all may leave now.

Aggie stepped up in front of Liza and Gant. —Why did you want to see us?

—To give my condolences to the Tower's most famous recent (and famously recent) inmate.

—Why did you really send for us?

—To give my congratulations to Gant on winning the heart of my semi-estranged twin sister.

—Semi-estranged? shouted Liza.

—It's nothing personal, said Leo. —But I just haven't heard from you in a minute.

—I have been busy with studying, Oxford, and this man here [she motioned towards Gant]. And I only recently learned about you being Pope.

—How recently? asked Leo with his eyes narrowed.

—Why did you bring us here? pressed Liza until Aggie nodded.

—I'm having a bit of difficulty trying to come up with a miracle to give this populace, admitted Leo.

—Miracle? laughed Gant. —Nobody can do those…

—Is Aggie a medium? asked Leo.

—I believe so, said Gant after looking at Aggie quickly. —But being a medium does not a miracle make.

—Ah, said Leo. —But we can make one because of that I should think. No?

Gant sighed shortly. —What did you have in mind?

—Aggie? said Leo as he looked over at her and smiled, —could you be a dear and send a thought into my head?

—Mediums don't do that, said Aggie as she looked at the floor.

—Oh really? Leo chuckled. —Because I've heard otherwise, from the previous Pope himself.

You're being intractable. It won't serve you well in the future, Leo suddenly thought as Aggie looked up and stared at him.

—But it serves me very well now, replied Leo.

Gant and Liza looked at Aggie accusatorily.

—You didn't, said Gant desperately.

—He needs a miracle, said Aggie. —I think we can help.

—Can you feed thoughts into my mind? asked Leo.

—You already know that I can, Aggie responded.

—No, but can you let me have that power, clarified Leo, —to where I can transfer thoughts into other people's minds?

—How many people did you have in mind? said Aggie nervously.

—My entire laity, smiled Leo.

—Like, everyone who's Catholic? coughed Aggie.

—Yes, said Leo, slightly malevolent, —everyone who's Catholic.

—Wait, Aggie replied quickly, —capital-C Catholic, or lower-c catholic, like universal?

—Yes?

—We'd need another medium, I'd need to be close to you physically while you transfer the thoughts, and we'd need a non-medium to bridge the gap between mediums and not, independent of the new one – that's you.

Leo looked out the window and then at Gant. —There's a partition we can use. As for the non-medium aspect, we can use Gant.

—I'm not doing it, Gant said suddenly.

—You don't even know what I'm going to say…

—I know it will be completely unhelpful for the development of mankind.

—Are we assuming it develops now? laughed Leo.

—I think it does, said Gant.

—Then wouldn't it make more sense to let me perform this miracle and see how the world resolves it based on how it would develop? The world knows about these powers – it supplied them.

Gant cursed, said that made sense, and agreed to help them.

—Now we need another medium, said Leo, who shook his head and said it was just his luck to come this close to a miracle.

Aggie looked at Liza and thought *you're a medium, Liza. Why don't you speak up?*

Because then my brother wins, and I don't want him to win.

You're jealous of what he had with Gant?

Liza's mind was silent in response, and Aggie accurately took this as an answer.

He was with Gant a while ago, and they've both clearly changed, maybe Gant more than Leo — because of all the power that's been thrust in Leo's face recently. You need to forgive your brother for what was out of your control anyway, and offer your help because it will make the world a better place, I'm sure of it. I know what Leo will say.

You know what he'll say?

Yes.

What is it?

It's good; you'll see.

Liza nodded at Aggie and then told Leo she was a medium too, causing Leo to almost drop his scepter.

—Send a thought into my head then, said Leo. —Prove you're a medium.

I forgive you, Leo suddenly thought, as if he was saying it to himself but he knew he didn't think it and that it came from his twin sister after all these years.

Leo dropped his scepter and fell to his knees in front of the *Pieta* and wept until his miter dropped onto the floor and landed between him and the other three.

Gant stepped forward, handed Leo back his miter, and said he had a population to address.

Leo stepped out onto the Basilica steps to address the multitude that had gathered in St. Peter's Square, putting his scepter to his side, adjusting his miter, and staring straight ahead of him at the Obelisk.

If one were to look behind the doors to the Basilica, you would be able to see (from left to right) Aggie, Gant, and Liza – with Aggie holding her arms out until they were touching the door, Gant placing his hands against his head so the center of his palms could align with his temples, and Liza holding her arms out and touching the door as well – none of them speaking but all of them in a deep, meditative concentration that nothing could have broken.

But as it was, the portion of the laity that had gathered in the square stood motionless, waiting for the highest elected official of the Catholic Church to say something to them, to let them know that everything would be fine, despite Napoleon's meddling and despite rumors that were going around that the great general would invade Russia and need more troops.

For a while the slight wind circling through the square was all that was audible, until a dove cooed, left its perch on top of the Obelisk, and fluttered away with everyone's eyes glued to it –except Leo's, whose eyes stayed focused ahead of him at the Obelisk itself. Leo cleared his throat and the crowd simultaneously turned their heads from the dove to Leo, who spoke into their minds using the ability of Aggie, Liza, and Gant but saving the words solely for himself and his followers:

I cannot predict the future. That task is beyond my capability. But I have been granted immediate clemency from some force to say the following words. We are so much more than what the past or futurity holds for us, and we're no longer slaves to the present. In fact, we will become less like slaves to the present than we were before. But the double-edged sword of this is that we will no longer serve the past and future in the same way. We will fight tooth and nail with the past and future, all while ignoring the present because we are no longer subservient to it. We are in an abusive relationship with Time itself, with the concept of time as it holds us captive from all that we can achieve. And we are in a failed marriage with Religion. The two relationships coexist only because we allow them to and do not own up to the damage we are causing the relationships, as well as the damage they are causing us. We think all our terms for understanding human sexuality and gender will get us somewhere definable, when the only thing being defined is how much we can define something, the act becoming some sort of cyclical reason to never examine what we need to examine. Well I'm here to tell all of you — around the world — that we must be absolutely modern in our thinking. For the first time in history, people will be more readily keeping track of what we do on a daily basis, and with this comes accountability, not with a god of any sort but with each other. It must be our duty to try to maintain the health of one another, not through systems but in spite of systems, not to try to outwit the systems but to define us outside of them for once. When I was a boy starting to become a man, I loved another boy who was already on his way towards becoming a man — or at least more so than I was at the time. He pushed me away from his presence, but his presence stays with me, and anything that leaves a mark like that is not only emotionally sacred, it is rather a mark of holiness that lingers long after the curtain closes on the physical or even emotional love. And it is this that I wanted to say to all of you gathered here and around the world — namely, that the world is moving a clip faster than anybody realizes, and there will be so many people who will slip through the cracks and I'm letting you know to not let them slip through the cracks. Instead, reform the systems that hold them down and attempt to resolve their hardships through rigorous reexamination of politics, religion, and economic matters. The only thing worse than not knowing what to do is knowing what to do and not doing it, and this message to the world — for modernity to be ushered into the world we find ourselves in now, it cannot be premature. It must be the premeditated thought process of a world that has seen the light once and for all, and that has allowed itself the slightest peek into the mirror of wherever its mind goes when it sleeps. It is for these reasons that homosexuality must no longer be considered a sin. It is among the emotional first fruits, and hard labor mentally and emotionally has been done over love between the same sexes already, so much so that to prematurely close the book on that chapter of our history and nature — to try to hide what we previously called "demons" — does an extreme disservice to the book and its overarching narrative, not to mention its narrative structure. So open the book and read till the page where homosexuality is legal everywhere and not a sin anywhere. I'm already there.

Leo looked away from the Obelisk and at the vast swath of people crowding St. Peter's Square to maximum capacity. He lifted up his scepter and guided it till it had pointed in every direction in front of him, christening the crowd. The crowd stood silent and motionless; no one dared do anything other than blink and breathe. Somewhere and somehow Dr. Eaves, Mr. Livery, Ruker, and Blintz heard Leo's interior monologue running in their heads like an incantation they wanted no part of performing – but perform they had to. And somewhere else, Ralph, Breton, Junie, and Tomothy heard it too, wondering if they were going insane until Ralph and Breton talked to each other, and Junie and Tomothy talked to each other – and eventually what everyone discovered was that everyone on earth heard the message and all it took was hearing more people say the message back and forth for the missive to make sense to anybody. It became a game of telephone – before it was invented – that allowed each person on the line to invent the game themselves. Napoleon heard it in a mixture of French and English and immediately asked if an English-speaking major in his ranks heard the same message in English, and the major certainly did. Everybody in the world collectively shuddered with the responsibility of new knowledge. Everyone didn't know what to do other than go outside and see if this had happened to anybody else, this weird occurrence that only they seemed privy to but quickly discovered that other people heard the same voice in their head. And several people wondered if it was God, but more often than not they ruled that out based on the tone of the message and the content of the message itself. Why would a god undercut its own operation like that? they wondered. And Leo would have agreed with them on principle.

Leo lifted up his scepter, knocked against the doors to the Basilica, and, after they swung open and revealed Aggie, Gant, and Liza, Leo's back became no longer visible to the crowd, none of whom left St. Peter's Square until the next morning.

Leo stepped back into the Basilica and hugged Liza, Gant, and Aggie in that order, saying that they did great and that he couldn't have asked for better help for the event.

Aggie said it was the least they could do, Gant said it was nothing, and Liza said she was always happy to help. Leo nodded solemnly before saying that they needed to catch the next train to Paris and that he would need to change into civilian clothes first.

When they boarded the train, Gant was curiously quiet, even with all the Tuscan villas being passed, even during the outskirts of Florence, even when they actually made a stop at Florence and the train station was for some reason holding an exhibition of artwork from the city's museum. Aggie couldn't help but look over at Leo with concern and thinking *can you do something?*

What would I do? How could I help?

I don't know; maybe talk to him?

You talk to him; I need to talk to Liza – we'll get another car and I'll talk to Liza there.

Leo suggested he and Liza get another car to catch up and hash things out, and Aggie said that her and Gant could play a card game, with Gant less excitedly assenting. Liza nodded and followed Leo to another car.

Leo walked into the car and slumped down.

—So what's new? he asked.

—What do you mean? Liza replied. —You know what's new.

Leo sighed. —How did you meet Gant?

—He was playing Benedick in one of the Globe's productions of *Much Ado.*

—That's a great role, said Leo approvingly. —I'm sure he was great in it.

—He was, but I'm going to be honest, said Liza finally, —I didn't really know how to approach you about this until the miracle you laid out for the world to see. I kept thinking, "is this the brother that I grew up with?" until I realized that everybody changes over the course of their life, and also that we hadn't grown up together ever really, not since we were very little. And it was this that I clung onto when the miracle happened and it was all laid bare.

—What I said needed to be said, said Leo.

—But are you the one to say it?

—Who else will? said a slightly exasperated Leo. —The world is not moving fast enough in the direction it should be going in.

—Is history not dialectical? asked Liza. —Not in a Hegelian sense, more in the sense of things being able to be returned to normalcy before the inevitable occurrence speeds the world's progression up for a microsecond – for a yard or two – and then we wait for the next change?

—I don't have that long, Liza, said Leo, —and you know that. I cannot rest until this is resolved in some way or another.

—You cannot wait for the luxury of having other people resolve your problems for you – that's for you to do.

—And I suppose I should just sit on my arse and let the world pull me down along with it?

—No, but you could be at peace with yourself independent of the world. That's what your lack of faith is taking away from you…

—I didn't know you were religious, gasped Leo.

—Learn something new every day, said Liza bitterly.

—But what does faith have to do with anything systemic going on in the world right now. It seems fairly ancillary.

—That's what I'm saying, sighed Liza. —It is ancillary, but that's the beauty of it: you get to examine your life independent of those systems.

—But those systems prop up those in power only by utilizing the natural inclination towards religion.

Liza couldn't argue with him about that and decided to drop the line of inquiry.

Leo wasn't having it, though. —And if you think all the fairly recent religious wars were about something *ancillary* being *protect-ed* than you're out of your fiking gourd. All religion has been is one cheap trick trying to outdo another cheap trick, and the peace it brings being ancillary to the systems around it (which I still don't believe) won't make a world of difference against what's going on around that peace anyway.

Liza sighed and said there was no getting through to Leo.

—There's no getting through to you either, Leo smiled back.

—Good, said Liza, —then we're on the same page.

—Just like old times, said Leo.

Once Leo and Liza left, Gant realized he didn't want to play cards, and Aggie realized that she didn't want to teach him.

—So what's the deal? said Aggie eventually, the sentence trailing upward in pitch to where Gant knew she was concerned.

—How do you mean?

—We've been passing historic sites… Surely you have something to say about them?

—Not really, said Gant, oddly demurring.

—Then what's the deal with you and Leo?

Gant sighed and almost got up to leave his seat before eventually sitting back further.

—There's nothing to say about that anymore.

—There must be something to say about it still.

—What happened was in the past, nothing more, said Gant slowly.

—But the past infects the future, doesn't it?

—No, said Gant with finality. —It infects the present, and, at present, I don't want to have this conversation.

—You can't or you don't want to?

—Both.

—I think you can, said Aggie. —But I also think the part of you that can't is overriding the portion that can – the portion that needs to.

—Are you really going to drag it out like this? asked Gant finally.

—I need to know what you were thinking while the miracle was occurring.

—I provided Leo the emotional backing for it, sighed Gant. —What more need be said?

—The emotional backing surely, replied Aggie, —but don't you think the miracle would've had a bit of a hitch if that emotional backing was disingenuous?

—If you're asking if I still love Leo, the answer is no, I do not.

—I'm only asking if you used to love him, said Aggie quietly.

—Of course I did! shouted Gant suddenly. —Is that what you want to hear, that I loved him at one small point in my life and then he left it like a star that went all the way across my field of vision? Of course I did, Jesus Christ. Why else would I have come back? Why else would I have helped with the miracle? Why else would I have done anything that I've done for the past few years if I didn't love Leo at one point or another?

—But did you marry Liza to be closer to Leo again?

—I'm not answering that, said Gant shortly.

—It seems like you already did, said Aggie.

—I married Liza because I'm madly in love with *her*, said Gant slowly. —Her twin brother being a former lover I wish to reconcile with desperately is just a happy offshoot.

—So you just want finality and closure with regard to you and Leo being friends again, not lovers.

—Correct, clarified Gant, —I just want to be in his life as a friend now, as someone who he still has an emotional connection to, nothing more, nothing less.

—That's all I needed to know, said Aggie as she sat back happily. —That wish of yours can happen easily, you know. You just need to make it happen soon.

—I will, said a somehow newly determined Gant, for once in the conversation happy that the discussion was taking place and not wanting instead to leave it immediately.

Liza and Leo returned from the other car, and Gant and Aggie greeted them with all the mirth the premature ending of a tough talk provides.

When they exited the train – directly between the Notre Dame and the Louvre – Leo said he had a feeling that Napoleon would be waiting for him at the Louvre, "where the art is." Then the other three remembered what Paolo had said to them before meeting Leo again, so they all said their goodbyes to Leo right then and there, so Leo could visit the Louvre and Gant, Liza, and Aggie could visit the Notre Dame.

In front of the Notre Dame, Leo said goodbye to everyone.

—Goodbye Aggie, he said, smiling sadly and hoping for a re-union as they hugged tightly.

He said goodbye to Liza next, saying he was sorry and that he forgives her too, words that made Liza cry during the similarly tight-gripped hug.

—Goodbye Gant, he said warmly, as Gant replied that they'd always be friends and that there was always a space for him in his heart, even today, even for the future.

Leo looked back at the three of them waving him onwards, and he departed for the Louvre.

When Liza, Gant, and Aggie made it up to the belfries of the Notre Dame, they watched him walk all the way to the Louvre, until he crossed its promenade and finally disappeared within its large doors.

2.

Napoleon had just been pondering on the English message he'd received internally from Pope Leo when one of his footmen came in.

—Sir, the footman said, —we are unable to bring back the Rosetta Stone from Egypt. Sorry for the inconvenience, sir.

—And why would that be? Napoleon glowered.

—Pope Leo's miracle has galvanized the Italian forces to combine their efforts to bring it to the Vatican, in honor of the miracle. Something about the Tower of Babel finally being restored, sir.

—That makes no sense, said Napoleon. —Tell them that if they want their Tower of Babel, they'll find it in hell and nowhere else, because such a thing can no longer exist. Wasn't Leo's message in English anyway?

—I believe some people heard it in their own languages, sir.

—Well I heard it in English, said Napoleon. —Mostly at least.

—Do you speak English, sir?

—Yes, grumbled Napoleon. —Mostly.

—Well then, there you go, … sir.

Napoleon glared at his underling for as long as it took him to pin the last corner of a Map of Europe inside his Louvre headquarters, where he'd been stationed for a year now. He stepped back and looked at his finished Map of Europe. It looked complete, except he was unsatisfied about only holding his little sliver because of the Confederation of the Rhine's strengthening, as well Austria's neutrality – why couldn't they just declare war on him? It would have made it so much easier, especially now that Russia was in his sights… The 400,000 troops being mobilized in France currently would pay great dividends once the route to Russia was cleared away, so at least there was that. Prussia and Poland were of course in the process of being ransacked and plundered and destroyed, so he kept that close to his heart in case he needed a quick pick-me-up. The Prussian army was much smaller than the French army, and they didn't stand a chance so far, but if Austria and Switzerland weren't neutral he would have been able to go *up north* into Russia and not fucking *sideways.* So Napoleon was in the process of blaming those two countries, and their high and mighty Neutrality, for his immediate military problems.

The footman asked if he could go, and Napoleon said yes, but only if the footman could tell him which military generals have invaded Russia from the west.

—I don't think anybody's done that, sir, said the footman.

—Good, said Napoleon. —Then we'll be the first.

The footman nodded, saluted, and left, and Napoleon gave a half-hearted salute back to him before he realized that he didn't need to salute. Usually his words just did that for him, but his brain was so scrambled today that he didn't mind taking the extra action, however limply it was done.

Napoleon paced around his war table, looking at the Map and then at the Table, at the Map and then at the Table, until he thought he would go mad from all this unnecessary deliberation. He decided to go look at some of the art they'd collected in the wing of the Louvre he was temporarily stationed in.

He decided to look at the *Tiber* statue he acquired from looting the Vatican a few years ago, back when Pope Pius VII was alive and in charge.

He always found the right side (left side facing) of the statue very odd until one looked down at the source of the River Tiber god's look to the side: Romulus and Remus sucking on the teats of a she-wolf as Tiber holds a cornucopia in his right hand, supported by his right shoulder, and an oar in his left hand, resting against his left shoulder. What Napoleon always found odd about the statue was never the Romulus, Remus, and she-wolf part – in fact he found that the most natural and in some senses obvious part of the statue – but what he found odd instead was the shape of the cornucopia, how lopsided it seemed, as if it was about to fall at any second. It was never in Napoleon's cards to guess at how the sculptor made it that way, the reasons why, but still he felt somehow angry that this one aspect of the statue could escape his grasp so completely. Even the oar made sense – at least it was buttressed by his left shoulder that was in recline; but the shoulder the cornucopia was on was too reclined towards the right side of the statue, like it would fall if the whole thing wasn't attached through the medium in which it was created, the stonework of the whole thing in other words.

The god looked attractive to Napoleon in a way that ruggedness can afford a man at any point in his life, no matter what age the ruggedness developed out of. It was the quality of the stone itself that brought out the crisp world-weariness inherent in the subject matter of this god with desperate, feuding siblings and a weary she-wolf mother underneath him, no matter how seemingly precarious the cornucopia was. And it was this that made Napoleon immediately wonder if the sculptor was making a point about the state of the Roman Empire at the time – that internal feuding and infighting would cause the gods to lose their grip on the source of its success before it was even founded, represented by the cornucopia. And Napoleon began to further wonder whether this Russia invasion would cause his Empire's cornucopia to fall in a similar way, without the stonework backing of his Empire. But then Napoleon was reassured once again by the strength of the Empire – that he was in fact taking all the necessary steps towards making sure *his* Empire would last longer and spread wider than the Roman one, in short that he would be the stonework of his own Empire, independent of a weakly-held and tenuous cornucopia.

As it happened, the Tiber statue Napoleon was currently look-ing at was separated by a partition from the Nile statue at which Leo had been looking at intently for the same amount of time that Napoleon had been looking at the Tiber one.

This time, the god was leaning to the left (right side facing), and Leo noticed that its left arm was resting on a sphinx and the cornucopia was so set between the sphinx, the god's arm, and the ground, that the stonework didn't matter such that even one of the cupids could rest its little body inside the cornucopia, the little shite. In fact, there were so many little shites that one found it odd that this god was able to tolerate all of them walking all over him in any way, shape, or form. They were climbing over his entire person, distracting him from all that needed to get done, and pre-venting any sort of progress in any sort of direction, such that Leo began to wonder if anything ever got done by this god in this god's world anyway. The little tikes were bearing down on his right arm, which was carrying grain it looked like, and even though some of them were distracted by a crocodile towards the facing-left side of the statue, they were still just littered all over him – throwing tan-trums, crossing their arms and looking at him in what seemed like severe judgment, and bearing down on him so that he couldn't do a thing, like some sort of divine Gulliver forever tied down by the weight and cares of the people.

Which made Leo immediately wonder if this was the purpose of the statue, to try to show all the negatives and slow progress that comes with democracy and all its trappings. Even though it was by a Roman sculptor, he would have been aware of all that can go wrong within a democratic setting such that he could make this rebuke and make it as loud as it is in the sculpture. He wondered what agency the little cupids had in actuality, besides making sure this god was restrained and not able to leave from leaning against the sphinx. The god looked positively beside himself, and Leo could understand why this god would look so unhappy – he had several beings on top of him, wrestling and causing havoc – and little beings in statues almost always stand for multitudes if there are this many in a statue, thought Leo. So what was the statue trying to say about democracy? Leo thought to himself. But it was hard to parse out without some sort of other statue to complement it and complete its message. Leo looked at the partition and noticed it wasn't a full partition, that it had another side, and so he went clockwise around the statue, past the Nile god's resting figure, just as Napoleon also walked clockwise around his statue, past the Tiber god's figure.

Leo looked at the Tiber statue, at the cornucopia above the two babies and she-wolf, and felt sadder than while he looked at the other one, even though the expression of this river god seemed less pained. He found it strange that the far-off look of this god seemed less invested even though the cornucopia looked more precarious. He found the twins Romulus and Remus to be the most fascinating part of this sculpture, especially since the far-off look and the oar suggested that this river god was less invested in the safety and well-being of his charges. One of the twins was looking at the other while the latter actively suckled, and Leo thought it a bit odd that only one of them was suckling – that the twin to the left (when facing the statue) even bothered to stop suckling to look at his twin – with what? with jealousy? Leo didn't have the answer to this statue as much, and it angered him severely.

Napoleon looked at the Nile statue with disdain – all these babies crowding around this poor river god who was trying to provide for them. It was insanity. The least the babies could do was be grateful for all that the god had done for them, but no they were just climbing on top of him and having a severe lark. The babies didn't even seem to appreciate how much sturdier the cornucopia was in this statue as opposed to the other one; Napoleon of course knew they couldn't see the other one, being stuck in their own stoneworked world, but he still thought they could have at least pretended, like the far-off look of the Tiber statue. So this was what the gods were rewarded with after the rise of democracy? thought Napoleon to himself. How quaint.

Napoleon began to grow bored with this exercise, and wanted to cross-reference with the other statue, so he went around the partition again, only to find Pope Leo right before him, but not dressed in any of his sacramental garb.

Leo turned around and jumped up into the air, but only slightly.

—You look like a young poet, laughed Napoleon. —Are you here to regale me with some of your verse?

—No, said Leo as he regained his composure. —I'm here to talk to you about these statues.

—Ah yes, said Napoleon, —the Tiber and Nile statues. I presume you want them back at the Vatican.

—Not exactly, said Leo. —More just curious as to how they strike you.

—I think the Tiber one reflects where I'm at right now better, so if you want the Nile one back, you can have it.

—Maybe later, Leo said quickly. —But I'm more just wondering why the Tiber one reflects your current situation, or how, rather.

—I believe it to be representative of where my kingdom is and where it is going in the future. We're not prepared to have the entire populace under our thumb as well as represented – that would be madness, as the Nile statue shows. Instead, I like to think my kingdom has happy subjects suckling at the teat of a she-wolf, with some of them occasionally looking over at another person in jealousy.

—Are you assuming then that half of your populace will become the founders of another empire?

—I think if someone grows up in my empire and wishes to start another, concurrent one that runs parallel to mine without interfering in my kingdom, I think I would welcome that. In fact, I'm almost positive I would.

—Is there somewhere else we could talk? asked Leo suddenly. —It's freezing in here.

Napoleon said they could talk on top of the Arc de Triomphe's molded scaffolding, which may be a bit drafty but would allow them to have an overview of the city.

Leo agreed and they exited the Louvre, shutting its large doors and walking down its promenade and into the adjacent street. Napoleon had thrown on a scarf to disguise himself, and nobody would have mistaken Leo for a pope the way that he was dressed – in rags from head to toe.

They got to the steps of the Arch and walked inside one of the colonnades. Napoleon walked up the stairs first, with Leo following. Napoleon opened the hatch to the roof, and immediately stepped outside and walked down to the other end of the tall edifice. Leo hobbled up and then put his forearms down onto the roof of the Arch and then finally stepped up onto the roof, feeling a bit dizzy from the climb and feeling the air to have changed slightly than from when he was on ground level. And the situation seemed to change along with the air.

3.

LEO enters from stage left.

NAPOLEON continues pacing around the Arch stage right.

LEO

I've never seen someone look so free.

NAPOLEON

That's an illusion. I'm being besieged by enemy armies left and right.

LEO

Illusion or not, you have power. People respond to that.

NAPOLEON

What do you want from me?

LEO

I want to continue having this conversation.

NAPOLEON

That's easier said than done.

LEO (smiling)
I'm counting on it.

NAPOLEON (adjusting his hat)
What do you think makes a good government?

LEO
I think the effective ruling of a population must have their say in how it's run, surely.

NAPOLEON
Really? I've always found that a quaint idea, not worth my time.

LEO
A good government knows what its people want and effectively delivers it to them.

NAPOLEON
And you think a population just automatically knows what they want?

LEO
Sometimes, yes.

NAPOLEON
And you think, further, that that same population knows what is best for them?

LEO
Maybe even that, yes.

NAPOLEON
But surely what they want and what's best for them don't always match, no?

LEO
They can match if the leaders are being transparent in the way that they govern.

NAPOLEON
So you think to be a fully developed modern leader one must at least pretend towards transparency?

LEO
Modern leaders have their pick of the political spectrum smorgasbord, with new ones added.

NAPOLEON
You think we will move past monarchies and representative bodies?

LEO
The world will shift its emphasis towards a de facto set of both, but only in name.

NAPOLEON
What will take the place of the monarchy, then? Representative bodies?

LEO
Some combination of the two, within and beyond the categories at the same time.

NAPOLEON
You mean an oligarchy, then?

LEO
Not necessarily. History will prove the merits of individual governments as they go along.

        LEO steps towards the edge of the Arch and looks down.

LEO
This is an impressive building.

NAPOLEON
It's not a building per se. It's an arch. (beat) Also, it's still being built…

LEO
Can it not be both?

NAPOLEON
It can be both only in the sense that a government can be both of the people and for the people. As in, it can serve the purpose of a building, like a government can enlist a representative body to perform its bidding, but it remains functionally (and for all intents and purposes) an arch, a statement of triumph dedicated to might, rulers, and military victory. No amount of sandpapering your words will change that.

LEO (smiling)
I like to think of architecture as fulfilling both functional and aesthetic ends, don't you think?

NAPOLEON
Architecture is whatever we make of it. Whatever we look at and perceive a building as, is what it is. We can't spin the wheels of history away from where they're turning.

LEO
We can certainly try to.

NAPOLEON
Then you're just assuming history will get worse – or even worse – repeat itself.

LEO
I'm assuming whatever role a pessimist needs to assume in these situations.

NAPOLEON
Whatever role you believe will fit the bill for your given population – the laity.

LEO
You know that's an almost-abolished concept, right?

NAPOLEON
What, the laity?

LEO
Yes.

NAPOLEON (laughing)
Yes, I know. I've been on the forefront of it. (beat) Why did you want to meet with me?

LEO
It is my presumption that we could help each other along – speed things up for history as it were.

NAPOLEON
I have no idea what you mean. History is taking place whether we want it to or not, whether we want to reverse it or not. Nobody can reverse the flow of time that leads to history.

LEO
You mean preventative measures can't be taken to prevent atrocities?

NAPOLEON
I'm merely stating the obvious: that it's impossible to change the past.

LEO
Or the future, I agree. But if the present is an amalgamation of the past and future, then what time is left for us to change?

NAPOLEON
I'm not changing anything. I'm content with things as they are. I have my armies, my military might, my kingdom.

LEO

Yes, but what if I were to tell you that your kingdom will fall very soon.

NAPOLEON

I wouldn't believe you, simple as that.

LEO

Well it's going to happen. I've been the harbinger of several things in my life, and this is one I feel very confident about, that your kingdom is on its last legs.

NAPOLEON

If that's the case, then I won't invade Russia.

LEO

Do what you feel you have to do, but I'm not sure that will help matters either.

NAPOLEON

And why is that?

LEO

Because I just sped modernity past your kingdom – through my miracle.

NAPOLEON

The Tower of Babel crock?

LEO

Yes. People won't forget that anytime soon.

NAPOLEON

People already have. Nobody is buying what the Church is selling, not even that.

LEO

People will buy because the market has not yet run out on it, and the coming age of modernity has not yet occurred, so I was just trying to speed things up a little, try to avoid any unnecessary bloodshed.

NAPOLEON

There has been unnecessary bloodshed already, in the past.

LEO

But at the rate technology is developing, there will be further bloodshed in the future, on a scale no one has ever seen before.

NAPOLEON

And you're saying your stupid little "miracle" is something that has sped human evolution past the point where technology advances farther than the human capacity for mercy?

LEO

I'm only saying that, after the miracle, there is no need for the distinction between a spiritual life independent of technology and a spiritual life that uses all the technology available to it – it gets people transcendence without the middle man.

NAPOLEON

Absolutely no one is looking for easy transcendence.

LEO

That's a lie and you know it.

NAPOLEON

People don't want to be spoon-fed transcendence.

LEO

Ah, but they do want to be governed with an iron fist. Makes sense: if people suffer, then they get their transcendence slower but more meaningfully.

NAPOLEON

I don't think suffering is a proper method for understanding transcendence.

LEO

I think it's one of the only ways to understand transcendence, aside from what I supplied people. If people lived under your rule for the remainder of their lives, there would be no need.

NAPOLEON

But you're saying people would achieve the result of the transcendence more slowly?

LEO

Yes.

NAPOLEON

In my opinion, you're speeding things up too much with this miracle. Human evolution can't handle a jump in its evolution of that kind of magnitude. Not only will people be initially resistant to it, but they will eventually realize what it means and that will be an even worse scenario.

LEO

And why is that?

NAPOLEON

Because then they will become complacent. The suffering won't even be an issue because peace will bring everybody to the brink of ultimate stupidity.

LEO

And you're banking on your empire being ruled with such an iron fist that people will have no choice but to suffer?

NAPOLEON

I'm saying they won't have any other options but to suffer, and that's if they're lucky. The unlucky ones will have the choice of whether to suffer or not, and they naturally won't take it and they'll grow complacent.

LEO

I don't think the pursuit of happiness is equivalent to complacency…

NAPOLEON

Ah, an America reference. I knew that would show up somewhere…

LEO

America will be at the forefront of this fight in the future.

NAPOLEON

What, the fight between a religious miracle and a kingdom on the verge of destruction?

LEO

No, religion will have nothing to do with it. It will be about avoiding the kind of government that you're suggesting, the all-seeing eye of your eternal gaze, the one that watches its back but only because it already assumes what's in front of it.

NAPOLEON

I don't understand.

LEO

I was sent on a journey to become the next Pope to try to usurp your power.

NAPOLEON

That makes no sense — we have separate loci of power.

LEO

My boarding school in England presumed (rightly I think) that your brand of toxicity — with its allegiances to masculine power structures – would take the place of the Church's brand of toxicity – with its allegiances to very different masculine power structures. They just wanted to make sure that one wasn't taking the place of the other, if that makes sense.

NAPOLEON
It would except the two systems seem mutually exclusive if you take both to be true.

LEO
And this will be a way that future leaders will enable your system to thrive, by using a version of religion in favor of it, one that blends in with your flavor of toxicity better than if they did believe it.

NAPOLEON
But you can have neither, surely.

LEO
That's for farther down the line in history than I can see.

NAPOLEON
Good, because I plan on running this kingdom until all of Europe is under my grasp.

LEO
Oh, about that. It doesn't seem like you will be able to if you invade Russia.

NAPOLEON
Hmm, then I won't invade Russia.

LEO
But none of that will matter if my miracle takes effect. It will make people see that they need to be truly represented.

NAPOLEON
And how is that?

LEO
It was a collective auditory hallucination. You don't think that will be common parlance within a few days?

NAPOLEON (cursing)
My men have already been talking about it.

LEO
And people will continue to talk about it, and it will make them realize that they need to be collectively represented. How do you not see that?

NAPOLEON
I see only what is in front of me right now.

LEO
Then you must be able to look past your hang-ups and realize that collective representation is what the world needs right now.

NAPOLEON
That is not what's in front of me – that's in the past or in the future.

LEO
Fine. If I can't convince you to not withdraw your Russia campaign without giving up the miracle, I will rescind it. I will use my papal glow to transform into a much older man, the historical Pope Leo, if you will promise to try to invade Russia and lose your military might and campaign, but effectively win the battle.

NAPOLEON
Won't that just put us on equal terms, i.e. won't that stack the deck against us both?

LEO
That's the point. I'm willing to make that sacrifice if you are.

NAPOLEON
Hardly.

But before Napoleon could even utter the word, Leo's body rose up in what onlookers would describe as "heat lightning," twisting and morphing about until Napoleon was very nearly blinded by the sheer magnitude of visible light radiating on top of the al-most-Arc de Triomphe. Leo's body undulated and seemed to go back and forth between dimensions, bending the fabric of time but perhaps not space – the space being taken up by this bizarre miracle-reversal Leo found himself in the middle of, flying in the air like a buffoon yet enjoying the ride still.

     LEO drops down to the top of the Arch again.

LEO
There. Now it's your turn. You must promise to maintain the course you were going with your military campaigns.

NAPOLEON
I most certainly will not.

LEO
Do it, or I will push you off this arch.

NAPOLEON
I don't believe that you will.

LEO
You're right, I probably won't. But let me tell you about how revered and reviled you will be after your death-

NAPOLEON
I'm listening…

LEO
  You will be so highly regarded that history will look upon
  you both favorably as a brilliant military general, and unfa-
  vorably as a tyrant. You will be noted for your blithe cruelty,
  as well as your humanity; you will set the stage for the future in ways untold until the telling happens from people in
  exceedingly high positions of power. Does that not sound
  good to you?

NAPOLEON
  I don't believe you.

LEO
  Why would a man of my age lie to you?

NAPOLEON (laughing)
  Fair point.

LEO
  Will you keep your Russian front in place?

NAPOLEON (nodding gravely)
  Yes, I think I just might.

LEO
  Very good.

    LEO suddenly has a pained expression and lurches forward,
            almost falling off the arch.

          NAPOLEON asks him what's wrong.

LEO
  I've been trying to talk to you for a while now, Napoleon.

NAPOLEON
  Why did your voice change?

LEO

This is Aggie Smith. Nice to finally make your acquaintance.

NAPOLEON (horrified)

What do you want from me?

LEO

Promise that women will be able to have their fair say in the world, in government, law, school, religion, etcetera.

NAPOLEON

I don't think even your friend (I'm assuming friend, yes?) Leo would agree with that, right Leo?

LEO

He would most certainly agree with it. He is a willing vessel right now.

NAPOLEON

Then Aggie, and I suppose Leo, what would you have me do to make that happen?

LEO

More political representation for women. The rest will follow, hopefully.

NAPOLEON

Surely more work will need to be done towards that end if that's what you're seeking, with law, school, religion, etcetera?

LEO

Political representation for now, as it will enable the others to take place. We don't want to move outside of history, like Leo said.

NAPOLEON

If history's not being moved outside of, then how is this happening?

LEO

This is the eternal present of the life of the mind. Witness it full and in the flesh.

NAPOLEON

I'm witnessing it now, and I'm absolutely horrified.

LEO

Don't be horrified. It will be over soon.

NAPOLEON (horrified)

You mean the vision, right?

LEO

Yes, of course we mean the vision.

NAPOLEON

Fine, fine, I'll invade Russia for sure, (beat) definitely. Just make the vision disappear.

LEO

Sure thing. (beat) It's gone now.

NAPOLEON

Yes I know.

LEO

But what a funny thing to have the air outside confirm what you already know…

And the older Pope Leo submitted to what he knew on top of the Arc de Triomphe, as Napoleon was first down the stairs of the colonnade: there could be no history independent of the flecks on the white rose, or in the irises of someone you love. It was a funny thing to have that confirmed as he stepped down into the Arch, knowing that he would never feel the same way about anything again.

Notes

Introduction:
Popes getting to choose their own names (4)
  —Popes throughout history have chosen their papal names, based on tradition and according to what their core values are, since 533, when Mercurius (named after the pagan god Mercury) chose the name John II. Since then, popes have chosen the name of a previous pope, a saint, or sometimes both, and often with inherent, implied messaging provided.

Part One:
Telepathy and its history (13)
  —Telepathy, and the occult in general, have a rich and well-established history in British culture. From its pagan roots, to Aleister Crowley, on up to its recent cropping up in light of Brexit-esque fears and rituals, the practice of witchcraft and its subsidiary modes has led many to cross the Atlantic in search of pagan enlightenment. One telepath in Britain in 2019 urged his followers to telepathically prevent Brexit. C.S. Lewis had a deep and abiding interest in occultist learning and phenomena, even after his conversion to Christianity.

Homosexuality and English boarding schools (27)
  —There is not time here to enumerate and list all the various sources of and history of the homosexual imagination within the English boarding school, but I will give

two examples, drastically separated by time period and medium, that posit the same trope and operate within the same schema: the E.M. Forster novel *Maurice* and the American film *The Imitation Game,* the former of which tells a semi-autobiographical story of forbidden love within the confines of the English boarding school system, and the latter of which describes the young love for a boy from the computer's godfather Alan Turing, while he was a child at an English boarding school in the early 20th century, a doomed love that would both provide the impetus for some of the greatest advancements of that century, as well as the cause of one of its most preventable tragedies (Turing committed suicide after being forced to undergo "hormone therapy" to cure his homosexuality.)

Part Three:
The Witchcraft Act of 1735 (82)
 —In 1727, Janet Horne was the last person executed for witchcraft, and the 1735 law made execution of and for witchcraft in England illegal. It also had the downside of making it illegal to proclaim one was practicing witchcraft in any way, shape, or form. This mainly took the form of persecuting self-proclaimed mediums, and the last person to be convicted under the act was Jane Yorke of east London in September 1944, for "pretending to cause the spirits of the dead to be present".

Internships (94)
 —The concept of an internship didn't exist until the late 1800's, and its first usage in Britain dates to 1879, for an assistant to a resident physician or doctor in training at a hospital (etymonline).

Female students at Oxford University (95)
 —Female students weren't allowed into Oxford until the 1870s. 1879 was the year when women's colleges were introduced to Oxford, starting with Lady Margaret Hall

and Somerville. In 1973, Balliol actually became the first of the traditional all-male colleges to elect a woman as Fellow and Tutor.

Female professors at Oxford University (97)
—The first woman to be appointed to a full professorship was Agnes Headlam-Morley in 1948, when she became the Montague Burton Professor of International Relations. Before that, Miss Ida Mann held the Margaret Ogilvie's Reader position in Ophthalmogy until September 1947 but held only the title of Professor.

Women taking the Oxford entrance exam (109)
—Women weren't allowed to take the Oxford entrance exam until 1885.

London's Globe Theater renovation (116)
—The Globe Theater was destroyed by a fire on June 29, 1613. A year later, a reconstructed Globe was built on the same site, but that was then closed, via Long Parliament's ordinance of closure for all London theaters, in 1642, with the governing body citing theater's incompatibility with the rule of law—this action was reinforced by another act in 1648 declaring actors "rogues" and issuing penalties for spectating a theatrical show put on in London. In 1660, the English Reformation brought Charles II into power, and he lifted the ban, but only two theater sites were operational at that point (the only two that had operational patents), not including the Globe. The Globe itself wasn't renovated until 1997.

Part Four:
Tourism during the Napoleonic Wars (160)
—"The Wye Tour was an excursion past and through a series of scenic buildings, natural phenomena, and factories located along the River Wye. It was a popular destination for British travelers from 1782 to around 1850,

and reached its peak popularity during the Napoleonic Wars, when travel (especially the Grand Tour) to Continental Europe was not an option." The Grand Tour was a custom from the 1600s through the 1700s, where upper-class men who'd just come of age (21) would tour Continental Europe (Wikipedia).

Trans-Siberian Railroad completion date (172)
—The Trans-Siberian Railway was thought up by Tsar Nicholas II in 1890, with the Russian government issuing an imperial rescript to get the railway constructed starting that year. It was finished 14 years later in 1904, with the completion of the Circum-Bakail Railway.

Part Five:
Arthur Rimbaud reference in Leo's speech (215)
—At the end of Arthur Rimbaud's *A Season in Hell* (1873), at a key point in the speaker's final missive from his own (very) personal hell, he breaks with his normal high pitch to deliver a seemingly out-of-the-blue yet also precisely pitched secondary missive, no longer to any beings that could influence where he is, but to the world: "One must be absolutely modern." (*Rimbaud Complete*, translation by Wyatt Mason, 2003).
Napoleon's Russia offensive (223)
—Tactically, as well as in terms of how it made Napoleon and his rule look for the European populace, this was Napoleon's greatest mistake and led to his defeat. Tactically, Napoleon misgauged the United Kingdom's desire to sue for peace – a move the French leader though imminent after he captured Moscow, thus pressuring Emperor Alexander I via his trade lines. The UK didn't sue, the Emperor didn't forfeit, and Napoleon ended up losing because of drastically high casualty numbers, horrific weather conditions, and an extremely low morale among his own troops. Towards the end right, before the retreat, the campaign lost many of its soldiers from desertion.

Construction of the Arc de Triomphe (228)
> —Commissioned after Napoleon's Austerlitz victory in 1806, the architects Chalgrin and then Huyot worked on it, with the foundations completed in 1808, and then in 1810 having the wooden mock-up and scaffolding completed. Chalgrin died in 1811 and gave the responsibility to finishing it with Jean-Nicolas Huyot.

Napoleon's reforms (238)
> —Napoleon's issuance of the French Penal Code of 1810 included crimes against the state, crimes against the person, and punishments for violations, misdemeanors, or felonies, but, like the French Penal Code of 1791, does not include those crimes "created by superstition", crimes which included heresy, sacrilege, homosexuality, incest, or witchcraft. In E.M. Forster's novel *Maurice*, the "Code Napoleon" is referenced as "France being a safe haven for gay men, or, as Maurice puts it, 'unspeakable(s) of the Oscar Wilde type.'" (Wikipedia).

Napoleon's legacy (238)
> —The Code Napoleon from 1804 set out the plan for civil law (not case law) in Napoleonic France and was to become very influential in establishing a firmer social contract upon which societies in Europe could operate. As such, many of the reforms he initiated provided more support to women, but they were still very much beholden to their spouses at least situationally. However, divorce laws were put in place, as well as laws allowing the women in divorce cases to maintain moveable belongings that were in their possession.

Napoleon's exile (239)
> —In 1815, after Napoleon surrendered to the British, he was brought to Plymouth Sound aboard the HMS Bellerophon. He was exiled to St. Helena, a British island in the South Atlantic, via HMS Northumberland, where he lived until he died.

Acknowledgments

I would like to thank Mallory Smart, Kevin Binder, and Bob Sykora for their help in my editing process for this manuscript, with a special shout-out to Mallory, who's been so supportive for the past five years, and has always spurred me on towards new heights in my writing and life. Speaking of which, I'd also like to thank my parents Larry and Jeri, my sisters Allie, Melissa, Megan, and my aunt Deborah. For research, I consulted the following books: *Church Papists* by Alexandra Walsham, *Church Reformation in Protestant Britain* by Alexandra Walsham, *Priests, Prelates & People* by Nicholas Atkin and Frank Tallett, and *The Antichrist's Lewd Hat* by Peter Lake, with Michael Questier. My influences stylistically for this book were regency romances, various satires, YA literature, and more specifically Thomas Pynchon, Brian Catling, and Arthur Miller. I consulted Langley and Belche's New Map of London (1812) for the locations of various time-period-specific London haunts for that era, courtesy the British Library's UK website.

About the Author

Blake Wallin is a writer from Atlanta specializing in poetry, fiction, and playwriting. A recent graduate of George Mason University's MFA program in poetry, he attended the 2018 Kennedy Center Playwriting Intensive as well as the 2018 Virginia Quarterly Review's Summer Workshop in Poetry. He is the author of two previous books, No Sign on the Island (Bottlecap Productions) and Occipital Love (Ghost City Press).